DEAD DUMMY

A DUPLICATE BRIDGE CLUB MYSTERY

BY

DOUG & SHERYL RILEY

For information, email Cozy Cat Press at:
cozycatpress@gmail.com
or visit our website at:
www.cozycatpress.com

COZY CAT
P R E S S

ISBN: 978-1-952579-28-8

Printed in the United States of America

10 9 8 7 6 5 4 3 2 1

For Augustus John

Chapter 1

I turned the key in the lock, causing the rabbit-foot that Mamaw had given me for luck to twist from the end of the key ring. I opened the glass door of the turn-of-the-century downtown building and stepped into what I hoped would become the reality that matched my dreams. I prayed it wouldn't reflect my nightmares.

The space looked the same as when I'd last entered the building. There were decorative tin tiles covering the ceiling, peeling paint and all. The walls were covered in stucco, with several open spots that showed the brick beneath. The floor of dirty walnut ran back eighty feet, built of wood from the old growth forests that used to cover this part of Alabama. The space was narrow, only about thirty feet wide, and empty other than for a high counter that had been pushed to the side wall, which held a cash register that could have found a place in a museum. It was a blank canvas.

I headed towards the rear of the space, my mind racing with plans that I could finally put into action. The counter would need to be moved out from the wall and pushed towards the back a bit, maybe three or four feet. The register I would keep, of course——it added to the old-world charm I hoped to invoke. I should probably get the floors done first, though, and I still didn't know what to do about the walls.

"Are you sure about this, Gracie?" asked Mamaw as she entered the doorway following me. "Starting a business makes me as nervous as a long-tailed cat in a room full of rockin' chairs. Is Alpine big enough to support a coffee shop?"

"Sure?" I answered. "No. But it's a little too late now." The small town of Alpine was nestled in the Appalachian foothills of northeastern Alabama and had been economically left behind after the original German settlers had used up the old growth hardwoods in the area to make intricate furniture. Now the town was blossoming again like a heritage rose growing in a culvert. Alpine was trading on the rustic beauty of the area to bring in tourists, and I hoped to leverage that increase in outside cash to make a go of Gracie's Grounds, a coffee house modeled after my favorite afternoon retreat in Paris.

"I reckon Ida would let you out of the lease. I can talk her around," replied Mamaw.

I turned to look at the woman who'd raised me since I was eight——well, her and Papaw. Mamaw was a few inches shorter than I was, with bright blue eyes that often sparkled with mischief. Today those eyes were clouded, and I knew that Mamaw was truly worried. "I have to do something, Mamaw," I explained. "The insurance won't last forever." For about three months now, I'd been living off my savings and the insurance policy I'd received when my husband had died in a plane crash. Pierre's death was part of the reason I'd scurried home like a whipped dog, although there was more than his death to the Event-That-Changed-My-Life. Anyhow, I'd licked those wounds and knew it was time that I made myself useful to society again. I couldn't spend every day at the Alpine Bridge

Club playing cards, not at thirty-three years old.

"I just wish your Papaw was still with us," she lamented. "He'd know how to help much more than I do."

I smiled, remembering the gruff man who'd often given me bear hugs that at times felt like they could break bones. "Your love and support are all I need, Mamaw. Besides, Evan Petrovich will do all the heavy lifting. He should be here any time and we can see if he thinks he can get the work done before Oktoberfest." That was critical, I knew. I needed to have Gracie's Grounds open before the annual festival, both for the revenue it would generate and for the advertising. It was going to be close——Oktoberfest was only a little over three weeks away.

"I don't like you spending so much money on this ol' place," complained Mamaw.

"I'm not spending that much," I replied. "Ida Bea promised to cover half of the renovation costs and she's waived the rent for the first two months. I really couldn't have asked for a more favorable deal." Unfortunately, it had taken me longer than I'd hoped to gain possession of the downtown space in the center of Alpine. The Strange family had rented the building for over eighty years, running a shoe repair shop called Cobbler's Corner. Only two octogenarian sisters remained from that once large clan. One of those two sisters——Mary Sue——had been opposed to closing the shop. Luckily for me, the other——Mary Jane——eventually prevailed. Only the counter and the cash register remained; the Strange sisters had moved or disposed of everything else. Well, either they had, or Ida had hired someone to clean out the space. Regardless, I was happy not to have to sort through the years of clutter the shoe repair shop had generated.

"I know Ida gave you a good deal," Mamaw said. "She's

still trying to make amends from the summer."

"That wasn't Ida's fault," I answered. At the end of July, I'd been unfortunate enough to discover a dead body at the Alpine Bridge Club. It had been a hectic few days, being questioned by the police under suspicion of murder. About the only good thing that came out of that period was reconnecting with Emily Huntsman——Stevenson now. She was an old friend from grade school who currently served as a police officer for the Alpine Police Department. I supposed running into my old high school boyfriend, Hank Waderich, was also a direct result of the investigation. I should count that too, although at times I didn't know if my reignited relationship with Hank was a blessing or a curse.

"Still, she feels bad about it, Gracie," Mamaw reminded me. "Her husband, Wilhelm, coming after you in your own house and all. I'm still amazed that everything turned out as well as it did."

So was I. I didn't like thinking back to that day and wished that Mamaw would let the past rest. Yet it had been the most exciting event to happen in Alpine in years——heck, maybe even this century. Gossip and speculation about that time continued even today, almost two months later. The Alpine Tribune had been running articles for weeks and desperately wanted me to give an interview. I refused every request, just trying to put it all behind me. Unfortunately, one of the reporters, Brandi-With-An-I Yugler, refused to take "no" for an answer. She'd tracked me down last week, yet again, in Margaret's Diner, seeking an interview. In comparison though, I had it easy. Brandi-With-An-I had harassed poor Ida too, even accosting her at Wilhelm's funeral.

I headed towards the back of the building and opened the door to the storage room, stepping into the tiny space. On the right, a narrow door led to the only bathroom in the building, a small area containing a porcelain sink attached to the wall and a chipped commode. The left side held a steep and narrow stairway, the first flight stopping about halfway up on a landing and then switching back for the second flight to reach the upper floor. Ahead was the back door that opened into the alley behind the building. I knew there was room to park one car, or room for a dumpster, but not both.

I heard conversation behind me and turned to see that Evan had arrived and was talking to Mamaw. The man towered over her, and you could see the muscle definition through his tight navy shirt. He could certainly give Hank a run for his money, even the Hank from his football-playing glory days. I felt a little guilty thinking it, even if it was true. I walked over and stuck my hand out. "Thanks, Evan, for coming over so quickly," I said.

He grabbed my hand, gave it a firm squeeze, and replied, "My pleasure, Miss Thies."

"Please, call me Gracie," I said. The smile Evan returned revealed a mouthful of straight white teeth, and a pair of dimples in his cheeks that I swore you could fall into. His green eyes twinkled like a snowflake in the sun, and his mop of unruly blond hair topped him like a spoonful of whipped cream on a slice of Margaret's pecan pie. I felt my heart quicken and knew I was blushing. I was with Hank now and didn't need a man like Evan Petrovich to cause me strife. My life was filled with enough trouble the way it was.

"Gracie, you really mustn't run up and down those steep stairs back there," interrupted Mamaw, motioning with a hand to the back of the building, but with a hint of malice in her voice. "It just causes you to flush so, and with your coloring..." she tsked.

"But…I…yes, Mamaw," I replied, the heat on my face growing. I wanted to curse my Irish red hair and pale skin. Mamaw had seen how I'd reacted to the man, and in her own way was just trying to protect me, or at least my reputation. Well, either that or she was giving me a warning of sorts. In a place like Alpine, rumor ran faster than a hog at slop time. And she'd warned me plenty about how affairs of the heart were of particular interest in this small town.

Evan snorted, and I flashed him a glare, causing that smile of his to fade a little. He pulled the clipboard he held in his left hand to his chest like a shield. "Well, Miss Thies, shall we review the work you want done?" he asked.

I nodded as I pulled my hair into a loose bun that I knew would fall again like leaves on an autumn day and proceeded to tell him my plans. I showed him where the counter needed to be moved, how I wanted to position and use the old cash register, and described the additional counters that needed to be made. I asked about the floors and if they should be done before or after the other work. We examined the bathroom, and he took some measurements with his tape, scribbling notes on his clipboard. Evan grunted a few times throughout, but otherwise kept quiet and thankfully didn't use that nuclear smile of his again. Somewhere along the line, Mamaw had interrupted, saying she had to leave or risk being late for her bridge game. I had waved her goodbye and replied that I'd see her tonight for supper. Afterwards, I finished by describing to Evan the feel of the place I wanted to invoke, not that I expected it would do much good. In my experience most Alpine residents——men in particular——didn't really understand the Old-World look until they saw it in person. And then I got to the heart of the matter, "And I need all this done by Oktoberfest. The espresso machine and other coffee equipment will be delivered late next week. I have the specifications here somewhere," I said, showing him the packet of papers I'd brought. "I want to have the grand opening before the festival."

"Before Oktoberfest?" asked Evan bleakly.

"Yes," I said.

"That's a pretty aggressive timeline," he replied. "We have to get the permits before we can start. And even if my crew could get the main work done in three or four days, the building inspector won't sign off quickly. And what about the health inspector? You still have to have a health permit, right? You can't just open a restaurant without a health permit."

"I need to be open for Oktoberfest. I need the revenue from that weekend to make a go of this," I said, gesturing to the space. There would be hundreds of tourists and they all had to eat and drink. It wasn't as if there were that many choices, not downtown at least. There was Margaret's Diner down the street of course——that was an Alpine fixture. And a new Chinese restaurant called Panda Garden had just opened two doors down. There were only a few other places downtown——Bill's B-B-Q and a seedy bar or two. None of them served the type of drinks I imagined: coffees, espressos, and lattes. "It's not a choice," I finished firmly.

"Hey," Evan replied, holding his hands before him in a gesture of peace. "It's not me holding you back," he said. "I can get the work done, at least I think I can. All except possibly for that bathroom, that's going to take some tinkering to get up to code. It's the town hall you have to convince. They're the ones that tend to delay these things."

"What if I got you that building permit today?" I asked, thinking furiously. I couldn't believe it was all falling apart before I'd even served the first cup. "When could you start and what could you get done by the end of next week?"

"I can have my guys start tomorrow," he said. "We'll have to start with the ceiling——that's lead paint up there, and it's peeling. You won't pass any health inspection until that problem is resolved. Moving the counter and building the add-ons won't take long. What do you want to do with the walls?"

"What do you suggest?" I asked. I hadn't even realized the ceiling was going to be a problem, how many other landmines did this old building contain? And what did it mean to bring the bathroom 'up to code'? I was afraid to ask as I figured the answer was not going to be to my liking.

"Your choices are to remove the rest of the stucco and leave the bare brick, repair the stucco, or just seal it and leave it as is. It all depends on the look you prefer," he explained.

"What's the cheapest option?" I asked, fearing the unknown costs that seemed to be mounting.

Evan pulled a claw hammer from the belt he had around his waist and headed to the nearest wall. He tapped a few times and I watched as flakes of stucco floated to the floor to reveal the antique brick beneath. I heard him grunt, and then he returned to the center of the space looking at the walls as if he was gazing at a Monet at the Louvre. "Well," he said, "the stucco isn't too hard to take down, but if it was me, I'd spend a few hours artfully putting a few more holes in it. Maybe even make the ones already here a bit bigger," he continued, using his hands to demonstrate a suitable size. "Not too many, mind; you don't want to degrade the stability of the rest of the stucco. Then I'd slap some fresh white paint on the stucco parts, clean the bricks, and seal the whole thing. The white paint will give you a bit more light in here. The brick alone will make it pretty dark otherwise. The building is too narrow for that, I think."

I closed my eyes and tried to picture what Evan suggested.

Once the image came, I knew at once that he was right. I hadn't thought about how dark the space would be without some white paint on the walls. If I removed all the stucco to reveal the brick, I'd probably need to paint the brick to lighten the space, thereby losing the antique look in the process. The three chandeliers from the ceiling wouldn't provide enough illumination, not with the front windows perpetually in the shade from the portico. "You have an eye for this," I said. "I like it."

He flashed me that killer smile, but somehow I resisted. Maybe the financial pickle I was in gave me an immunity of sorts. I had thought this was going to be easy——a little remodeling and then I could put my shingle out and run a coffee house just like the one off Mode de Blanc in Paris where I'd spent so many lazy afternoons. The reality was more troublesome than I'd thought. "And lighting?" I asked.

"Will the white stucco be enough with the three chandeliers?"

"Keeping the chandeliers sounds right. You can't get anything to replace them that would fit into the décor at a reasonable price," Evan added. "And I wouldn't touch that ceiling once we have it cleaned. That tin tile is just too precious to risk." Evan stared at the ceiling and paced the room looking upward from several different angles. "I'd add some wall sconces, I think. Maybe every six to eight feet or so. We'll have to rig the wiring, probably have a main line covered in conduit a foot or so from the ceiling all around the room with spurs coming down to each sconce and outlet. It'll add a bit of a modern touch, and we can make it match the stainless-steel machinery you have coming." The man was like a dream come true. He'd taken my vision and was transforming it into a workable plan. Every suggestion he had fit perfectly with what

I'd wanted. "That leaves the power problem, of course."

"Power problem?" I asked, a sinking feeling in the pit of my stomach.

"This old building isn't wired for the type of power you'll need," he explained. "You'll burn it out before the first cup is brewed. I wouldn't be surprised if this old place had knob and tube wiring," he laughed. "It'll all have to be replaced."

"I can't afford that," I said appalled. I could feel the tears forming——it was all falling apart before I'd even gotten started. I felt like I'd stepped into a cow pie while wearing my wedding dress on the way to the church.

"Hey now," Evan said. "Don't fret. It's not all bad. You have a simple rental agreement, right? No disclosures?" he asked.

"I don't know," I said wiping my eyes. I was furious with myself for playing the damsel in distress card, even if I didn't intend to do so. "I don't think so," I continued, thinking about the papers I'd signed. It was a simple thing, only about three pages long, and I didn't remember anything about problems with the property.

"Then there's nothing to worry about. The ceiling, bathroom and wiring, should all be paid by the owner."

"What?" I asked.

"The owner can't rent the place unless it's up to code, at least can't newly rent the space. Renewals are another matter, something about a grandfather clause. Anyhow, the ceiling paint is a health hazard, the wiring is a fire hazard, and as for the bathroom, well, I'll claim that it's a health hazard too. The plumbing needs to be replaced. The only thing you have to pay is cosmetic, the work on the walls and reconfiguring the counter with the add-ons. I'll talk to the owner——this is one of Ida Bea's buildings, right?"

"You would do that?" I asked, hope rising. If Ida had to

cover the lion's share of the repairs maybe I didn't have to have the shop open for Oktoberfest. I might be able to build the business more slowly.

"I'd be happy to. What do you plan to do upstairs?" Evan asked.

I felt embarrassed discussing it, not with what I'd learned needed to be done on this floor and my reaction to the costs. I knew my plans were more like dreams——a schoolgirl's fancy of a prince come to rescue her. I had learned there were no princes, not in Alpine or anywhere else in this world.

"I'd thought of converting the space into an apartment, you know, so that I could live above the business. Now though..." I said reluctantly, "...with what needs to be done down here."

"Let's take a look anyhow," smiled Evan.

I led the way to the back of the building and up the narrow steps. The second floor was bigger than the first, extending over the portico out front with a pair of windows that overlooked Main Street. There was a second entrance as well, a set of outside steps on the back of the building that led to the single parking space off the alley. A lonely window out the back wall provided some much-needed light. There were no side windows of course, as the building shared walls on either side with other downtown structures. Much like the downstairs, it was one large room with tall ceilings. While from the outside, the building looked like it was three stories, access to the top floor was through a pull-down ladder and the space was only about four feet tall, just big enough for some awkward storage and the heating and cooling units.

I explained my concept, wanting to keep the space open while still taking some square footage for a large bathroom and some closet space. I was fond of baths and knew I wanted a big tub. It might be a bit extravagant, but I felt that if I was going to renovate the space I might as well make it to my tastes. Evan made some suggestions and between the two of us we landed upon a floor plan that made good use of the limited natural light while still giving a decent flow to the studio apartment.

"Thanks for listening, Evan," I said after our conversation had waned. "I can see now what the space could become, and it would truly be wonderful. But I think with the work downstairs that needs to be done, I can't take this on as well. It helps, though, to have dreams," I smiled, still immersed in the vision. "I guess I'll just have to stay where I am for now."

"Aren't you living in a small house off Elm, the one with the green shutters?" he asked. I glanced his way, wondering how he knew that about me. My look must have startled him. "I've read the paper," he sheepishly admitted. Unfortunately, I knew, that said it all. Only a hermit would not have heard about the murder in the bridge club, and the killer's accidental death at the cottage this past summer. I had been at the center of it all——make that a deaf and blind hermit.

"Well...sort of," I replied. It was a difficult question to answer, and not one I relished going public about. Since I'd been accosted and almost killed there, I now felt uncomfortable whenever I spent any time at the cottage. The place didn't feel like home anymore, and I doubted it ever would again. I either spent my nights with Hank at the farm, or at Mamaw's Victorian. "It's...been hard," I continued lamely.

"I can imagine," said Evan. "It must be difficult after everything that happened."

"You could say that," I snorted. The one time I'd tried sleeping alone in the cottage on Elm had not ended well, at least unless you considered rushing to Mamaw's Victorian at 3:00 a.m. in a panic attack as well. "But it's not like there are a lot of choices in this town," I lamented. The rental market was brutal——finding the cottage on Elm had been a stroke of luck as rare as bidding to a solid grand slam in bridge.

"Exactly," replied Evan with a twinkle in his eye. He flashed me that nuclear smile and I felt the heat again on my face as an image of him shirtless in my arms flashed through me. "There really isn't much to rent within thirty miles. You almost have to go all the way to Gadsden to find a livable place." I banished all thoughts of the two of us together and focused on following his train of thought. How was the housing market related to me, this project, or the cottage on Elm? I was flummoxed. "So," he said, apparently taking my silence as permission to continue. "This is a little awkward, but...don't take this the wrong way... I mean if you're really using the cottage then fine...but could I sublease the house from you?"

"What?" I asked. Maybe I should've seen it coming, but his request left me floored, like someone had snuck up behind me and hit me in the back of the head with a hammer.

"I want to sublease the house on Elm from you, and in return I'll give you a deal on renovating this place," he explained, expanding his arms outward to indicate the space. "Say, completing it at cost?"

My mind raced. At first, I'd kept the cottage in case my memories of the attack faded, yet so far that hadn't happened. Now I kept it mostly to keep up appearances and as a place to store my possessions——that and because if I broke the lease, the penalty wasn't that much less than just paying the rest of the rent anyhow. However, if I subleased the cottage to Evan, I wouldn't have to pay the remaining months of rent on the lease and I could invest that money into the business instead, or into the renovations for the upstairs apartment. I could easily move my possessions up here, there was plenty of room, and I wouldn't be that much worse off than living out of the suitcase as I'd been doing. I might even be able to spend the night up here if I set up a bed. I smiled and asked, "When do you want to move in?"

Chapter 2

After seeing Evan out, I locked up and walked the three blocks to the courthouse, passing by my 1972 Mustang. I had bought the car on a whim in Atlanta when I'd returned to the states after Pierre had died. The Beast had been nothing but trouble, in and out of the shop three times already. If it weren't for the fact that my mechanic was an old friend of Papaw's whom I could trust, I would've been forced to sell the thing. As it was, I was tempted to sell it anyhow. I needed reliable transportation and the Mustang was anything but. The trouble was I just loved the look and feel of driving it, plus Hank liked it too.

Evan and I had decided I'd pursue the building permit while he went to speak with Ida about the renovation costs. We had agreed to rendezvous back at the building around 6:00 for an update and to refine the timeline. I felt lucky to find him available, although he'd admitted that business was a bit slow. Thinking back, there was something a little off about our conversation. It almost felt like Evan preferred talking with Ida about costs to the mundane task of getting the permit. I'd have thought that getting the permit was something that Evan, as the contractor, would have been more suited to doing.

I arrived at the courthouse and passed by the bronze statue of Colonel Wilber Corbert, which sat in the middle of the square in front of the imposing limestone structure. The accompanying plaque claimed that Colonel Corbert was an aide for Alabama Governor Andrew B. Moore when war broke out between the states, and then had promptly joined the rebel army, eventually gaining the rank of Colonel. I figured the statue's existence had more to do with the last name than with whatever deeds the Colonel had accomplished. The Corbert family was well known around these parts for their wealth and political connections. In fact, my new landlord had once been a Corbert herself before taking her husband's name. With what had happened this summer, I wondered if Ida regretted doing so.

I entered the courthouse and passed through a metal detector manned by a sleepy-looking woman in blue——even little ol' Alpine had a detector these days. A hall stretched in either direction with marble on the floor and carved wood paneling that spoke of a richer time. Solid oak doors lined the hall with little brass placards sticking out above each that named the offices beyond the entry. I glanced left and then right, eventually deciding that the Department of Code Enforcement and Permits was the most likely, at least it had 'permit' in the title. I walked to the entry, my steps echoing in the otherwise empty hall, and saw that the door was ajar. Peeking in revealed a small room with threadbare carpet on the floor and three more doors with glass windows that led further into the structure. A small reception desk dominated the scarce square footage, where a willowy woman in a royal blue dress with flowing gauzy sleeves sat pecking at a keyboard. I coughed to make my presence known.

As she turned my way, a large silver pendant with a shiny ebony stone set in the center swayed with a flash as it settled on her bosom. She was younger than me, with flowing dark hair framing a round face accented with a pink stripe over her left ear. "Blessed be. How may I serve you?" she asked.

"I need to get a building permit," I said. "Is this the right place?"

I felt the hair go up on the back of my neck when she stared blankly into the space on my right. She paused, and then in a melodic, if somewhat dramatic voice, began, "Your aura is the color of flame, seek and you shall find. The Goddess Brighid smiles upon your strong will."

"What?" I asked, feeling a bit unsettled in my stomach, like someone had walked across my grave.

"Be reassured," she sighed, and then with a small shiver and a smile, her eyes met mine. "Your goddess has led you correctly," she continued in a much more normal voice. "I have what you seek." The woman stood and opened the top drawer of a file cabinet. After riffling a bit with the files, she produced a packet of papers. "Complete the necessary items on these pages and when Tommy returns, if the stars align, he'll sign it," she explained. "Of course, you'll have to make a monetary offering. Checks only, personal is fine."

"Tommy?" I questioned. I looked around the room. The doors to the three offices had names stenciled on the glass. The only one I recognized was Tommy Hilgeman, a widower who played bridge at the club most afternoons, often badly, and who scowled bitterly when he produced bad boards against me and Mamaw. Tommy fit better in the fifties than the present day. Then again, Tina seemed to be a throwback to——well, I didn't know when.

"Hilgeman," the receptionist answered as she waved

vaguely towards the door with his name. "Tommy Hilgeman, a name suited to his occupation. I am Tina Thompson, also known as the One Who Sees." Tina brandished the papers in her hand and offered them to me with a flourish that made her long sleeves flutter like wings.

"Gracie Thies," I said, taking the papers from her.

"You have seen the White Lady, Goddess of Death," she replied, mouth open in awe. "You defeated her servant. I must know, you must tell me, the insight will expand my mind, allow me to see and be more than I am." Her eyes sparkled like Tinker Bell sprinkling fairy dust on the Lost Boys. "Tell me of the time you faced the White Lady's disciple."

"Uh…" I replied, examining the form I held and ignoring her demand. It was simple enough to fill out, just detailing the work that was to be done and by whom. It looked like you were supposed to attach some architectural drawings for bigger projects, but Evan had said the job was small enough not to need it. We weren't doing anything structural.

"The Blessing of the Perpetual Flame, that must have been instrumental in how you persevered and survived the encounter. Could you feel it? In the depths of your soul?" Tina asked. "Did your flame spirit rise up to defeat him? You must tell me."

"How soon can I get this filed?" I asked. I wondered if it was an act, or if Tina really was playing with a deck missing a few cards.

"Perhaps the pixies intervened; they are attracted to ones of fire like you," continued Tina, looking at me hopefully. "Do sweets and candies vanish from your home without your knowledge?"

"Do I just need his signature?" I asked. "That and the check, of course." I figured I'd discovered why Evan was avoiding this office. I was a little surprised the likes of Tommy put up with such an eccentric.

"To be brushed by the White Lady and yet survive," Tina sighed, and then shook herself out of her preoccupation. "Pixies cannot help you, your fate depends on the whims of Tommy, and he is not here." Tina collapsed into her chair, and her face drooped as her eyes grew large like a puppy begging for a bone.

"What do you mean by the 'whims of Tommy?'" I asked.

"You need to procure a contractor," Tina sighed. "Tommy will demand such to move with speed. Have you made those arrangements?"

"I've hired Evan Petrovich," I answered.

Her eyes grew. I'm not sure how, but now they looked like full moons at harvest. I felt a chill down the middle of my back; this was almost worse than the voice she'd used when I'd entered, maybe because this time it felt real. "By the Goddess," Tina muttered, "the Eye of Fate shines upon us." She trembled in her chair, and her face blanched. "I did not see. I name myself, and in my folly and arrogance claim power beyond my grasp. Cethlion is refusing to bless me. I am She Who Sees Not."

"Is there something I should know?" I asked carefully.

Tina shook her head negatively, and then muttered, "I shall not intervene, by the Goddess's will, I shall not." Tina turned back to her computer, a determined look on her face. "May the Goddess Brighid protect you." She started to peck at the keyboard, devoted to the computer screen as if I was no longer of any consequence.

I paused, trying to figure out what had just happened. Evan was almost painfully attractive, and Tina seemed to have an unusual way of interacting with others. Could she be intimidated by Evan's looks? "Evan is a handsome man," I offered, trying to coax something more coherent from the woman.

"He is who and what he is," she replied cryptically. "Tommy is most likely playing bridge, ah, but you would know that——would you not?——with your history. I am sure you know where he may be found," she continued in an impatient tone.

"Tina…"

"I cannot help you further," she interrupted. "Best to face the Fates quickly. Tommy will expect the form complete, with the name of the contractor given. Perhaps your fire spirit will blind him and light the way where others fear to trod." She refused to even look at me.

I shook my head and left, wandering back the way I'd come. Something about Evan had set Tina off and I had this nagging suspicion it would cause me grief. Could it be as simple as I was a woman and Evan had a reputation with the ladies? Mamaw always warned me about getting involved in romantic entanglements in a town like Alpine. That was grist for the rumor mill, and prime grain at that. Only after I passed back through security did I realize I'd forgotten to ask about the health permit. I thought about returning, but I was hungry. The one cup of coffee I'd had this morning was not going to be enough.

I reached the sidewalk on Main and looked eastward towards the bridge club. I could see the building in the distance and knew that there was a good chance that Tommy was there right now playing bridge. As tempted as I was to march over immediately and demand his signature, I still hadn't filled out the thing. It would be better to wait until the end of the session anyway, and this way I could get that bite to eat. Instead, I turned left and headed back towards the Mustang. I would drive over to Margaret's, get an early lunch, fill out the paperwork, and only then head to the club to catch Tommy before the bridge game ended.

I got to the Mustang and turned the key. Thankfully, the Beast started without trouble. I made a U-turn and headed towards Margaret's, passing through the intersection of Maple and Main. My mind turned back to the stormy July afternoon when the Mustang had stalled in that intersection due to high water, and I'd been rescued by Hank. That day had sparked the flame again in our smoldering relationship.

Hank and I had plans for tonight, although I suspected I'd be a bit late on account of my meeting with Evan. I vowed to try talking to him again about our future before other things distracted us. I wasn't opposed to those things, I just wanted more than the physical side. If we were going to be together long-term, we needed to resolve some issues, the most pressing of which was what to do about Hank's father——Harry. Harry had lost both legs below the knee in a car accident a few years ago, and the curmudgeon used that to manipulate his son. Hank doted on the old goat to the point where I felt I was second fiddle. It wasn't fair, to Hank or to me. Heck, it wasn't even fair to Harry.

I pulled into the lot at Margaret's and found a spot near the front door. It was early yet and Monday, so I wasn't surprised to see the lot held only a handful of cars. The diner itself was a simple square building covered in windows, built much later than the rest of downtown. I entered and waved as Margaret called for me to sit anywhere. I headed towards my favorite booth in the back, tucked away to be less visible from the door, where I'd have the room to spread out. I sat and began the arduous task of filling out the paperwork.

"Whatcha' have there?" asked Margaret with pen and pad in hand. She was older than me, about the age my mother would have been. She had graying brunette hair tied back into a loose bun and wore a wrinkled white apron covering a light blue dress.

"A building permit to renovate the Cobbler's Corner into a coffee house," I replied without looking up.

"A coffee shop," replied Margaret. "What would you want to do that for?" she asked. "Owning a restaurant is no easy task, believe me. Sometimes I feel I live here."

"So do I," I laughed, glancing up. "I must eat here twice a week or more. I'll have the chicken salad and a Diet Coke," I continued, not even looking at the menu. I knew it by heart. Margaret shuffled away without saying a word and I continued filling out the form. From what I could tell, the permit itself was more of a formality than anything else. As long as nothing structural was happening, and the contractor was licensed, then getting the project started should be as easy as finding a Crimson Tide fan. Well, maybe not quite that easy. You couldn't throw a snowball in Alpine at Christmas without hitting a Tide fan, not that there was ever any snow at Christmas in Alpine.

"So, Miss Thies," said a voice that caused me to inwardly cringe. "How did it feel to find Wilhelm Bea in your house?" asked Brandi-With-An-I Yugler, claiming the seat across from me. I threw her an unwelcoming glare, but she didn't notice or possibly didn't care. The woman was busy studying the papers spread out on the table before me.

"None of your business," I snapped, gathering the forms and trying to stack them neatly. I didn't need Brandi-With-An-I in my business, old or new.

"The police report said you were found naked, in the tub,

with poor Wilhelm Bea shot dead at your feet. I have a source that claims the two of you were having an affair."

"What?" I screeched. Knowing better but not being able to help myself, I added, "Who said that?"

All I saw was a satisfied smirk as she continued, "And this source says you flirt with all the single men at the Duplicate Bridge Club, your own personal hunting grounds. Perhaps you'd also flirted with a few of the not so single men?"

"That's a lie," I seethed. It had to be Clovis Jones. The retired farm hand had it in for me, and the "personal hunting grounds" comment sounded just like him. He was a menace at the bridge club, causing strife both at the table and off. "You print something like that, and I'll sue you for liable."

"So, I have you on the record then," said Brandi-With-An-I giving me a Cheshire grin.

Crap, I didn't want to give her anything, but I didn't see how I could just stand by and watch my reputation go down the gutter. I knew what that was like in this town. "Fine," I said. "On the record. I did not have an affair with Wilhelm, or anyone else before you even ask."

"I never believed it myself," she said conspiratorially. I knew she was trying to tame me, like a horse-trainer breaking a filly. Soon she'd act like we were fast friends just gossiping. And then it would appear in the paper, for all to see. I was having none of it. "It's just when some folks hear that you were naked, and him an older man, well, tongues will wag. He didn't...try anything with you... did he?"

"Other than try and make me write a suicide note? Other than try and kill me? Nope, he was a perfect gentleman," I snapped. Margaret came and slammed down my salad and Diet Coke, almost hard enough to chip the plate. I glanced at her and got an icy stare that she passed between me and Brandi-

With-An-I. She apparently didn't like the reporter any more than I did. She set the check down and left without a word. "Why don't you find someone else to pester?" I asked. "I really don't want to discuss it anymore. What is past is past, as my Mamaw would say."

"Oh, come now. We were just chatting. Nothing to be concerned about," meowed Brandi-With-An-I. You could almost hear her purr as she sat patiently waiting for me to speak. If she knew me better, she would have known that silence was a poor tactic——I'd had to deal with Mamaw through the years. I just smiled and ate my chicken salad. "The people of Alpine want to know," she offered eventually. "If you don't tell your tale, then someone else will. Maybe not in a way so much to your liking."

I continued eating, refusing to say another word. Maybe the woman would finally take a hint and leave. After another pause, she continued, "You were found alone with two dead men, both prominent citizens, and both were shot. That's quite a coincidence." I remained silent and watched as the vein in her neck began to pulse. I wondered if my refusal to talk was putting a touch of grey in that perfectly coifed blond hair of hers. She probably had it colored. "You know, someday you may want to have a friend at the paper. Give me an interview now and I can be that friend." She paused and smiled expectantly. I gave her my glassy stare. I figured if it annoyed Mamaw, maybe it would annoy Brandi-With-An-I as well. It was better than claiming that pixies had come to my rescue. I wondered how I could point her towards Tina Thompson; the two would mix like water and oil. "Come on, Miss Thies, I have you on record anyhow," she said. "You should just tell me your version of events."

I took another bite of the chicken salad and gifted her with an ironic grin.

"I don't know why Emily Stevenson defends you," she barked. "From what I can see, you're a narcissistic prom queen who thinks she's too good for this town and the people in it."

"Emily? What does she have to do with this?" I asked. As soon as I spoke, I regretted it. The reporter was trying to bait me, and I fell for it.

"So, the princess deigns to speak to mere mortals after all," replied Brandi-With-An-I. "Emily says you were almost comatose when they found you in the bathroom of the house on Elm. How did you get in such a state?" I gave her my glassy smile again and got a frosty stare in return. After a moment, Brandi-With-An-I stood in a huff and marched away like a rooster in a henhouse.

I finished my salad and drank my Diet Coke. I looked for Margaret to get a refill, but for some reason could not attract her attention. I finished filling out the paperwork and glanced at my new cell phone for the time. If I left immediately, I should arrive at the club a little before the end of the game. I dropped a ten spot, more than enough to cover the bill with a little extra, and then hurried away, waving to Margaret as I went.

The Mustang roared to life, and I headed down Main past my future abode and eventually parked in front of the Alpine Bridge Club under an old oak tree. The massive old Carlyle hotel stood vacant across the street. Work had not resumed on the renovation after Edward's death. It was the lack of funds for renovating the hotel that had instigated the events that had led to Edward's murder by Wilhelm Bea. There was speculation that an investor from Birmingham was interested in the project, but at the moment the structure was abandoned.

I entered the club and saw that the session was still in

progress. I waved to Mamaw and nodded to Gladys, the club manager and director of our games. Gladys had been particularly supportive these last few weeks, as if somehow I'd arranged for Wilhelm Bea to attack me in my own home and thus had personally removed her from suspicion of murder. I scanned the room and found Tommy, playing with Howard Ellis as he usually did, and walked over to stand near his table like a kibitzer watching an expert play at Nationals. I needed Tommy's signature, and by God, I wasn't going to let the man out of my sight until I got it. An aura of fire indeed.

I saw Tommy putting his bid cards back into the bidding box——it had been a competitive auction that Tommy had won. From the bidding, it looked like the high cards were basically split. Otis Greer, the club president, was on lead and after hesitating finally offered a low trump. When Howard displayed his cards as Dummy, I scanned Tommy's hand and compared. I could tell it was going to be close. Tommy won the opening lead and pulled trump, ending in his hand. That looked like a mistake to me——Tommy needed to develop a side suit in Dummy and entries were going to be an issue. Play progressed and as I had thought, Otis used a hold-up play to kill the Dummy. Tommy ended up down one.

"That was close, Tommy," offered Howard. "Sorry about the dead dummy." I couldn't help it, but a derisive snort escaped. That was bad play, not a dead dummy.

"What do you want?" snapped Tommy, giving me a glare with enough heat to boil a mess of greens.

Inwardly I winced; I needed this man's signature and here I was agitating him. I knew he got short when things went poorly at the bridge table. Why couldn't I have kept my mouth shut? "I need your signature on a building permit," I admitted sheepishly.

"Let me see that," he growled, taking the form from me and turning to the back page to sign his name like John Hancock on the Declaration of Independence. "You have a contractor lined up?" he asked, shoving the crinkled form back at me.

I grabbed the signed permit and answered, "Evan Petrovich."

"What!" Tommy screeched, standing, causing everyone in the club to stare. "Give that back," he said. "I'll not allow that bastard to work in this town again," he continued trying to grab the papers in my hands. I pulled them away even as I felt the heat on my face from embarrassment. One simply didn't act this way during a bridge game.

"Excuse me," called Gladys, heading our way. "Quiet now, or I'll have to sanction you, Tommy. There are people still playing."

"She just tricked me into signing something I shouldn't," Tommy said. "This is town business."

"I did not," I interrupted. "I just asked for your signature. It's not my fault you didn't ask about the details."

"Well, you should have said something. That form isn't legal," he said.

"Yes, it is," I snapped. "I have your signature."

"That doesn't matter," he said. "You don't have my approval."

"Yeah, she kinda' does," offered Otis sagely. "You've signed it, Tommy. Whether you meant to or not, Petrovich has the permit to do the job."

"Over my dead body. Not after what he did to my Sandra," seethed Tommy.

"Stop it!" cried Gladys, glaring at the two of us. "Gracie, take your papers and leave, and shame on you for bringing your personal business in here. And Tommy, you still have a board to play. I suggest you do it and stop interrupting this game."

"But she…" started Tommy.

"Enough!" fumed Gladys. She turned to the room and said, "I'm sorry, folks. Nothing to see here," she intoned soothingly as everyone looked on. I glanced around, realizing we had an audience as if we were the Jets and the Sharks from West Side Story. "Please go back to playing."

Tommy glared but remained silent. I scowled and turned away, making my way through the club as quietly as I could. Gladys kept her frosty gaze locked on me, and I knew whatever goodwill I'd generated with her had vanished. When I passed Mamaw's table, I saw her shake her head. I felt wrongly blamed but knew there was nothing I could do about it. Anything I said now would just interrupt the game again.

I left the club and drove back to the courthouse. I wanted to make a copy of the permit and file it before Tommy got back from the bridge game. With how he'd acted, I had no desire to have another confrontation with the man anytime soon. I did wonder what had happened between Evan and Sandra. That must have been what had alarmed Tina Thompson earlier. She must have known how Tommy would react to Evan's name, and wanted to avoid any backlash.

I entered the courthouse through the same door as earlier in the day and made my way to the Department of Code Enforcement and Permits. I slipped in to find Tina studying a large leather-bound book. I couldn't see the title, but the pages held ornate calligraphy. When she noticed me, she quickly stood, grabbed the book to clutch to her chest, and pulled her rolling chair in front of her like a barrier before an attacking army. "I foresaw your return. There was nothing I could do. The righteous anger of Tommy is not something I can deflect.

No spell suffices; the darkness swells in him."

"You could have warned me," I replied, shutting the door behind me to have a bit of privacy. I was tempted to give her a piece of my mind, after the trick she'd pulled.

"Yes," she deflated. "I should have. I have wronged you. I have been blessed with the sight, and as such must use my power for good or risk losing my gift from Cethlion forevermore. There must be a way for me to make amends. Perhaps I can suggest another contractor, one whose fortune is waxing, not waning."

"No need," I replied smugly. "I just need to file my signed permit. You said a personal check would suffice."

Tina spun her chair and sat like she was trying to take a seat in a dark movie theatre while holding popcorn and watching the film. The leather-bound book thudded as it landed on the desktop, released from numb hands. Tina peered into my face, a look of awe in her eyes. "Your fire spirit is indeed powerful, more than I could see."

"Why is Tommy so upset with Evan? What happened there?" I asked, handing her the papers. I almost felt guilty, having provoked such a reaction, but I knew I hadn't done anything wrong.

Tina quickly examined each page, chuckling over Tommy's signature on the last one. "Everything is in order here," she said, placing the forms in a machine tucked in the corner to make copies. "Tommy's eldest daughter is married to him," she said in a surprisingly normal way. "And Evan recently moved out. Tommy thinks his daughter's reputation has been ruined and seeks vengeance." She paused before continuing, "He's ignorant about relations blessed by the Goddess, shrunken and deformed by the White Lady's premature claiming of his wife. I have tried to lead Tommy into the light, as have others, but——alas——all has been for naught. He is beyond reach."

"So, Tommy is Evan's father-in-law?" I confirmed.

"Yes," explained Tina, her voice growing ghostly. "My Third Eye has seen it. Tommy is a gnarled tree in the wasteland, his only two fruits landing pitifully in the rocks, finding no sustenance for growth. The tree sways in the wind, branches twisting and groaning. The sun fades and all is darkness," she continued waving her hands like she belonged on a stage.

"What?" I asked.

"Tommy wants grandchildren," sighed Tina, returning to a more normal tone. "His youngest is unmarried and thus far, Evan and Sandra haven't had any children. He's been pressuring Sandra, and now it looks like Evan and Sandra are splitsville."

"I see," I said. It explained so much. "So that's why Evan wanted me to get the permit, to avoid a run-in with his father-in-law, and why he wants to sublet my cottage." Evan must be living out of a suitcase just like I was.

"He does?" asked Tina. "I have not been blessed with a vision of this. Your spirit is indeed powerful. I need to seek Cethlion's guidance before the tree is cracked by the strong winds or burned by flame."

"What?" I asked, exasperated. "Why can't you just say what you mean?"

"The Goddess Cethlion grants me visions, and I must describe what I see. Besides, it is obvious enough. If Tommy believes Evan left Sandra for another woman, that will drive his anger. I must consult the Goddess to see if there is a way to keep his anger from destroying him."

Before I could reply, the door behind me flew open with a crash. I jumped and bumped the desk, knocking over a small vase of snapdragons. Tina howled and grabbed for the leather-bound book as water from the vase threatened it. I was bumped from behind and heard a curse and a crash as the intruder dropped whatever he had been carrying. I stumbled into the desk more fully, causing the vase to roll and fall, breaking upon impact, glass spreading across the floor like pebbles on a beach. I froze, as did Tina, and gave a sigh of relief when silence reigned.

"Sorry, Miss," croaked a voice behind me. I glanced over my shoulder, seeing a gangly man clutching a half dozen architecture tubes with three or four others around his feet. The tubes twisted like batons, and the man was at best a novice majorette. I quickly grabbed a tube as it fell, earning a grin of thanks from the awkward man. I took another, and he was able to corral the remaining tubes. "Let me put these down, and I'll just slip out and see if a janitor is available to help clean up this mess. I'm such a buffoon," he lamented.

The man dashed to an office, the one with Clyde Petersen stenciled on the glass, and I heard another bang and a curse from inside. I exchanged a look with Tina, who was still clutching the leather-bound book like it was her only child.

"I have attracted the eye of Dwynn," Tina moaned. "I failed you, and the Goddess protects me not. Look at this mess."

I picked up the remaining tubes on the floor and handed my collection to the man as he reappeared. "I'll need that update on the permits for the Carlyle," he said to Tina as he headed back into the office to deposit the drawings. "The folks in Birmingham want to move forward."

"Tommy has not finished his review, Clyde," exclaimed Tina to his retreating back.

"The Mayor will not like to hear that!" yelled Clyde from his office. "We need that paperwork ASAP," he continued from his door. "And Tina, the Mayor has heard more complaints. You need to tamp it down. I know he's your uncle, but even his patience is limited."

"I cannot forsake my gift!" Tina pleaded.

"I know, I know," replied Clyde, holding his hands up like he was calming a nervous pony. "No one is asking you to. Just…have your visions at home maybe…and try not to talk about goddesses or spells at work."

"I'll try," she said quietly. "I've been working with Ms. Thies this morning, and everything has been just fine," she said with a hopeful glance my way.

Clyde turned to me, raising the eyebrow over his left eye inquiringly. I said something noncommittal, and he grunted as he headed into the hall, muttering about finding the janitor.

"Thank you," mouthed Tina silently once Clyde had vanished. "Clyde is a good man, an honorable man, but not always an understanding man. And he is a bit clumsy," she sighed. "I am in your debt."

"Think nothing of it," I said. I then asked about a health permit and learned that Marion Vinner handled that for the town. Her name was stenciled on the third and last glass door in the office. Tina claimed that Marion was a stickler for details and would not sign off easily. At least that was what I think she said, translating Tina talk was a bit of a challenge. There was also something about Tommy and Marion, but for the life of me, I couldn't decipher what. I figured the Wangs had just obtained a health permit to open Panda Garden, so I knew where I could go for less cryptic advice.

I finished up my business, got a copy of the building permit, and said my goodbyes when Clyde returned with the janitor. Tina offered a "Go with the blessing of the Goddess," which earned her a sharp look from Clyde. I still had several hours before I was due to meet Evan, and I'd promised Hank I'd check on Harry today while he was in Gadsden. Hank had taken a job down there to earn some extra cash to help pay off the lien on the farm. It meant long drives and less time for us to be together, but that was better than his alternative means of earning some cash.

The drive to the farm was uneventful, and I spent the lion's share of the afternoon with the ol' coot. The man was doing much better than when I'd first visited the farm after returning to Alpine. The booze was mostly gone from the house, and Harry was more likely to be in his wheelchair puttering around, than in the recliner before the television. The man could even fix himself a meal now. Yet Harry was still homebound, and it was hard for him to maneuver in the old place. Hank had mentioned wanting to build a ramp from the front porch to the sidewalk so that Harry could at least wander the house yard, but Hank had not found the time.

The sun was a golden ball in the west as I headed back to town for my meeting with Evan. I pulled into a spot next to a dark SUV, outside the place I hoped soon to call home, and unlocked the door. It looked no different than this morning, although to me it felt like progress had been made. I turned on the lights and placed the building permit on the counter next to the cash register. I grabbed the hammer that Evan had left at my request and contemplated the walls. I didn't want any particular pattern to the bricks showing through from beneath the stucco, but I knew I wanted more brick showing. I began to widen a hole in the stucco, causing debris to fall and dust to fill the air.

Before I knew it, I began to sneeze. Dust was everywhere and my eyes felt like I'd spent the afternoon in a pool with too much chlorine. I could not stop myself, sneezing every few seconds with no ability to control my body. My arms flailed as I staggered, and I swung the hammer like a Viking warrior gone berserk. Then someone grabbed me from behind, pinning my arms and plucking the hammer from my grasp before I caused permanent harm. I sneezed one last time, almost tossing my rescuer, as I slowly regained control of my body. I turned and looked up into the green eyes of my savior——Evan Petrovich. My heart threatened to beat out of my chest, and I knew there was heat on my face. At that moment I heard a noise at the front door. Turning I saw Hank on the other side of the glass. His face was solemn, but there was murder in his eyes.

ChaptER 3

I woke early the next morning in the bed that had been mine since I was eight, the bedspread a colorful design filled with pastel butterflies I had picked out at age ten. I glanced at the dressing table, seeing the old pictures of Hank and me that I'd taped to the mirror during high school. I knew this situation was just temporary, a momentary setback that would vanish as my life became more settled, but it was still depressing.

I got out of bed and sorted through my suitcase, which I'd temporarily placed on the window seat. I found a pair of jeans that didn't look too dirty, and a green blouse I knew Hank liked. I gathered the necessities and headed to the bath for a shower. I could hear movement downstairs and knew that Mamaw was up and had coffee going. I'd brought over my machine from the cottage that brewed the single cups of flavored blends from individual plastic capsules, but Mamaw still seemed to prefer her old coffee pot. I wondered again if I'd misjudged, and if the Alpine palate was not ready for the coffee house I imagined. Certainly, if Mamaw was any guide, business would be slow, possibly to the point of glacial.

My cell buzzed as I started the water in the tub. It was Evan

Petrovich. After what had happened last night, I wasn't ready to speak to the man, so I let the call go to voicemail. While the water warmed, I sat on the edge of the tub and reflected upon how much I missed the claw foot at the cottage, and about the events of last night.

When I'd seen Hank in the window, I'd rushed out to speak to him, quite literally leaving Evan in the dust. Hank had turned away by then and was marching back to his truck like——well——like the pissed-off boyfriend he was. I'd grabbed his arm and had turned him to face me as I'd said, "Hank, where are you going? I thought we had a dinner date tonight." I'd flashed him a grin and could remember putting a hand to my hair to add a little bounce. I'd felt the grit and dust from the stucco.

"Who's he, Gracie? Look, never mind; I don't want to know," Hank had said, shaking his arm free.

"Hank, nothing happened."

"That's not what it looked like to me."

"I was sneezing from the dust and couldn't help myself. Evan grabbed me to keep me from harm. I should have used a mask, but I didn't. It was my fault," I'd explained.

"That's a statement I can agree with. It's your fault," he'd snapped.

"Hank!" I'd replied, letting a little of my Irish temper loose. "How dare you turn this into something that it isn't?"

"I saw you, Gracie, in his arms. I saw the look on your face," he'd said. I remembered how he'd frowned, the look of hurt in his eyes. "Look, I'm tired and don't want to fight. Not right now. I'm going home."

"But Hank…" I'd tried.

"You go home too," he'd interrupted, opening the door to his F150.

I'd called to him then, saying that nothing had happened, but Hank had ignored me. He'd gotten into his truck and pulled away as if I'd become invisible, leaving me standing on the street with hands clenched at my sides, holding in my anger. The man had been a stubborn fool, just like his father.

I'd returned to the building after the fight, where Evan and I'd had a stilted conversation, him apologizing and me stating that it wasn't his fault. Eventually, he'd left too, promising to start on the renovation early the next morning. He'd said he had some calls to make beforehand to have his men ready. I'd then spent my pent-up rage pounding on the walls, this time with a mask. Afterwards, I hadn't even swept the floors, leaving the mess and heading back to Mamaw's for the night. I'd spent another hour talking to Emily on the phone, telling her what had happened and generally complaining about my life.

The bathroom was steamy by the time I came out of my reverie, and I hopped into the shower. When I got out, I saw I'd missed another call from Evan and one from Emily. I got dressed and headed down the stairs checking my voicemail. The first was from Evan saying I needed to come downtown immediately, his voice shaky. I wondered what was wrong, my heartbeat quickening, and tapped on his second voicemail. In this one Evan's voice was calmer, but the content was more worrisome as he explained the police had arrived and wanted to speak with me. The last voicemail was from Emily, telling me in her own colorful way to answer my damn cell phone.

I reached the bottom of the steps and called to Mamaw in the kitchen, telling her that the police were looking for me. When I entered the space, I saw Mamaw sitting calmly at the table with a cup of coffee in hand and chatting with an officer in blue.

"I think they found you, dear," replied Mamaw, the policeman across from her standing as she did so. "You remember Bert, don't you? He was the nice young gentleman who escorted me to the station this summer for interviewing." I remembered Bert all right. I remembered him telling his partner to arrest me when I yelled to Mamaw about her gun being used to murder Edward. I remembered being slammed into the patrol car and having my arms twisted behind my back. Luckily, I sustained no permanent injuries, just a bruise or two, and damage to my ego.

"Ms. Thies," added Bert in an overtly official voice. "Chief Doeppers would like to have a word with you. He sent me to fetch you." Bert Lancaster was about my height with dark hair, parted to the side and stiff like the meringue on a pie. His navy shirt was slightly wrinkled and appeared to have a ketchup stain on it.

"Am I under arrest?" I asked more out of curiosity for how he would react than anything else. Bert had always struck me as a bit tentative, although his partner, Officer Yancey, had been much more aggressive. Thankfully, she'd taken a job down in Birmingham a month or so ago. Yancey and I had not gotten along.

"Well…no…but you're wanted for questioning," he said, ending much more forcefully than he'd started.

"Then I can get a cup of coffee first," I said, passing him by to grab a cup from the cupboard.

"I think Chief Doeppers is anxious to speak with you. You better just come along with me," Bert replied moving towards the back door.

"I'm sure the chief will want coherent answers," I explained, pouring coffee from the pot Mamaw had made. "And for that I need a cup of coffee first."

"She really does, Bert," inserted Mamaw. "Until she has that first cup, she's like a bear waking early from hibernation."

"Well, maybe you can bring it along," offered Bert, his gaze shifting from me to Mamaw and back again. I could see a bead of perspiration on his forehead. I remembered how Mamaw had treated him this summer, while Yancey had been escorting me to a jail cell. I began to feel a little bit sorry for the man.

"I'll drink it in the car," I conceded, heading for the door, and waving goodbye to Mamaw. Her nose was twitching, and I knew she'd be on the phone before the back door had closed. Mamaw was a central node in the Alpine gossip network, and this was too juicy not to pass along. I just hoped she'd spin it so that I didn't come off too badly. "Can you tell me what this is all about?" I asked Bert as we walked to the patrol car.

"I'll leave that to the chief," he replied, I could almost hear the relief in his voice.

Bert meandered through the neighborhood until he turned onto Main heading towards downtown. We passed under the banner advertising the start of Oktoberfest, and as we approached the building in which I hoped to open Gracie's Grounds, I saw several patrol cars parked out front with lights flashing. Bert pulled into a diagonal slot in front of the Pole & Arms and escorted me into the building, keeping a firm grip on my upper left arm. While I might not be under arrest, I wasn't exactly free either.

I entered the building and saw a crowd of officers milling about. There was a crumpled body in a pool of red on the floor to the left, a bloody hammer nearby. I felt my stomach drop, and quickly looked away before the sight unnerved me. I was not fond of blood. I saw Emily further back in the space, standing near Evan and two men I didn't know, but from their dress I suspected they were employees of Evan's. I nodded her way earning a worried grin as reward. A flash on my left pulled my eyes back to the body, and an image of a policeman parting graying hair for another officer to take a picture seared my mind. My world darkened and I felt my knees become rubber as I imagined brain matter splattered among all that red on the floor.

When I regained consciousness, I saw Emily's worried frown. She was hovering, using a collection of papers to blow some air towards my face. "What happened?" I asked, sitting up.

"You fainted," answered Emily, a note of relief in her voice. "Weakling."

"That's not fair," I sighed.

"You fell over like Sleeping Beauty when she pricked her finger on the spindle," she laughed.

"I did not," I said, feeling a blush on my face. "And I think you've been watching too many Disney movies."

"Yeah, well Eliza Anne is at that age. You up for answering a few questions?" she asked in a more professional tone. If Emily was done teasing that fast, I knew things were serious. Okay, I knew things were serious the moment I saw the body.

Emily helped me up and led me towards the back of the room where Chief Doeppers was stationed, sitting on a folding chair and holding court like a king. The man looked little different than when I'd last seen him this summer. His blond hair was still thinning, his middle-aged paunch was still growing, and his brown eyes still looked like they carried the weight of the world. Doeppers and I had a checkered past. I had spent the majority of my adult life believing the man was a crooked cop. Only since earlier this summer did I realize that Doeppers was an honest man. I still found it hard to like him though.

"Miss Thies," he intoned, turning to a fresh page on the little notebook of his that he carried everywhere. "I have a few questions for you."

"Who got bludgeoned?" I asked before he could say another word. I saw the skin tighten around his right eye, the only indication that I'd annoyed him. I knew I should behave and just answer his questions. But I also knew that I'd be here for hours no matter what I did, at least if my experience this summer was any indication, and he'd pester me with questions the entire time while answering few of my own. I just wanted to get in the first lick.

"Get that thing bagged," growled Doeppers to the men by the body. I watched as an officer, hands covered in rubber gloves, used just a finger and a thumb to lift the bloody hammer and place it in an opaque plastic evidence bag. I knew my fingerprints would be all over it. It was the same hammer I'd used on the walls the night before. Afterwards, the officer with a camera began taking pictures of where the hammer had been. "When were you last in the building?" Doeppers asked, returning to his questioning.

"Last night," I said. "I was here with Evan Petrovich until about six or six-thirtyish, and then he left and I stayed to work on the walls. I used the hammer, just so you know. I admit that. I locked up before eight and headed to Mamaw's house."

"And you spent the rest of the night there?" he asked. I was surprised he was ignoring the murder weapon; maybe he wanted me to forget about it.

"Yes. Mamaw can verify it. I had leftovers for dinner, meatloaf. And spent an hour talking to Emily on the phone afterwards. She can vouch for me."

"When were you on the phone?" he asked. "As precisely as you can remember."

I sighed and answered. He asked what we talked about, what I'd said to Mamaw last night, when I went to bed, and what I'd watched on television. He asked if I'd locked up last night, and who else had keys to the building. He asked what I'd done besides beat the walls senseless. I swore the man even wanted to know when I had my last bowel movement. And with each answer, he'd scribble, scribble, scribble in that little notebook of his. I knew it was part of his process. He'd compare my answers to those provided by others looking for inconsistencies and lies.

"You said you were working on the walls. Doing what? Looking for hidden treasure?" he smirked. I smiled back——the man thought he had a sense of humor. I explained how I planned to turn the space into a coffee house, and how I wanted the walls to look. He snorted again at that but wrote it down anyhow.

"Do you know Tommy Hilgeman?" Doeppers asked. He was staring intently, as if searching for a reaction.

"Was Tommy the victim?" I asked.

"Why do you ask?" he said.

"Why did you?" I echoed.

"Please just answer the question," he said.

"Yes," I replied. If Tommy was the victim, I had some explaining to do, as did Evan. This could get a little dicey. "Tommy's a bridge player, and as you probably know, he issues building permits here in town. I needed his signature for the permit to renovate this place."

"So, you have a permit?" Doeppers asked.

"Yes, a copy of it should be around here somewhere," I said looking around. "I left it last night. It's supposed to stay on the premises in case it's needed."

"When did you see Tommy last?" Doeppers asked.

I explained about the confrontation yesterday at the bridge club, and what I could remember about what was said. Doeppers' eyes lit up, and I knew I'd just put Evan on the suspect list. With the rumors floating about, he would have made the list regardless of what I said.

As I was finishing my tale, I heard a screech and stood to look towards the street. I saw a platinum blond in her late 20's rush to the door from a navy SUV, pulling driving gloves from her hands as she did so. The woman burst through the door and shoved her way to Tommy's body, dropping to her knees and wailing. Bert had tried to grab her but had been a little too late. Then Doeppers was there, pulling her away and guiding her to the other side of the room, issuing soothing noises. I hadn't even realized the man had passed me by, he'd moved so quickly.

With the addition of the hysterical woman, I knew my interview was over for the moment. However, I also knew that if I tried to leave, someone would just stop me. Doeppers liked to keep everyone close until he had all his questions answered. I walked over to where Emily was standing with Evan and his two employees. One was a Latino man about my age with dark wavy hair and clean skin. The other was a pimply teenager, skinny as a rail, with a mop of dark hair that needed combing. My inner mother itched to tell the boy to stop slouching. "Who's the woman?" I whispered to Emily with a subtle nod to the newcomer. The blonde seemed calmer now, but her weeping hadn't stopped.

"That's Sandra Petrovich," offered Emily quietly.

"You shouldn't have stopped me," seethed Evan. "I should be allowed to comfort my wife." I glanced his way and shuddered. The man looked as angry as Samson in the temple of the Philistines before the walls came tumbling down.

"You know you can't talk to her, not until we get this all sorted," replied Emily. "Besides, after your shenanigans, if she gets her paws on you, we just might have a double homicide."

"Listen," Evan said. "Sandra and me, we've had our problems. But that doesn't mean I don't care for her."

"Chief Doeppers won't stand for it and you know that. Just keep your pants on and let him sort through this mess," replied Emily.

I saw Evan and the Latino man exchange knowing glances while the teenager picked his nose. Again, my inner mother itched to admonish the boy. "I don't believe we've been introduced," I said, indicating the two men.

"This is Manny," offered Evan. "He's the foreman when I'm not around. That's Douglas over there. Douglas, stop that!" said Evan.

"What?" replied Douglas, wiping the snot on his pants, causing Evan to sigh.

"Hola," offered Manny with a smile almost as devastating as Evan's. "It is——how do you say?——a pleasant."

"Pleasure," I offered with a smile. "My name's Gracie, Gracie Thies."

"My English is not so bueno," he grinned.

"Humph," snorted Emily. "You done yet?" she asked. "Got them there introductions done and all?"

"Emily," I replied. "It doesn't hurt to be polite."

"Well, you just got to be careful, Gracie. One of these three coulda' done it."

"Nunca," said Manny.

"Never," added Evan indignantly.

"Whatever," said Douglas rolling his eyes.

"Listen, all I'm saying is it's best to keep the barn door locked up tight. And by that, I mean your traps. Keep your mouths shut," said Emily glaring at each of us.

I sighed and turned my attention back to the room at large. Doeppers had taken Sandra aside so that her back was to the body, and was asking her questions, his little notebook out as he scribbled away her answers. A few other officers were still taking pictures of the scene, but I could tell that they were almost finished.

My stomach growled, causing Emily to look at me sideways and roll her eyes. I grinned sheepishly, thinking how I'd missed breakfast this morning and had only had the one cup of coffee. The coroner arrived with a gurney in tow, and I averted my gaze to the back of the building while they examined the body. I didn't want a repeat of my earlier fainting spell. I saw sunlight on the floor of the storage room through the open doorway and deduced that the back door must be propped open. That made me wonder how Tommy had gotten in here in the first place, I'd closed everything up tight before I'd left last night.

"Was everything locked when you got here this morning?" I asked Evan, still keeping my eyes averted from the grisly scene near the body. I didn't want to chance seeing any blood, especially if it spurted.

"Manny and I came together, and we parked in front. Douglas arrived after us," answered Evan.

"Yah, we come together, Señorita," corroborated Manny.

"The front door was locked, and I used the key you gave me to gain access. That was when we discovered the body."

"Stop talkin'," barked Emily. "No comparing notes."

"I was just wondering," I said, earning a glare from Emily.

"When we saw the body, I called the police immediately, and then I called your cell. I called your cell again after the police arrived," complained Evan.

"I said to stop talkin'," interrupted Emily. "If you don't keep your traps shut, I'll hogtie ya' and put an apple in your mouth like I was serving ya' for Thanksgiving dinner." Evan exchanged a glance with Manny and rolled his eyes like Emily had earlier, and Douglas before her. We had a regular eye rolling party going on.

My stomach growled again, and this time it was loud enough to attract the attention of not only Emily, but Evan and Manny as well. "Emily," I asked, "how much longer is this going to take? I'm getting hungry."

"You just can't stand here quietly, can you?" she snapped. "You just can't wait and let Doeppers do his job? You gotta' flap your tongue like some goose after the gander."

"Goose...gander?" asked Manny confused.

"I was just asking a question. I missed breakfast is all," I complained.

"She just means that Gracie talks too much," explained Evan.

"Like a Kardashian," muttered Douglas.

"Enough," Emily yelped. "Evan, you go stand next to the wall there, and, Douglas, you stand against that there other wall. Manny, sit. Right here," she said pointing downwards. As the boys followed her directions, Emily grabbed my arm and dragged me towards Doeppers, muttering into my ear. "Keep your damn head down, Gracie. Let Doeppers do his job and stay out of this one." Emily pulled me up to the Chief who'd just asked Sandra a question about where she'd parked last night.

"Further down Main. Daddy had parked in this direction," she answered with a sniffle.

"Jon," interrupted Emily. "I can't keep those nitwits from yappin' and Gracie here has a stomach growl that can be heard in Texas." Almost on cue my stomach growled again. "Can we release any of 'em?"

Doeppers turned a steely gaze my way and snorted. He didn't look happy at being interrupted. "Emily, take Gracie down to Margaret's and feed her," he said. "Then hightail it back here. I should be done with Mrs. Petrovich by then. I have a few more questions for Miss Thies. There are other details I still need." As Emily dragged me away, I heard Doeppers call aloud, "Bert, go back and keep an eye on those three. And keep them from talking!"

Emily pulled me out the front door and a flash blinded me as I stumbled. Once my eyes recovered, I saw Brandi-With-An-I, camera in hand, smirking like she'd just caught a record-breaking catfish.

Chapter 4

"Brandi," said Emily. "Damn, girl, you nearly blinded me. Whaddya' think you're doin' sneaking around like some peeping Tom outside a high school girl's window?"

"Just getting the front-page photo for tomorrow's Alpine Tribune," she laughed. "I can see the headline now—— Alpine's very own 'black widow,'" she said using air quotes.

"You can't print that," I said miffed. The menace followed as Emily pulled me down the sidewalk; apparently, we were walking to Margaret's.

"Wouldn't she have had to marry 'em?" asked Emily.

"True, I suppose," pondered Brandi-With-An-I. "Maybe 'Alpine's Grim Reaper' would be better."

"You print anything like that, and I'll sue," I snapped again, pulling my arm free from Emily's grasp. Why wasn't Emily chasing her away? Technically, I was in police custody and should be under their protection. I didn't want to mention that aloud though and give more ammunition to that scoundrel who claimed to be a reporter. She was worse than a horsefly at a picnic.

"Oh, just shut your trap," growled Emily to me. "You've

caused enough fuss already."

"Ooh, what did she do in there?" asked Brandi-with-an-I, a cat ready to pounce.

"None of your business," I squawked. Inwardly, I cringed——I sounded like Mamaw when the neighborhood dog had gotten into the trash. And all the outburst bought me was one of Brandi-With-An-I's patented smirks.

"Would you two stop," snapped Emily. "Y'all are worse than when Eliza Anne was teethin' while Jon Junior had the chickenpox. I survived that and I'm not going to put up with it from you two."

"She started it," I complained, pointing to Brandi-With-An-I. "I just want to be left alone."

"As if!" she retorted. "Princess here comes marching back into this town after a mysterious hiatus in Europe, stumbles upon a dead body, is caught naked with a second body, and now is connected to a third. And when I ask for a quote, she clams up and won't give me one."

"That was not my fault," I said. "I had nothing to do with any of them."

"Well, it sure looks fishy to me, Princess Ariel," replied Brandi-With-An-I smugly. Apparently, I was a mermaid now.

"Stop, you two," Emily said, turning around to look at both of us at once. We were standing side by side, stopped on the sidewalk with no one around. "Brandi, I have known Gracie since grade school, and we have been friends ever since. Hell, she's more like a sister to me than Tammy ever was. And Gracie, Brandi here was my only friend when I first divorced Jon. It was not easy divorcing the police chief in a town this size. She actually introduced me to my Henry, though I'm not sure if that was more of a favor to him or to me," she laughed. "You two are my best friends. I just wish you could try and get along."

I looked from Emily to Brandi and then back again. I guessed she wasn't all that bad, just pushy. I supposed as a reporter she had to be, and as a woman reporter in a small town especially. I took a deep breath and then said, "I'll try." I hoped I wouldn't regret it.

"Me too," said Brandi reluctantly. "But I'm still putting that photo on the front page," she continued as she began walking again, pulling Emily with her.

"Brandi!" I cried, hurrying to catch up to the two.

"Tell me," said Brandi. "Does the chief have a suspect? Does he know who killed Tommy Hilgeman?"

"Even if I knew, I couldn't tell y'all," snorted Emily. "And how did you know it was Tommy?"

"Don't print that picture," I said. "I'm warning you."

"Oh hush," said Brandi to me. "I have my sources. How was he murdered? It was murder, right?"

"Damn, girl, y'all are pushier than Jon Junior at the fair. The chief will give ya' a statement soon enough," Emily said. "And if those sources are who I think they are…"

"Bah, that man is more boring than watching the Tide play Vandy," said Brandi. "And slower than molasses. I need something now. How was Tommy killed?"

"And get Jon pissed at me? Again? I swear that man would fire me if he could, and that's mostly because of you."

"Blunt force trauma. To the back of the head," I said. I'd read enough mysteries to know the proper words, even if I didn't like thinking about the blood. "Now about that picture."

"Really." said Brandi glancing my way with a little smirk. "How interesting. And will you corroborate that, Emily? Off the record, that is."

"What have I caused!" cried Emily with hands raised to the air.

"Well, you said you wanted us to be friends," said Brandi, pulling me to her so she could place an arm around my shoulders and act all friend-like. I shook her off me like a hound dog trying to dislodge a flea.

"Like two rats in the hay barn, you two," laughed Emily.

"More like a cat and dog, I think," I said.

"Don't mix your pickles, Schatzi," said Brandi.

"What?" I asked, looking at her.

"It was a phrase my German teacher used in high school. She said it whenever we mixed our metaphors," she explained. "In German you would say, Mischen Sie nicht ihre Gurken, Schatzi."

I rolled my eyes to Emily, and she laughed, causing Brandi to snort, and that made us all laugh. We hurried across the street and walked through the parking lot into Margaret's Diner where Emily led us to a back booth. We each picked up a menu, although I already knew what I'd order. A pair of eggs over easy with grits would hit the spot just right. Margaret came and took our order, glaring like we were barefoot and shirtless. I wondered what Brandi had done that caused Margaret to act so rudely. And who orders a kale omelet with chives? Was that even on the menu? I just hoped Margaret would return to her friendly self the next time I came in with Mamaw.

"Wonder what's got her panties in a wad," pondered Emily.

"Brandi," I muttered under my breath.

"Gracie," stated Brandi at almost the same time. "Now, Emily, give me something, off the record of course," she continued, pulling her own little notebook out to take notes.

"What?" I asked, confused. Why had she mentioned my name?

"I got nothin' for you," stated Emily.

"But I need something by press time," lamented Brandi.

"Wait a minute, what did you say about Margaret?" I interrupted.

"Nothing important," Brandi said to me. "Now, do you know the time of death? Did it happen last night?" she asked Emily.

"You need to talk to the chief," stated Emily.

"You think Margaret is mad at me?" I asked.

"Is she always this dense, or only after a murder?" Brandi snidely asked while gesturing to me.

"Brandi, you promised to play nice," chided Emily.

"Wait a minute," I said. I didn't need Emily to fight my battles with Brandi-With-An-I. "Margaret hates you, not me."

"Oh, don't be ridiculous; Margaret and I go way back."

"Why would Margaret be mad at me?" I asked.

"Because," Brandi explained in a huff. "You're opening a coffee shop just down the road from the diner. You're going into competition with her, and Margaret doesn't need that right now. It's tough enough to keep a business going the way it is."

"I've never seen the place open without her," offered Emily thoughtfully.

"But I'm not really going into competition with her. The coffee house will be completely different from the diner," I explained.

"Well, you have to convince Margaret of that, not me," replied Brandi. "Now about the murder. Inquiring minds will want to know."

"There's nothin' I can say," Emily replied exasperated.

"Y'all just havta' wait for Jon's official statement."

"I can't miss tomorrow's deadline," Brandi reasoned. "The gossip mill in this town will have chewed it up and spit it out by then."

"Mamaw is on the phone already," I said with a smirk, causing Brandi's face to bleach white. "Started this morning."

"Emily, please," begged Brandi. "Give me something. Don't make me go to my other source."

"What other source?" I asked, intrigued.

"Brandi is talking about Bert," replied Emily with a laugh. "She doesn't want to have to go flirt with him again."

"Last time it cost me a date in Gadsden at the movies," Brandi shuddered. "He wanted to hold hands. The man has sweaty palms."

"And afterwards?" Emily asked with a gleam in her eye.

"I don't want to talk about it," answered Brandi, quickly shaking her head.

Margaret came with our orders, and the omelet Brandi had ordered looked better than some of the breakfast items I used to get on Mode de Blanc in Paris. On the other hand, my two eggs were closer to hard fried than over easy, and the small pile of grits was cold. Crap, Brandi had been right.

We ate in silence for a few minutes; well, I mostly watched the other two eat as there was little on my plate that was appetizing. When we finished, Brandi left a twenty on the counter, saying she would cover Emily's eggs on toast. I dropped a five, just enough to cover the cost of my meal with a little extra. Brandi huffed upon seeing my lack of an adequate tip, but I wasn't about to give Margaret a bonus for such a poor excuse of a breakfast.

We started walking back downtown, towards what I hoped would become Gracie's Grounds. It didn't take Brandi long to start in again. "About the murder," she asked. "Can you tell me anything?"

"There is nothin' to tell," said Emily. "Well, nothin' that y'all don't know already."

"Okay then, how about just confirming the facts I do know so that Larry will let me print them," she said hopefully.

"Larry?" I asked.

"She means Larry Thigpen, the owner and editor of the paper," replied Emily.

"He wants a reliable source for everything that appears in print, and if it's anonymous, he demands two," complained Brandi.

"Sounds reasonable to me," I replied.

"But damn inconvenient," laughed Emily. "Go ahead and shoot. Jon will just have to deal."

"Okay, Tommy Hilgeman was found dead in Cobbler's Corner this morning," she ventured, sounding like she was composing the story in her head.

"Not Cobbler's Corner," I objected. "Call it the future site of Gracie's Grounds."

"As if anyone would know where that was," Brandi snorted.

"I will confirm that," said Emily. "About Tommy, that is."

"And the cause of death was blunt force trauma to the back of the head," continued Brandi with a thankful glance my way.

"It appears so, but there's no coroner's report yet," added Emily.

"Duly noted," said Brandi. "And the place was locked when the body was found, right?"

"Is that a question or are you looking for confirmation?" asked Emily.

"A question," Brandi admitted sheepishly.

"I locked the place up tight before I left last night," I

offered. "And Evan Petrovich said the front door was locked this morning."

"Ah," said Brandi triumphantly. "Can you confirm the front door of the building was locked before the body was found?"

"Brandi," Emily said. "You can't print that. Jon will have a conniption fit. I swear he will haul your ass in and sit you down like a toddler who's eaten too much candy on Halloween. And Gracie, you need to learn how to keep your mouth shut."

"But I thought you wanted us to be friends," I said with a grin.

"I've changed my mind," she replied. "I think I liked it better when you two were nipping at each other's heels like a pair of Chihuahuas."

We arrived back at the future site of Gracie's Grounds. Brandi looked frustrated when she was barred from entering, which somehow made me feel a bit better. The body was long gone, and someone had thoughtfully put a tarp over the area where it had been, covering any lingering red. I hoped the floor wasn't ruined by blood and gore. There were only a few people remaining. Bert was watching Manny and Douglas, while Doeppers was interviewing Evan. Doeppers looked our way and stood, and I heard him tell Evan as he approached us that he would return shortly.

"Miss Thies, I just have a few more questions and then I think you will be free to go, for the moment that is," Doeppers said to me. "Officer Stevenson, will you please keep Mr. Petrovich company." Emily gave me a rueful smile, and then went over to where Evan was sitting. Doeppers led me out of earshot of the others and then asked, "You said earlier that you locked up the building and headed home, around 8:00 p.m., correct?"

"It may have been a little before that. I don't remember. I

did call Emily though on my cell from Mamaw's house. That was pretty soon after I got home."

"I see," he said scribbling in his notebook. "And tell me about your closing up procedure."

"I don't really have a process yet. It's still all new to me," I explained. I shut my eyes to think about what had happened the night previous. "I locked up the back first, and then turned off the lights. I remember needing to use my cell as a flashlight to light the way so that I didn't trip over the mess on the floor. I left by the front door, locking it behind me."

"I see," said Doeppers scribbling in his notebook.

"Wait, the floors!" I said, making a connection. "These floors should be filled with dust and stucco debris. Somebody has swept in here."

"Who had keys to the building, Miss Thies?" Doeppers asked annoyed. Apparently, he didn't like anyone making deductions but him.

"I don't know," I said. "I just gained possession yesterday and I haven't had a chance to change the locks yet. I gave my second set of keys to Evan Petrovich. I'm sure Ida Bea has a set, but I don't know who else. Maybe the Strange sisters—— Mary Jane and Mary Sue. They owned and operated Cobbler's Corner for years in this space. I'm not sure of any others." I made a mental note to ask Ida to have the locks changed, and that needed to happen soon. The question was, who would have come in here after me and swept the place? Did it have anything to do with the murder? And how did Tommy Hilgeman end up here anyhow? Could the murderer have set a trap for the man?

"You mentioned earlier having a building permit for the renovation work, and that Tommy had signed it. May I see it?"

"I left it on the bar over by the cash register. Didn't you find it earlier?" I asked. I hadn't seen anything of the paperwork since last night.

"There were no papers near the register, Miss Thies," Doeppers said intently.

"Look," I said. "I had the signed form and filed it yesterday. You can ask Tina Thompson at the courthouse. She should remember me. Or ask Otis Greer. He was there when Tommy signed it." Could Tommy have broken in to steal back the building permit and been attacked? But then who would have swept the floors?

"I'll speak with both of them," replied Doeppers, scribbling away. "I hope you realize that until I can verify some of the aspects of your statement that you will remain a person of interest."

"Yes," I sighed, remembering the ordeal from the summer. "And that means no leaving town without speaking to me first."

"And furthermore, any discussion of what you witnessed here or what happened last night will be considered interference in my investigation," he said. "No talking." When I nodded, Doeppers continued, "I'm glad you understand. We'll be finished here shortly. You should be able to proceed with your...work...on the walls by tomorrow afternoon. We will use Mr. Petrovich's keys to lock up before we go." The man nodded to me and turned, flipping through his notebook, and heading to speak with one of his officers. I had been dismissed.

I looked towards the back of the space. Manny looked worried, as did Evan; Douglas just looked bored. Evan and Manny kept exchanging glances, and they wore almost matching grim expressions. I hoped that no one on Evan's crew had committed the crime, but I didn't know any of them from Adam. I supposed any one of them could have murdered

Tommy, either working together or separately. With what I'd learned yesterday, Evan had a motive. Tommy was trying to drive him out of business by refusing to issue building permits. And something had happened between Evan and Sandra, causing Tommy's ire to begin with. There might be enough there. If Manny depended on the business for his own livelihood, then indirectly he had been threatened by Tommy as well. Could Evan have made a copy of the keys for Manny? Evan said Manny was the foreman when he needed to be elsewhere. Did that entitle Manny to a set of keys? If so, did Manny get his keys yesterday and did he come by to check out the work site? Had he decided to sweep the floor, was confronted by Tommy, and in the resulting argument had committed murder?

And what about Tommy? He'd been willing to use his position in town for a personal vendetta against Evan. Was that a one-time thing, or was that part of a pattern? I remembered from this summer that Edward Schultz had threatened to sue because of construction delays on the Carlyle. Those delays had contributed to Edward's cash flow problems and eventually contributed to his murder by Wilhelm Bea. Had those delays been caused by Tommy?

I sighed and stopped the woolgathering. I had nothing upon which to build a theory and besides, it was none of my business. I would do as Emily had suggested and keep my head down. I would let Doeppers and the police solve this one. No point in sticking my neck out and getting it chopped——well bludgeoned——in this case. I shivered, thinking of the bloody hammer smashing down upon me. I needed to get out of here before my imagination got away from me.

I left the building and looked up and down the street. Thankfully Brandi-With-An-I was nowhere in sight, but neither was the Mustang. It was then that I remembered I had arrived in the patrol car with sweaty-hands Bert. I considered going back into the building and asking for a ride but decided to try Mamaw instead. Of course, I got a busy signal. My stomach growled and I tried Mamaw's cell instead. No luck, but I left a message. I was hungry and wanted another cup of coffee. Margaret's was out; I wouldn't be eating there anytime soon. That left Bill's BBQ or Panda Garden. Okay, that really just left Panda Garden. Bill's BBQ was not a place I enjoyed, too much protein and testosterone for my tastes. I walked down the block past the Pole & Arms and towards the courthouse. Thankfully, the restaurant opened at 11:00 on weekdays, and so I only had to wait about five minutes before the doors opened.

I entered and waved to Mr. Wang, the owner and operator. He gestured to the dining area with a wide grin that showed his yellowing teeth. I picked a booth about halfway down against the side wall and sat facing the front. Hanging above the table was a panorama scene of the Great Wall of China, somehow lit from behind so that it glowed, and the seats were scarlet red upholstery with subtle patterns of Chinese characters in a slightly deeper hue. Chopsticks sat on the table to my left and regular cutlery was on my right with a menu between. I picked it up and began studying. While I had visited Panda Garden a handful of times already, I didn't know the menu quite as well as the one at Margaret's.

"How I help you?" asked Mr. Wang in broken English.

"Can I have chicken-fried rice and a Diet Coke?" I asked.

"Yah," he said nodding, jotting a number in Mandarin on his pad.

As he turned, a thought occurred to me and I asked, "Mr. Wang, did Tommy Hilgeman dine here last night?"

"Mr. Hilgeman?" Mr. Wang asked, turning to me and

flashing those yellow teeth. "Yah. He here with daughter. Had crispy duck and muko muko Tsing Tao beer."

"When did he leave?" I asked, curious. Tommy must have eaten here just before being murdered. Crispy duck had been his last meal. I decided to avoid duck for a while.

"Yah, he ate late. Bad spirit. No good. Not like crispy duck," Mr. Wang said, his smile fading with the memory.

"But when did he leave?" I asked.

"Bad man. No good," continued Mr. Wang, shaking his head negatively with an exaggerated frown on his face. "You good woman. No yell. No complain. Happy, Yah?" he said patting me on the shoulder and walking away.

So, Tommy had eaten here last night, and had been drinking. Could he have gotten into a drunken brawl with someone? No, that didn't make any sense with how and where the body was found. And how did Tommy get into a locked building? Someone else must have a copy of the keys, and that someone might be the murderer.

My cell rang and I pulled it out to see Mamaw was calling. I hit talk and before I could say anything, Mamaw had begun, "Gracie, are you all right?" she asked. "I just got your voicemail."

"I'm fine," I said. "Just stuck downtown. I'll need a ride home later."

"Oh dear, and what happened with the police?"

"It's not good, Mamaw." I said. "Tommy Hilgeman——"

"——is dead. Yes, I heard," she interrupted. "Found bludgeoned, a baseball bat to the back of the head."

"Really?" I said. I knew better than to correct her, not with what Doeppers had said. "How did you hear?"

"Oh, Gladys Chisholm told me. And after that awful row you had with him yesterday at the club."

"How did Gladys know?" I asked, intrigued. It always amazed me how much Mamaw could learn through the rumor mill, when it didn't scare me to the tips of my toes, that is.

"Oh, I don't know dear, you know how gossip flies in this town. Maybe it was the coroner. They're neighbors you know," Mamaw explained. "So did the police hear about the incident at the club? Is that why they wanted to speak with you?"

"Actually, Tommy's body was found at Gracie's Grounds," I said.

"Oh, no," said Mamaw. "Oh, Gracie. You simply must halt these plans of yours to open a coffee shop. I'll call Ida immediately and just tell her to tear up that lease. You can't build a business there now. How morbid. What will people think?"

"Mamaw, you play bridge in a building that had a murder not three months ago. Remember, I discovered the body," I said.

"Well, that's different, dear," she said.

"How?" I asked. I mouthed a thank you to Mr. Wang as he placed my chicken-fried rice and sweet tea in front of me.

"Because you're my granddaughter," she said indignantly.

"Listen," I said. "I just got my food. After lunch I'm going to walk to the cottage and do some packing. Can you come by later this afternoon and pick me up?"

"You mean you're finally going to move in here?" asked Mamaw excitedly. "I think that sounds wonderful. This old house is just too big for just one person."

"Mamaw, I said I was packing. That doesn't mean that I plan on moving back home."

"You aren't moving to the farm, are you? I know you and Hank are close, but, Gracie, it's just not done. What will people say?"

"I'm going to eat. My food is getting cold. Bye now," I said, hanging up before Mamaw could get another word in.

I ate my lunch in silence, noting that Mr. Wang only had a few patrons. I hoped that didn't signify a lack of a lunch crowd generally. If so, Gracie's Grounds might be as doomed as Pompeii. Unfortunately, Mr. Wang wouldn't answer any more of my questions, and so I left fairly quickly after finishing. I passed by my shop on the way to the cottage and dashed under the covered portion to peer in the front door. The place was empty, but still had police tape across the doorway to restrict access. I didn't know if that meant Chief Doeppers was ready to release the scene or not. He'd said they'd be finished tomorrow afternoon, but maybe he'd finished more quickly than he'd thought. That or maybe they had taken a lunch break. I sighed and continued my walk towards the cottage. Even if Doeppers was done, there was nothing I could do at the moment. It was Evan and his men who needed to gain access.

And that reminded me of the missing building permit. I would need to visit the courthouse and see if Tina could make me another copy. I stopped, thinking of heading in that direction now, but then started walking again towards the cottage. My copy of the permit might still appear, and if not, I could always stop by tomorrow. Besides, I didn't really need the permit until Doeppers released the murder scene. Better to spend my time now packing up the cottage.

I walked down the block and passed Margaret's Diner across the street on my right. I'd have to find the time to have a frank conversation with Margaret and see if we could somehow find peace. Alpine was too small of a town to have feuds, and, besides, I didn't like Chinese food that much.

I continued walking, thankful that it was not too hot at midday. I reached the corner of Main and Elm and glanced to the

Bea residence. Ida lived in one of the more impressive Victorians in this historic town, with a wrap-around porch on the north and east sides and a round turret at the northwest corner. The upper floor had cedar shingles in a slate grey, while the bottom floor was pale-yellow. I didn't see her sedan in the circular drive and wondered where Ida had gone. With what had happened three months ago, and that menace of a reporter badgering her, Ida had become little more than a recluse. She only ventured out to a few safe places. At least that's what Mamaw had told me.

I turned the corner and walked the remaining distance to the cottage. As I approached, I saw Hank's F150 sitting in the drive.

Chapter 5

"Nora told me where I could find you," explained Hank, standing in the open back door. "I stopped by her house first and she said you were over here packing." Hank had been waiting in his truck and had followed me to the house when I'd passed by without a word. After the way he'd treated me last night, like some hussy who'd swoon at any man flexing a muscle, I wasn't ready yet to talk to him. Instead, I started unloading the kitchen cabinets. And then I realized I hadn't thought of packing materials, so all I was really doing was making a God-awful mess. "Gracie, what are you doing?" When I ignored him and continued to fruitlessly unload another cabinet, he tried again, "Please, Gracie, talk to me."

I turned and stomped my foot, suddenly feeling like a toddler pitching a tantrum. I banished the image and took a deep breath to settle myself; laughing now would not be good. Hank needed to learn he could not treat me the way he did last night, not if we were to have a future together. "So, you want to talk now? What about talking last night?" I asked as calmly as I could. I wasn't exactly calm, but maybe he wouldn't notice.

He flinched, so I knew he'd heard the irritation in my voice.

I hated that my Irish heritage made me so easy to read. Then he began, "Look, I'm sorry. I shouldn't have reacted that way. I was tired and was caught off guard. Who was he anyhow?"

"We have to be able to talk, Hank," I said. "Really talk. I don't feel like we talk at all anymore."

"It's been hard, Gracie," he said. "Everything is such a mess at home. And now..." he said, waving his arms at the dishes I'd unloaded.

"Don't you think I know that? Don't you think it's been hard on me as well?" I asked.

"Okay," Hank said. "I get it. Let's talk now. Who was that last night?"

"I'm not about to start that conversation. We have bigger fish to fry," I said. I was not going to let him turn this all back on me. I had nothing to be ashamed about, even if Evan's nuclear smile could cause a nun to swear off her vows. "What are you going to do about Harry?"

"Pop? What about him?" Hank asked confused.

"All you do is take care of him and work. And the work is to try and pay off the lien on the farm. Something that Harry caused, by the way."

"What do you want from me?" snapped Hank, hitting the door frame with a fist. "He's my father."

"He's a grown man who should be responsible for his own actions," I replied. Hank was coddling the old goat. Running himself ragged while Harry did nothing but complain.

"The man lost his legs. What do you expect?"

"I expect Harry to act like the adult he is, legs or not. When was the last time he left the house?" I asked.

"Gracie," Hank said, "you know how he is."

"How you let him be," I let slip. I began again. If only I could make Hank see the truth. "Hank, Harry has to be able to live his own life, and you yours. We need to move on." If only Hank could understand how dysfunctional his relationship with his father was. He just needed to give Harry the chance to take care of himself for once. He needed to let Harry gain back his pride.

"So, this is all my fault. Is that how it's going to be?" snapped Hank. "It's how I 'made him.' Well, I didn't cause the accident that cost Pop his legs. And I didn't seek comfort in another's arms, either."

"Oh, don't you dare, Hank," I said, seething. "This is about you and your father; it has nothing to do with me."

"Doesn't it though, Gracie? Doesn't it? We were surviving just fine until you came along. And you're the one pushing now, aren't you? How can this not be about you?"

"You call what I found this summer surviving? Harry was drinking himself silly most days and you were growing marijuana to make ends meet."

"At least ends were meeting," Hank stated. "And now what? I'm trying to work the farm while holding down two jobs, one down in Gadsden. I never get to see you, and when I do, I find you in the arms of another man."

"You just can't let that go, can you?" I snapped.

"Who was he, Gracie?" Hank asked.

"I think you should leave," I said. "Go see your father; you seem to prefer him to me!"

As soon as the words left my mouth, I regretted them. It sounded too much like an ultimatum, too much like the jealous woman I'd become. I prayed that Hank would balk, would refuse to go. I wanted him to demand to have a life, a life with me. I wanted him to choose his love for me over his father.

I didn't get what I wanted.

"Fine, have it your way," he said, turning and leaving from the doorway.

I rushed to the back door but didn't chase Hank down the drive. I felt my chest tighten, my lungs short of breath, as tears began to flow from my eyes. Hank turned to look back at me once, when he opened the door to his truck, but he didn't say anything. His eyes met mine and through my tears I could see my pain reflected in his. The moment passed though, and his mouth hardened into a grim line. And then he was gone.

I retreated to the kitchen table and sat with my face in my hands as the tears came. Why had I pushed Hank so hard about his father? How had I expected him to react? The man was under tremendous pressure, trying to raise money to make the mortgage payments on the farm. If only Harry hadn't gotten into that accident with Clovis Jones, and if only the resulting court case hadn't gone so poorly with the large judgment. The excessive award included funds for a permanent injury Clovis did not have. During the summer I'd gotten hold of a video of Clovis that proved he'd lied. Hank had appealed the judgment, but there had been no action yet. Hence, Hank was stuck in limbo, and me there with him. Why couldn't I have been more patient?

I stood, wiping the tears away, trying to put the fight behind me. There was nothing I could do now. I'd just have to talk to Hank later, after we both had calmed down. We could still build a life together. This was not the end, at least I hoped it wasn't.

I felt as wrung out as a farmhand after a day tasseling corn. Dishes covered half the counters, the doors of empty cabinets hanging open. I didn't feel like packing anymore, but I felt like being around people even less. I walked to the smaller of the two bedrooms and stared at the bookshelf that held the sparse collection of paperbacks that I'd not yet had the chance to read. I needed an escape, and so picked up a dog-eared Agatha Christie that I'd purchased at the used bookstore during my last trip to Gadsden. I'd read it first years ago when I'd discovered my love for mysteries in high school. It was a Hercule Poirot, the one where he and three other detectives were invited to a dinner party with four murderers. During a friendly game of bridge after the meal, the host was murdered, and it was up to Poirot to discover the identity of the murderer before anyone else got killed. I retreated to the couch and curled up with the novel, but couldn't find the escape I sought. Too much had happened, and I felt like I had no control over my life.

I sat there, brooding, for I didn't know how long before Mamaw came for me. She entered without knocking, as was her custom. Mamaw knew immediately that something had happened——the woman could read me——and so I told her everything. I told her about the fight with Hank, and how he'd misinterpreted what he'd seen last night. I told her about my inadvertent ultimatum, and how Hank had reacted. She held me as I cried, muttering soft noises about how everything would turn out for the best. In time, I recovered, and we retreated from the cottage, locking and leaving the place the mess I'd made of it, almost like a reflection of my life.

The sun had fled by the time we returned to the Victorian in Mamaw's Buick. For dinner we had pot roast with cooked greens and peach cobbler that Mamaw had mixed up earlier in the day. I wasn't in the mood to talk, but Mamaw filled the silence with the gossip she'd heard that day. The phone had apparently been ringing nonstop, with several of her friends appalled that their little town had had two murders within such a small timeframe. And that was on top of the usual goings-on, of relationships forming and breaking.

"I feel so sorry for Sandra," Mamaw said, starting in on her dessert. "First her husband walks out on her and then her father is murdered. He's seeing another woman; I'm just sure of it. And being motherless no less, so the poor girl just has no one to talk to."

I muttered something noncommittal as Mamaw continued, "And Gladys is just beside herself. She wants to hold a memorial game for Tommy, just like we did for poor Edward after his murder, but Tommy wasn't as popular at the club as Edward was, well before folks knew what Edward had been up to, of course," Mamaw continued, a clear reference to the money that Edward had stolen. "Anyhow, Gladys is afraid that if we hold a memorial game that no one will come. I told her that was just silly; folks in this town would honor Tommy no matter how much of a rascal he'd been. It is, after all, a chance to play bridge."

I nodded, knowing it was expected. Mamaw was in a groove like the needle on a record, a broken record——I swore she'd started repeating herself.

"Ida agrees, of course. Speaking of, Ida has been through so much, don't you think, the poor soul? Not as much as you, mind, but imagine her husband murdering her bridge mentor and now a second body appearing in one of her buildings. She's beside herself, thinking she may be cursed or some such nonsense like that."

"Ida?" I asked. This was too much to take, not after the day that I'd just had. "Ida has been through so much?"

"Well, I said you'd been through more," she responded dismissively. "But you know, dear, Ida is much more fragile than you are. She'd just begun trying to get back out after all that had happened, and with that pest of a reporter almost stalking her. I told Ida to talk to a lawyer and get a restraining order. I'm about ready to call Larry Thigpen myself and complain. As editor, he really should have better control over his reporters," she continued.

"Look, Mamaw, I'm bushed," I said standing. I didn't want to hear more about how Ida's life had been disrupted. What did the woman think I'd been through? A mere tumble into Cacanaw Creek getting my hair wet? After all, it was Ida's husband who'd tried to murder me to cover up his own crime. "I think I'm going up to bed."

"At 7:00? Don't be ridiculous. Besides, we have a few things we need to discuss," Mamaw said on a more somber note.

After the years growing up in her household, I was all too familiar with the tone of voice Mamaw had just used. I knew this was not a discussion that I could delay. Mamaw was now on a mission, everything before this had been preliminary, noise to fill the silence. I sat dejectedly, knowing that "resistance is futile" as Jean-Luc Picard had once said on one of my favorite Star Trek episodes.

"Oh, stop sulking," Mamaw said, laughing. "It's not that bad. Coffee?" she asked, standing to make a pot.

I nodded and tried not to squirm like I had as a child. I knew full well that Mamaw could be like a bulldog with a bone, and I clearly was that bone tonight. I had a sudden urge for a cigarette, the first time I'd felt the pull of my addiction in a long time. I was almost two months free of the habit. I wondered what the trigger was: seeing a body, the fight with Hank, or the impending verbal drubbing by Mamaw. Maybe it was all three.

"Now, I know you had plans to move in with Hank," Mamaw primly began. "Well, that is clearly a pig without mud now. And you haven't slept in that house of yours in months.

It's time, honey, to move back home. Permanently."

"I had no plans to move in with Hank," I said confused. I knew Mamaw would have disapproved, not that her opinion would have stopped me. Deep down I knew I would have, but Hank had never asked.

"No need to save face with me, Gracie," Mamaw said. "I saw the dishes pulled out of the cabinets. I was there this afternoon holding you as you cried over that man. I always feared he'd hurt you again, like back in high school. As I've always said, 'what's past is past.'"

"This is not high school," I said. "And Hank and I have grown beyond that." I didn't want to talk about those days, and how because of Hank and his cousin John, I'd taken a drug rap at seventeen for marijuana possession. At least all I'd gotten was community service. At the time I was appalled, and it had ruined my reputation. Now I knew it could have been much worse.

"He chose himself and his family then, as he did today. You said so yourself, Gracie. People don't change."

"Let's back up a step," I said, not wanting to discuss my love life with Mamaw now——well, really, not ever. "I was not planning on moving in with Hank, and I am not moving in here either." I told her then about my conversation with Evan, and how he was going to convert, at cost, the space over the coffee house into a studio apartment. I told her Evan wanted to sublease the cottage, so that I could not only save on rent but also have a bit more cash flow to help get the business started. I explained that I was packing so that Evan could move in that much earlier. I admitted I would still need to stay here with her for a little longer, but that it would be short term until the space above Gracie's Grounds was habitable. Mamaw remained silent throughout, gradually turning whiter than a moonshiner hearing sirens.

"Oh dear," Mamaw muttered, after I'd finished.

I could tell something was wrong, like in bridge when the opponents leave in a low-level double. At the table you just know the cards are going to break badly. "Mamaw, what did you do?" I asked.

"Well, did I mention that Hank stopped by today looking for you?" she asked softly.

"No, but Hank told me that you told him where to find me," I said.

"Well, we had some words," Mamaw admitted. "And... after I told him where you were and what you were doing, I might have mentioned that I disapproved of you two shackin' up. You should have seen him, Gracie, the man looked like I'd hit him between the eyes with a two-by-four."

I groaned. Inconceivable. I felt like that little Sicilian in the Princess Bride movie trying to escape from the Man in Black, except I wanted to escape from my life. "Mamaw, on the phone I distinctly remember telling you...crap, all I said was that I was not moving home, didn't I?" Mr. Wang had delivered my chicken-fried rice right before I'd had the chance to tell Mamaw my plans. All she knew was that I was packing.

"Exactly!" crowed Mamaw. "And I know how hard you've looked for someplace else you could rent. If only Ida's carriage house was habitable. And so, the only logical deduction was that Hank had asked you to move to the farm with him."

"Mamaw, how could you?" I cried realizing now what had happened. No wonder Hank and I'd had a row. I thought back on the conversation; it was seared in my mind. I tried to see what Hank had seen, and it was not pretty. He saw me packing and must have been wondering what I was planning. He had mentioned that the farm was a mess, was he trying to gently tell me that I was not welcome? And he had wanted to know about Evan, searching for an explanation for what he'd witnessed the night before. That I remembered all too well. And all I'd done was push him on Harry. He really must have felt caught between his father and me. As he'd said, from his perspective, it had all been about me.

"I'm sorry," Mamaw said. "I didn't know. I thought...it doesn't matter," she admitted. "I shouldn't have said anything. I knew better, but Gracie, I worry about you and him. I'm not sure Hank is the man for you."

I took a shuddering breath. There was nothing I could do about Hank right now, but I could address a problem with Mamaw, one that was long overdue. "Mamaw, I want to be perfectly clear," I said, using words I'd rehearsed in my mind for months now. "I love you and respect you, but I cannot have you second guessing my choices like this." I could see the words hit her, like a hurricane punishing the Gulf Coast. "I have to live my own life, warts and all. You have to trust me enough to let me make my own decisions, even if they turn out to be mistakes," I said. I felt as anxious as a schoolgirl going to her first dance.

"But, Gracie, I saw what happened between you and Pierre. I don't want to see something like that happen to you again," she cried, wiping her eyes.

I knew then that I could never tell Mamaw the truth, what I'd discovered after Pierre's death, the Event-That-Changed-My-Life. If she learned that ugly truth, she would question every one of my decisions regarding men for the rest of her life. "What happened between Pierre and me happened, and I will not say that all those years were good ones, but it was my choice. It made me who I am today. Would you take that away from me?" I asked.

"Gracie," she shivered. I took Mamaw into my arms, comforting her as she had me earlier in the day. It lasted only a minute, but it felt like we'd passed a trial of sorts, had made it into a new country. "I'll try," she whispered.

"That's all I can ask," I smiled, hugging her for a moment again.

"Well, then," she said, wiping her eyes. "Well, then...let's see." she said trying to get her bearings. "I guess that means finding a new contractor."

"What?" I asked.

"Well, if you're going to open Gracie's Grounds and live above the coffee house, you'll need a contractor for the renovations," explained Mamaw.

"But I've hired Evan Petrovich for the job," I said.

"Didn't I mention it? Everyone is saying Evan will be arrested for murdering his father-in-law."

Chapter 6

The rest of the evening was spent in fruitless speculation. Mamaw and I spent another hour hashing out what she'd heard, and debating the merits of one theory over another on who committed the murder. It felt like being stuck on the Arc De Triomphe roundabout in Paris, unable to get off and repeatedly covering old ground. Eventually, even Mamaw had had enough, and I retreated upstairs to a fitful night. I dreamed of falling off the Eiffel Tower, with Hank watching impassively just out of reach. I didn't need a psychology degree to interpret that nightmare.

I woke groggy and irritable, and seeing the front page of the Alpine Tribune the next morning only made matters worse. I so wanted to scream my rage, but I knew Mamaw, sitting across from me at the kitchen table, would not approve. The headline wasn't 'Black Widow' or even 'Alpine's Reaper.' The headline read 'Alpine's Own Body Magnet' with accompanying picture in tow that the shrew, Brandi-With-An-I, had taken the day before. Emily was in uniform, holding my arm like she was the only thing keeping me upright, and I looked ready to swoon with my arm raised, partially covering my eyes from the sun. It was as if I was some flighty seventeenth-century lady who'd just seen her beau.

"Well, the article isn't that bad," intoned Mamaw gently, taking a sip of her morning coffee.

I quickly scanned the piece, seeing how my newly discovered nemesis had drawn parallels between Edward's murder and Tommy's. She'd even managed to sprinkle in how Wilhelm had died in my presence, as well as the detail that I was unclothed at the time. The article made me out as some weak-kneed, frightened wallflower flustered by the sight of death, and fainting as if the dead pulled me with them. How had she learned how I reacted to blood?

"This isn't bad?" I asked Mamaw. "She says here, and I quote, 'Gracie Thies has been discovered with three dead bodies, and twice fainted from the shock.'"

"Well, it could be worse," Mamaw said. "She could have made you out to be some vampiric hooligan, like a Mexican celebrating the Day of the Dead."

"Mamaw, the Day of the Dead is a celebration of life. It's not anything morbid," I explained, irritated. I could tell by the look on her face that she disagreed, and before I had a chance to say anything else, my cell rang. I grabbed for it and saw that Emily was calling. "I should take this, but we'll talk more about this later," I warned Mamaw.

I took my coffee and headed back upstairs to get ready for the day while I spoke to Emily. She began with an apology, saying she had no idea that Brandi would write something like that, let alone print it. I told her it wasn't her fault, but that I wanted nothing to do with Brandi from now on. She said she understood, although I could tell she was disappointed that the two of us were unable to be friends, and then we moved on to other items. She asked about my row with Hank, and I asked how she'd heard about it. She laughed at that, reminding me that little in this town could remain secret for long. I explained it was a misunderstanding, and then told her about my plans to convert the second story of the building downtown into a studio apartment. That led naturally into asking about Evan, and if he was a suspect.

"Aw, honey. You know I can't tell ya nothin' about the investigation. Jon would have my hide," Emily said.

"Look, I'm not trying to interfere. I just need to know if I should be looking for a new contractor," I explained. It would be a shame to lose Evan for the job. He'd understood what I wanted so well, but then again, if he was a murderer, I didn't want him.

"Hogs' tits, girl, no one can read those tea leaves," Emily said. "Maybe he done it, maybe not."

"Well, what am I to do then?" I asked, exasperated. "Mamaw says the gossip mill has Evan pegged for the murder." That was the most popular theory. Then again, some thought that it was a random killing or otherwise tied to his work for the city. A few speculated it was a romance that had gone bad.

"Damn, girl, you should know better by now than to listen to a bunch of old biddies. Half of what I do is run down those false leads for the chief. It's like chasin' hens in the farmyard. Girl, what ya' need to be askin' yourself——do you trust him? Do you think he done it?" Emily asked.

I thought then of what I knew of Evan, that nuclear smile, but more important than that, the way he looked when Sandra came crying into the shop and collapsed at her dead father's feet. Whatever had happened between the two of them, I knew that Evan still cared for Sandra deeply. He wouldn't have caused that hurt in her, not purposefully. Evan was not the killer. I knew that like I knew that the sun rose in the east. "No, I don't think he did," I told Emily.

"Well, then," Emily replied. "it sounds like ya' don't need a new contractor."

"Thanks, Emily," I laughed, somehow feeling a bit better. "I needed that. Any idea when the chief will allow us back into the building?"

"What I heard was that the chief 'spected to be done by this afternoon," she said. "That was yesterday, a'course. Maybe things have changed since then. Listen, I'm due at the station and Eliza Anne still needs a bath. I gotta' go, I just wanted to call about the paper and all. I still can't believe Brandi wrote that about ya'.'"

We said our goodbyes then, and I eventually crawled into an old pair of jeans and a flower-print blouse. At first glance the floral pattern looked benign, but a closer look revealed poisonous thorns amongst the blooms. It suited my mood.

I said my goodbyes to Mamaw and headed out for some peace. I could not spend another morning gossiping with her——my mental health couldn't take it. There was no reason to go by Gracie's Grounds. I knew the place would still be off limits, but I could continue with packing up the cottage. And that meant getting packing materials. My best bet was to see if Peter Teegarden had any spare boxes at Old Town Auto. I jumped into the Mustang and headed out that way. While I drove, I called Evan on the phone to discuss logistics. I first confirmed that he was still planning on doing the renovation, and then I moved on to the topic of subleasing the cottage. We agreed to meet at the cottage around lunch so that he could begin to make his own moving plans.

The trip out to Old Town was quick enough, and after I asked prettily, Peter was happy to set me up with a few spare boxes. We had this flirty thing going, Peter and I, although we both knew it was just for fun. At least, I thought Peter knew that was all it was. He was too young for me, and I had Hank, at least I hoped I still did. While there, I took the opportunity to pick up a couple of canisters of fuel additives for the Mustang. The Beast demanded the lead additives, otherwise it would spit and sputter like an asthmatic running a marathon.

On the way back, I drove through downtown, passing by my future coffee house, which unfortunately still had the police tape blocking the entrance. On a whim, I stopped to peer through the windows. A tarp covered the floor where Tommy's body had been. Otherwise, the place was as empty as I remembered it. I sighed, hoping that Chief Doeppers would release the scene this afternoon as he'd promised.

As I stepped back to the Mustang, I realized I'd forgotten to pick up packing tape for the boxes. With fingers crossed, I stepped into the Pole & Arms, the place that Wilhelm Bea used to own and manage, to see if the store had anything suitable. Mamaw had told me Ida planned on keeping the place open. It was a fixture of this town, and I figured that I might as well meet whomever Ida had found to run the place. We'd be neighbors soon enough after all.

I hadn't been in the store since I'd moved back to Alpine, but I didn't recall it ever looking quite this shabby. The collection of fishing rods and gear along the east wall looked in disarray and I swore a few of the rods were tangled. The gun racks mounted on the west wall had empty spots, missing inventory, and the glass display cabinets were covered with a scattering of loose pamphlets hiding the revolvers and smaller guns displayed beneath. The center of the space held the gardening equipment, and if there was an organizational scheme to the eclectic mix, it escaped me. It looked like the place had received little care since Wilhelm's demise.

There were only a couple of customers, carefully picking their way through the narrow aisles, and one worker standing back by the cash register staring at her phone. The only person I recognized in the place was one of the Strange sisters—Mary Sue, I thought. I could never tell the two apart unless they were together. Both were in their eighties, frumpy, with short grey hair. I'd first met the sisters at the bridge club several months ago. They had run Cobbler's Corner with their brother Junior before he'd passed. Now I didn't know how either spent their days when not at the club. I waved, but either Mary Sue didn't see me or chose not to. She hadn't been in favor of closing the store to make room for Gracie's Grounds. I sighed regretfully and wondered if there was a way to make peace. I decided to give it some time and made my way back to speak with the worker Ida had hired.

"Hello," I began, drawing the woman's attention. She was in her early twenties, thin, with a poof of blonde hair that reminded me of an eighty's sitcom. "My name is Gracie Thies, and I'll soon be your neighbor. I'm opening a coffee house next door."

"Ooh, like, that'll be nice," she smiled warmly. "Will you, like, have free Wi-Fi?"

"Probably," I answered. Thankfully there was a display covered with impulse buy items, including duct-tape. I grabbed a couple of rolls and placed them on the counter.

"Well, I hope the signal is strong enough to, like, reach over here. The reception is awful," she said. "Oh, sorry, I'm Cheryl."

"Have you been working here long?" I asked, paying for the tape after she rang it up.

"Like about a month. It's only me and a few others," she

sighed. "It's boring. Well, other than like there was a murder yesterday."

"Yea," I sheepishly replied. "That happened at my place."

"Ooo, like, do you know who died? I heard it was like Sandra's dad."

"The victim was Tommy Hilgeman, and he had a daughter named Sandra. How do you know Sandra?" I asked, intrigued. I couldn't imagine the distraught woman I saw yesterday being friends with the woman before me today. They didn't seem to have anything in common.

"She, like, sat for me when I was little," explained the woman.

"What was she like?" I asked. While I didn't babysit during my high school years, I knew several girls who had.

"Nice, sweet like. But she was boy crazy, that one," Cheryl continued. "Always, like, talking about this boy or that one. Her dad was like strict, and I think Sandra babysat to get away. If she wasn't talking to me about boys, she was, like, on the phone to one of 'em or, like, one of the girls in her posse of friends. She, like, snuck a boy in one of the times she was supposed to be watching me. My parents came home early and caught her. They didn't use her much after that," she explained. "Tell me, what kind of drinks are you going to serve?"

Cheryl smiled appreciably at my descriptions of the planned offerings of Gracie's Grounds, and promised to tell all her friends. As I was finishing, a customer interrupted, asking about a spinnerbait lure for smallmouth. Cheryl looked as puzzled as I was, and just waved vaguely towards the east wall. With the state of the store, and her apparent lack of interest in learning the merchandise, I wondered if Cheryl would last long enough to enjoy my free Wi-Fi. I glanced back as I was leaving and saw that the woman was back studying her phone.

I got into the Mustang and continued down Main. There were several cars in the lot at Margaret's Diner, and I knew I needed to make peace with Margaret at some point. At the corner of Main and Elm, I saw Ida sitting on her front porch and waved, earning a wave in return. I turned onto Elm and soon pulled in front of the cottage.

The kitchen was the mess I had left it. I taped up the boxes from Old Town and began to make some order of the piles. It didn't take too long before I was ready to move to the smaller of the two bedrooms. When I passed the bath, I couldn't help but let my eyes drift to the nickel-sized indention in the cast-iron tub. The dent had been caused by a bullet from Wilhelm's gun when I'd been hiding in the tub, the same bullet that had ricocheted and killed the man. Maybe pixies had intervened to save me, as Tina had posited. I shivered and hurried on.

I was packing up the books in the smaller of the two bedrooms when I heard the knock on the door. I got up, brushed some of the dust from my pants, and headed to answer it. It was Evan, of course, today in khakis and a cute navy golf shirt that was tight enough that I could see his pectoral muscles. The man was ripped. I grinned, earning one of his nuclear smiles in return. I felt the heat on my face and perhaps a bit elsewhere as I stepped back to let him in. It took Evan only a few moments to scan the place. The cottage was not large.

"This is nice, Gracie——exactly what I need," Evan said. "It looks like you've started packing already. You have quite a bit to move considering how small this place is."

"Actually, that was one of the things I wanted to talk to you about. I don't think I'll need everything in the studio above Gracie's Grounds. Not with the floor plan we've discussed." I'd have to downsize a bit; the studio would only be about two-thirds the size of the cottage. I showed him the furniture I wanted to keep, and the pieces I didn't need anymore. I'd keep the bedroom set, of course. A girl had to sleep, after all. I wanted most of the kitchen gear, the couch and an end table, the bookshelves too. And I had to keep the cedar chest that Mamaw and Papaw had given me on my wedding day. The thing had traveled to Paris and back; heck, it was more worldly than most folks in Alpine. That still left several pieces of furniture, none of which I needed. "So, is there anything here that you could use?"

Evan looked contemplative and took his time examining the pieces remaining. He selected a few items, saying they'd work until he got something better. A part of me felt insulted, even though I'd used the same reasoning when I'd moved back to town and furnished the place from leftovers of Mamaw's, supplemented by what I could find at a used furniture store down Gadsden way. It amazed me sometimes how one could get used to an old piece that was just supposed to be temporary. I shook my head and smiled——maybe they'd last longer than Evan realized. Then he turned to me and said, "So how much do you want?" gesturing towards the items he'd selected.

I offered them for free, but Evan laughed and flashed that nuclear smile of his, making me a bit weak in the knees. The man could level an Amazonian city with a look. He said that he could not, in good conscience, accept. I figured, despite the truck he drove and the SUV that was Sandra's, he was stretched cash-wise. I knew from Emily how hard it was to go from one household to two. And he was already doing me justice by renovating the studio at cost. I needed a price that would sound fair, and I really didn't even know the right range.

"Who do you have lined up to help you move?" asked Evan before I could say anything.

"Well, I..." I just petered off in a smile. My initial reaction was to say Hank, but I wasn't quite sure where the two of us were at the moment. And with Hank's work schedule, I didn't know if he could help me in a timely manner anyhow. While I could move the boxes in Mamaw's Buick, I had no way of moving the furniture. "Are you thinking trade?" I asked hopefully.

Evan laughed in return, and we made a plan. We decided I'd divide everything in the cottage into three piles: the items moving to the studio, the items to move back to Mamaw's, and the rest of it. Evan committed to moving the first two and would take what he wanted from the last before sending the rest of it to the Goodwill out by Old Town Auto. It felt like a win-win.

With the business taken care of, I walked Evan to the front door. As I was seeing him out, my phone rang, and I saw it was Emily's number. I motioned for Evan to wait on the front step while I answered it. I got the news I was hoping to hear—Doeppers had released the crime scene. I was so excited I didn't think straight and grabbed Evan in a hug telling him the news. Once I realized what I was doing, I released him feeling the heat on my face. Evan looked somewhat bewildered, perhaps even shocked, and after an awkward moment, we made it past my blunder. He flashed me his nuclear smile and said he'd call his team and head straight over. I watched as he left, fishing his cell phone from a pocket. I heard him speaking Spanish and figured he'd called Manny.

I waved to Ida as Evan drove away. She was walking the little Pekinese she'd bought to keep her company after the mayhem with Wilhelm. I earned a smile and a wave in return. I knew Ida would be happy to gossip for a bit, but I wanted to finish the work in the cottage and quickly turned away. I figured I'd give Evan and his crew a bit of time to get organized before stopping by the coffee house.

I made short work of it. Now that I had a plan, it was fairly easy to separate the belongs in the cottage into the three designated piles. The only one I really needed to be careful packing and labeling was the one heading to Mamaw's house. I knew she had some space available on the second floor. Mamaw didn't go upstairs anymore and had converted a sitting room on the first floor of the Victorian into a bedroom that she could use, but I didn't feel right just dumping a bunch of boxes up there. I wanted everything stored carefully and neatly labeled so that if I needed to find something in a hurry, I could. The items heading to the studio didn't matter so much. Those would be unpacked in a jiffy once the renovations were complete.

I finished with the sun hanging low in the west, an hour or so before supper time. I gave Mamaw a quick call on my cell to let her know that I'd be heading to her place after I stopped by the coffee shop to see how the work had progressed. I didn't really figure anything had happened yet, but I had high hopes that Evan had started something in the couple of hours he and his crew had been working. Mamaw seemed distracted about something, maybe even distraught. I tried to pry it out of her, but she wouldn't budge an inch, only saying she'd talk to me later in person.

The Mustang roared when I turned the key——I just loved that sound. I could have walked but wanted to head straight to Mamaw's from the coffee house. I pulled from Elm onto Main and drove towards downtown. The lot at the diner was pretty full, and I thought again about how best to approach Margaret. I had an idea of sorts that had occurred to me while packing, but wanted to run the numbers to see if it would work like I'd hoped.

Evan's pickup was parked in front of the coffee house as well as a beat-up old Civic, but otherwise the street was mostly deserted. Downtown was dead. I wondered if it would pay to stay open this late. I pulled in beside Evan's ride and saw that the lights were shining not only on the first floor, but also on the second floor where the studio apartment would be. At least it would be quiet at night.

The front door was locked, which I found strange, and I saw no one working through the window. I figured they were all upstairs and used the key on the rabbit-foot keychain to give me access. I marched on through the first floor to the stairs in the back, the only progress of sorts was a scattering of tools on the floor. Apparently Evan had decided to start on the studio first.

I thought I heard voices as I hurried up the steps two at a time, feeling it a bit more than I thought I would. I knew I needed to exercise more often, and I had the time, I just hadn't had the motivation. When I reached the top of the steps I almost gasped in shock.

Evan had his arms around another with romantic intent, and it wasn't Sandra. Evan was with Manny.

Chapter 7

My gut said to leave, and for once I listened and fled down the steps and towards the front door and freedom. I heard Evan call my name, but I ignored the man and kept on going. I wasn't exactly running, but I wasn't out for a country stroll either. Unfortunately, he caught me before I made it out of the building, grabbing my arm to stop me. I'd have to deal with what I'd seen; and do so before having had a chance to process it.

"Gracie, let me explain," Evan said, releasing me once I turned to face him. "I didn't mean for you to see that."

"Hey, no big deal," I said, feeling myself blush under his gaze. I didn't know if I felt embarrassed from seeing Evan with another man, or whether I was just embarrassed by intruding upon a private moment. All I knew was that my face was as red and hot as a Hoosier after a week at Gulf Shores. "What you do and with whom is none of my business," I continued, holding my hands up in the universal symbol meaning "no foul." I saw Manny out of the corner of my eye, waiting nervously on the bottom step.

"I didn't know you were going to stop by," Evan said. He

flashed his nuclear smile, but it no longer affected me in quite the same way. I didn't know if my body was reacting to what my brain had learned, or whether I was just less susceptible in my current state. "Once I sent Douglas and Shane home, I thought Manny and I could have a few moments to ourselves," he explained.

"I get it, no problem here. I didn't mean to intrude," I said. I still wanted to get out of Dodge, run like a deer when a hunter's trod cracks a tree branch.

"Can't we just talk about it?" he asked, pleading with his eyes.

I sighed and settled myself. I gave Manny a tight smile of recognition as he slowly meandered our way, earning a head nod in return. I guess with what I'd seen, I knew why Evan and Sandra were having marital problems. It also explained the lack of children, well maybe. It could be that Evan swung both ways. "Are you bi?" I asked. I was not up to speed with the lingo for the LGBTQ+ community, but I thought I had that right. "Wait," I amended. "I'm sorry. It's none of my business."

Evan laughed nervously, and I could feel the tension in my shoulders lessen. Somehow it made me feel a bit more comfortable knowing that Evan was as disconcerted by this conversation as I was. He flashed his nuclear smile again and this time I could appreciate it for what it was. I began to suspect that he used the look as an unconscious defense mechanism, like a nervous twitch. "No," he said. "Manny is, but I'm an old-fashioned straight-up American as apple pie gay man." I glanced to Manny and he smiled sheepishly.

"But you're married, right? To Sandra," I said. "Why?" I asked, confused. "Doesn't she know?"

Evan grimaced, as if the thought of his wife pained him. "Sandra and I, well, it's complicated."

"I'm sorry," I said. "I don't need to know." I was curious, but also sympathetic. Mamaw had poked her fingers into my own affairs of the heart too often for me to pry into another's unwanted.

"No, that's okay," he said. "In fact, I'd like to talk to someone uninvolved. The last few weeks have been rough."

Evan turned to Manny then, and said something in Spanish. I spoke fluent French after my years spent in Paris, and had a scattering of Spanish, but they spoke way too fast for me to understand. I got the gist though, once Manny used his broken English to say good night.

"I told Manny to go on home and I'd see him later," explained Evan. "Can we get a cup of coffee at Margaret's and then go somewhere to talk?" he asked.

"Margaret and I, we aren't in a good place right now," I admitted. "Maybe just a walk instead?" I offered.

"Sounds fine," Evan said.

It took only a few moments to lock up and secure the building. We headed away from Margaret's, towards the courthouse and the statue of Colonel Corbert. I saw a few cars pass as we walked together silently. I was not going to start the conversation; this was Evan's story. I glanced his way, and saw a contemplative look on his face.

"I grew up in a small town about three hours from here in Tennessee, and realized in high school I was gay," Evan began. "At that place and time, it was not something that I felt comfortable revealing, and so I kept it pretty quiet. My best friend, Jennifer, figured it out before I did, and she helped me through the rough patches. She also helped me keep it secret."

"How?" I asked.

"Well, we 'dated' off and on," he said, using air quotes. "I took her to prom; she was my beard." I'd heard the term before, so I knew what Evan meant. Evan and Jennifer had acted like they were in a romantic relationship to put off suspicion of Evan's true predilections. I'd read somewhere that Betty White had done the same thing for Liberace.

"And Sandra?" I asked. "Does she play that role now?"

"In a way, but that's gotten a little more complicated," he admitted.

"How so?" I asked.

"Sandra used to be pretty wild, a real party animal like Bluto in Animal House, nothing like her little sister Cindy. She butted heads with her dad during high school, when he tried to restrain her without much luck. Her mom was gone by then, of course. Well, in college she got in a little deeper than intended. There was an incident, and Sandra was hurt pretty bad."

"Oh my God," I said. "I didn't know." We had missed each other in high school; Sandra was well after my time. "What happened?"

"She was used by several...dirtbags," Evan said angrily. "It changed her," he admitted. "We got closer afterwards. I only pieced together what happened after we graduated, with the tidbits Sandra felt comfortable sharing. Her dad, Tommy, never suspected anything like that had happened to one of his daughters. Sandra kept it pretty close."

"She didn't tell the cops?" I asked.

"No," Evan said. "There was alcohol involved, and you know seeking justice can be like living the whole thing over again. Sandra didn't want to go through that."

"And so, you grew closer," I said.

"Yes, sharing a trauma like that can ease the burden."

"I don't think I really understand. How did this lead to you and her...?"

"Afterwards, Sandra was put off by men, at least by the

physical part. And well, I bat left-handed," he grinned. "I wasn't interested in that with a woman, and Sandra found my indifference appealing. Dating gave Sandra the space to heal, and it gave both of us an acceptable public face."

"Listen," I said. "I get that you both could gain from that type of arrangement, especially after imagining what Sandra endured, but how does that lead to a marriage?"

"Well, the marriage thing just happened. After you date for a while, it's expected. We both had what seemed like good reasons. Frankly, it's easier to get business after marrying into a community like Alpine than as an outsider. And well, I felt more comfortable with Sandra at my side than without. Sandra wanted the security, I think, and freedom from her family. I do love her, just more like a brother than a husband."

"And Sandra?" I asked. "How does she feel?" I could understand Evan's reasoning, small towns could be insular, and at least until recently Evan clearly preferred to hide his sexual peccadilloes. I didn't blame him. He did live in Alabama— rural Alabama. Not that a lot of places would probably be much better.

"She loves me as well, as least I think. And her dad got what he needed——a son-in-law who could take care of his oldest daughter. It fit, for a while at least."

"Does Sandra know you're gay?" I asked directly.

"Of course, she does," he replied indigently. "I mean, how could she not?"

"You've said those words? You've told her straight-out that you're gay just like you did earlier when you told me?"

"Well," Evan admitted. "No. That's something I've only learned how to do recently. It's something Manny has helped me with. I mean, he's Mexican, for goodness sake. Do you know culturally how difficult it is to be oriented differently as a

Mexican? He's had to deal with a lot more prejudice in life than I have, even in my worst nightmares. He got arrested once, when he was attacked after visiting a gay bar, and even served a bit of time for it. That's one brave soul," admitted Evan. I could almost hear the admiration in his voice, the infatuation of new love. "And I've told Sandra, straight out, that I loved her, but I was not interested in having sex with her."

"Okay, so what happened between the two of you?" I asked. We'd reached the courthouse square, the sun setting in the west made the shadow of Colonel Corbert stretch and grow like a vengeful spirit ready again to fight the War of Northern Aggression. When I gestured about turning back, Evan nodded.

"Tommy, before he was killed, had been pushing Sandra on the whole grandchild thing. He wanted grandchildren while he was still young enough to enjoy them, and Cindy's unmarried, and has moved to Atlanta for her job. We'd been fighting a lot about it. Sandra said she wanted to try, even after I told her I wasn't interested. It wasn't like she wanted to have sex with me either, not after what had happened to her in college. We'd only be doing it to appease her father, and that wasn't a good enough reason to try and change what we had going as far as I was concerned. We talked about adopting, but that's a whole other can of worms. It got to be a problem. Sandra and I fighting at home, Tommy treating me like I had a head of lice. When I moved out, Tommy said I wouldn't work in this town again. I figured he'd calm down after a while. I mean, not working would hurt Sandra just as much as it hurt me. Sandra has helped some with the books for the business, but hasn't had a paying job since we got married."

"So, the breakup had nothing to do with you and Manny?" I asked.

"No, of course not. I mean, Manny and I grew closer after I'd decided to move out. I guess I knew I was ready to move on with my life, but the breakup had more to do with the pressure to have children than anything else," claimed Evan.

We walked in silence for a while, and I wondered if Evan was being completely honest with me or perhaps with himself. Evan had moved ahead pretty quickly with Manny. Oh, I believed he still cared for his wife; I'd seen the look in his eyes when Sandra was mourning the loss of her father yesterday, but he clearly already had feelings for Manny as well. It was easier to close one chapter of your life when you had an inkling what the next chapter entailed.

We had made it back to the coffee shop, and I watched as another car passed by on Main. We were two of only a few people on the sidewalk. I could see a frumpy elderly lady walking away in the direction of Margaret's, and a man on the sidewalk across the street. "Listen," said Evan, grabbing my hands and drawing my attention back to him. "I need to ask a favor. I'm still working on coming out. It's not an easy thing for me to do, and I've got to think of the business. There will be some folks who will no longer be inclined to hire me."

"But perhaps a few others who would be more so," I offered with a smile. I knew where this was heading.

"Perhaps," sighed Evan. "So, what I wanted to ask was, could you keep what you saw to yourself? I don't need folks speculating, and with Tommy's death there would be too many idiots thinking the two were related. Maybe, after this has all settled, I can figure out how to move forward. I can figure out how to come out."

"What if it's related?" I asked.

"How could it be?" Evan replied. "What I have going with Manny has nothing to do with me and Sandra, let alone what happened to Tommy. It was probably just some wacko looking for money for dope anyhow."

I thought of my own secret, the Event-That-Changed-My-Life. I knew what it was like to have something so formative be unknown to those around you. Everyone seemed to have a secret——Sandra and what had happened to her in college, Evan's sexual orientation, my history in Paris, even Hank if you counted the marijuana he'd grown for his cousin John over the summer. Those secrets shaped us. Yet Evan had shared his secret with me, if only accidentally. And Sandra had shared her ordeal, over time, with Evan. Hank had shared his secret with me as well, but I had told no one.

Evan had said that sharing made life easier, and I believed him. Why hadn't I told Hank what had happened with Pierre? Maybe Hank had sensed that reservation somehow. Maybe it wasn't just the situation with Harry that was holding the two of us back. When he'd repeatedly asked about Evan, it made me feel like Hank didn't trust me, but then again, had I trusted Hank?

I looked into Evan's eyes, seeing the fear there. He flashed that nuclear smile and I grinned in return. I could keep his secret. Somehow it made me feel warm inside upon seeing his relief when I told him so. He smiled again then, not the nuclear one but one that felt more natural——a genuine smile. I watched as he climbed into his truck and drove away.

It was much later than I realized, and I knew Mamaw would be worried. No need to check the coffee house now. I pulled the Mustang keys out of my purse, but when I got to the driver's side of the car, I knew I wouldn't need them. Someone had knifed both tires on that side.

I cursed like the proverbial sailor and pulled my cell from my pocket to call Mamaw. I needed a ride. I thought about calling 911, but figured the local police were busy enough with trying to solve a murder. The cops couldn't do anything anyhow, and I didn't want to spend the remainder of my evening filling out paperwork at the police station. I'd wait until tomorrow to report the vandalism.

After catching Mamaw on the phone, I had to apologize three times for not calling earlier and causing her to worry. When I told her about the slashed tires, it brought on an even longer explanation. Mamaw was upset, more so than what seemed warranted by the vandalism. Hanging up, I sighed. I was plum dead tired. I wanted to curl up with a glass of Merlot and a good mystery book. I missed my claw foot at the cottage, well, not that particular tub, but the long baths I used to take where I could soak to my eyebrows. I wondered who'd knifed my tires, and if it was random vandalism or if I'd been targeted. Evan's truck hadn't been touched and it had been parked next to mine. I figured someone was sending me a message; I just wished I knew what it was.

I knew Mamaw would be a few minutes longer, and suddenly I felt a little leery about just waiting on the street. I didn't want to face the person who'd slashed my tires. I switched from car key to shop key and opened the glass door to Gracie's Grounds. When I turned on the overhead lights, I felt as nervous as if my partner had just unexpectedly jumped to Seven No-Trump. The place was not the same as it had been when Evan and I had locked the door before our walk. The tools that had been scattered on the floor by the east wall were now all lined up in a row like good little soldiers marching to war. And the papers and plans that had been on the counter up against the west wall were stacked in one neat pile instead of four sloppy ones. Someone had spent a few minutes straightening up in here.

As my hammering heart calmed, I realized that Manny had probably returned looking for Evan and had cleaned up while he was here. It was the only logical explanation. I mean, I knew the space had housed Cobbler's Corner, an old-time shoe repair shop, but that didn't imply there were little elves in the walls coming out at night to make shoes and do light housekeeping.

While I waited, I examined the blood stains on the old-growth wood floor where Tommy's body had lain. It was an ugly brown now, not the flowing crimson that caused me so much trouble. Evan had assured me that it would be unnoticeable by the time they refinished the floors. I wondered again who had killed Tommy. Evan seemed to think it was a random act of violence, but then why did it happen here instead of out on the street? And the murder weapon was one of convenience, the same hammer that I'd used on the walls earlier that night. If someone had robbed and killed Tommy for whatever cash he had, then wouldn't that person have had their own weapon? No, whoever had killed Tommy had done it in the spur of the moment, grabbing the most convenient weapon available. This was not a planned murder like what had happened to Edward this summer.

I had read enough murder mysteries to know the killer had to have motive, means and opportunity. Tommy had caused grief for many with his handling of the building permits for the town, not just Evan. There were numerous folks around here who had motive. And the means was obvious enough. This case looked like it boiled down to opportunity. Somehow Tommy and his killer had entered my coffee house, and then Tommy had died. The key to solving the mystery was in figuring out what had happened that night.

I heard a honk and went to the front to see Mamaw's Buick.

I waved, quickly doused the lights and locked up. There was no reason for me to try and solve any murders. As Emily had said, this was a matter for the police.

I felt as if a burden had lifted when I sank into the passenger seat. This had been a long hard day, and I was ready for it to end.

"Gracie," Mamaw growled. "I've told you over and over again that you cannot get involved romantically with a married man. That is just not done in this town."

I could almost feel the weight settle back on my shoulders; the day was not done with me yet.

Chapter 8

"Mamaw, there's nothing between me and Evan," I repeated for the umpteenth time. The short ride from downtown to the Victorian had been tense, and the dinner afterwards was worse. Now that dinner was over and the dishes were cleared, the argument continued. "I know what you've heard, but all of that can be explained."

"Ida saw you, girl," Mamaw said. "She saw you huggin' that Evan Petrovich. And what in the world was he doing at your place anyhow?"

"I explained all of that," I said again. "Evan is subleasing the cottage on Elm and he wanted to get a feel for the space. The hug was an accident. I'd just heard Chief Doeppers had released the crime scene and in my excitement, I hugged Evan. It was innocent."

"Hmph," growled Mamaw. "And after I spent my day trying to heal that rift between you and Hank. He told me about seeing you and Evan together."

"I still can't believe you went to talk to him. I thought we agreed you'd stay out of my relationships."

"Don't you get all high and mighty with me, girl," snapped

Mamaw. "You and your 'accidents' seem to always involve falling into that Evan's arms," she huffed. "I saw the way you looked at him. I was there, you know, before the game on Monday."

"Mamaw," I sighed. "There's nothing between me and Evan," I repeated. I so wanted to tell Mamaw that Evan was gay. If only I hadn't promised to keep his secret. Yet I worried that even if I had not made that promise, Mamaw would think I was lying, especially after the way this discussion had gone. She certainly had not believed much of what I'd said. "Now, I want to know why you tracked down Hank today. You had no business getting between the two of us."

"Gracie, my sweet girl," Mamaw said. "'Cause I care about you. 'Cause I did you two wrong and I needed to fix the error of my ways. How was I to know you'd moved on to another man?"

"I have not moved on!" I cried. "Evan and I are just friends; he's my contractor, for God's sake."

"Don't you take the Lord's name in vain. I raised you better than that," snapped Mamaw. "And child, I've warned you about messing with married men. That type of thing just isn't done around these parts. The phone has been ringin' off the hook about you and that man."

"Mamaw, tell me what Hank had to say." I was tired of denying, and Mamaw seemed to be winding down on her accusing. We both knew we weren't going to see eye-to-eye on it.

"Oh, girl," sighed Mamaw. "His feelings are as confused as a Northerner at a crawfish boil. Hank doesn't know his up from his down when it comes to you. And Harry—I know you said it was bad, but I didn't realize how much so until I saw for myself."

"He's better than what he was this summer," I said. "Harry, I mean."

"I can't imagine what that was like. That house is not suited for a man in a chair. Those floors are uneven, and I swear he can barely maneuver that chair of his from the front of the house to the back. And he can't get down from the front porch. What if there was a fire?"

"Hank said he was going to build a ramp, but he hasn't found the time."

"Umph," sniffed Mamaw. "Hank has too many irons in the fire if you ask me."

"He's trying to pay down the lien on the farm that they had to take out when Clovis sued Harry. Hank does detailing at a few car dealerships and has the full-time job down in Gadsden, in addition to the work on the farm."

"Harry needs more care than what Hank can provide," stated Mamaw.

"I know," I murmured. The situation at the farm was dire. I'd told Mamaw that, but she clearly didn't understand until she'd seen it herself. There was not a lot we could do about it, however. Not now.

"There's really nothing between you and Evan Petrovich?" Mamaw asked. "For real?"

"There's nothing between me and Evan. We're just friends," I said firmly.

"Okay, okay," said Mamaw. "I believe you," she continued, but the glint in her eye spoke to her doubt. "But it's not only me you need to convince. It's Ida Bea you need to talk to, as well as a few others. And Sandra, of course."

"Sandra?" I asked puzzled. What did Evan's wife have to do with this?

"Well, girl, she's the wronged party here. By the looks of it, you broke up her marriage. Folks don't take kindly to that type of doings around these parts," explained Mamaw.

"Evan was separated from Sandra long before any of this," I said indignantly.

"As if that matters. Most folks will just think you were better at hiding it 'til now," Mamaw stated flatly.

"That's crazy," I replied, but then I thought about what Mamaw had said. I knew she was right. I was in a pickle, like stretching to bid in bridge only to find yourself unaccountably at game. "Mamaw," I sighed. "What am I going to do?"

"Well, first thing is that you can no longer afford any more 'accidents,'" she said. I could hear the quotes. "You keep someone reliable with you whenever you deal with that man." So, I needed a chaperone——just great. "And you need to go and talk to Sandra, explain what's going on there, before things get more out of hand with her."

"What do you mean, get out of hand?" I asked.

"You can't afford new tires every few days," Mamaw said.

"You think Sandra slashed my tires?" I said, shocked. "I figured it was Clovis."

"Skeeter? Why would he do that?" Mamaw asked.

I told her about the trip out to The Barn with Clovis, something I'd kept to myself until now. I told her how he'd threatened me when I fled, after overhearing him talking about Edward before we knew the identity of the killer. I told her how I'd obtained a videotape of that night, and how Hank was using it to counter-sue Clovis. Clovis had said he'd make me pay, and if he'd learned of the video, I knew he'd follow through.

"Skeeter Jones," Mamaw said. I could see the fire in her eyes. "Maybe he had something to do with your car tonight. It would be in his character." Much to my relief, Mamaw had soured some to Clovis over the past few weeks. When he'd first started coming to the bridge club, Mamaw and most of the other ladies almost swooned over him.

"Everything seems to be going sideways. Did I tell you about Margaret?"

"Margaret?" she asked.

"Apparently, Margaret is upset that I'm opening Gracie's Grounds. She sees it as competition."

"Ah," Mamaw replied. "You'll have to handle Frank then too."

"I know," I said. Frank ran the local Piggly Wiggly and was married to Margaret. "I have a thought on how to take care of that," I said.

"Well, you got some fences to mend, child. I'll do what I can to keep the gossip mill from burying you. You should give Emily a call as well; she's the worst gossip around these parts."

I almost laughed but stopped myself in time. Mamaw claiming that Emily was a gossip——it was like the pot calling the kettle black. I said my good nights and was finally able to head upstairs to bed. I saw Mamaw pick up the phone as I left the kitchen. While on the steps, I heard Mamaw greet Ida Bea. I knew she was already working to counteract the gossip that was floating about me.

I needed a break from talk and decided to investigate whether my idea for handling Margaret and Frank would hold water. I pulled out my old laptop and reviewed the financial forecasts I'd made for Gracie's Grounds. I made a few estimates and ran the numbers. Not only did it look like it might work, but if my projections held, I might be in a stronger financial position. I printed out a few pages and tried to put something reasonable on paper. After I was unable to stifle my third yawn, I decided what I had was good enough.

I changed into an old T-shirt of Hank's, an extra-large that I'd borrowed one night for sleeping while at the farm. After the necessities, I lay in bed contemplating my day. I fell asleep almost before the lights were out.

The sun was shining when I woke the next morning and I felt well rested. My dreams had been Pollyannaish—where Gracie's Grounds was a phenomenal success, and I was able to franchise the label across the state. I showered, shaved my legs, and chose a teal sundress that I'd been lucky to find at the Goodwill in town. It hit just below my knees and had a pleated skirt with a square neckline. A little light makeup and I was ready to face the day.

Mamaw was drinking coffee while reading the Alpine Tribune when I entered the kitchen. I poured myself a cup and asked her if the paper had anything interesting. Mamaw pointed to an article on the murder bylined by Brandi-With-An-I. I perused it quickly, happy to see my name wasn't present. According to the article, Tommy had been on the city council for over a decade and oversaw all city permitting, handling the construction permits himself. I did learn that the permitting for the Carlyle, the old hotel that sat across from the bridge club, had been controversial, causing some infighting on the city council. Tommy was survived by his two daughters, a brother who lived in Anniston, two nephews, and a niece. His wife had died in an auto accident over a decade ago, and Tommy had not remarried. I wondered if Tommy had an entry in Emily's little black book of eligible bachelors. While Emily was happily married, she kept a tight list of who was with whom in this town, with particular interest in who was available.

Mamaw told me her Buick would be free this morning. She'd called Ada Mae to arrange for a ride to the bridge club for the 10:00 a.m. game. However, she said she'd need the car in the afternoon. That left me with a little over four hours, and I had a sundry list of tasks before me.

My first stop was the police station to report the vandalism with the Mustang. I detoured downtown and saw Evan's truck parked beside my Beast as well as a few other vehicles. It looked like nothing else had happened to my car overnight, which was the purpose of the detour. I wanted to stop and check on the renovation progress but decided I shouldn't as I didn't have a 'chaperone.' The drive to the station was quick, and when I went inside, I was pleased to see Emily manning the front counter.

"Lookin' pretty spiffy there, Gracie. You got a date later with a certain hot contractor?" Emily smirked. "And here I thought you were pining for Hank the Hunk. I guess you got someone else to steam your greens."

"Emily!" I laughed. "Stop that. There's nothing between Evan and me, believe me on that one," I stated emphatically. "And Hank and I will work things out."

"Hm, well, that's not what I heard," Emily said. "I heard that you had a little love nest going over there on Elm. Meeting men for who knows what kind of business," joked Emily.

"Well, you heard wrong," I said. "And I don't need that kind of talk about me."

"Just teasing, hun. Whatcha doin' here anyhow? I can't tell you nothing about the investigation. You just let us handle it and deal with your own affairs. Ha! Get it, you and affairs."

"Look, Emily, I'm here on business. Someone, and I don't know who, knifed the tires on my car last night. I can't prove it, but I think it was Clovis Jones."

"Here, let me get the forms." she said with a sigh. It took us about a half hour to finish the paperwork, and Emily and I spent another half hour trying to figure out who else might have vandalized the Beast. Emily was not convinced that Clovis had it in for me, but she also hadn't been there that night at the Barn, nor had she heard any of the snide comments he'd made at the bridge club. She offered to fill out the request for a restraining order, but it would have to be signed by a judge, and my suspicion aside, we had no proof. I already knew that the police really couldn't do anything, but at least now there was a record on file. If I could ever prove Clovis did it, I'd have the paperwork in place to take legal action.

As I left the station, I saw Brandi-With-An-I talking with Bert Lancaster over by a patrol car. They were facing each other, and Bert was looking down longingly into Brandi's eyes as she fervently spoke. I snickered when I saw that Brandi's hands were clasped in Bert's sweaty ones, and I couldn't help but smile. When Brandi saw me watching, she dropped Bert's hands as if burned, and crossed her arms over her chest in a practiced sort of pout. She flashed me a look, and I knew that if glares could maim, I'd be on the ground clinched in pain. Bert started talking then, drawing Brandi's attention. I wondered what detail from the case would appear in tomorrow's paper. I hoped Brandi didn't charm Bert out of a job.

Next, I headed out west of town towards the interstate where Don Talcone had his service station. Don and Papaw had been inseparable as youths, and I fondly recalled some of the stories Papaw had told me when I first moved into the Victorian after my parents had passed. Don knew the Mustang well, too well considering how many times I'd taken it to the station since purchasing the Beast. I figured Don would know how to solve the tire problem, and I could trust him to make me mobile as cheaply as possible. As I pulled in, I was not expecting to see Clovis Jones' shiny new pick-up, nor the man himself talking to Papaw's friend.

I was tempted to turn around and head back to town, but Don had seen me in the Buick, and I did need him to take care of the Mustang——the sooner the better. Mamaw and I couldn't share her car for too long without stepping on each other's toes. I gritted my teeth and threw the Buick into park. When I approached the two men, Don gave me a welcoming nod while Clovis proffered a smarmy stare. Don looked as solid as ever, hard like the old stump in the backyard of the Victorian. Clovis's mustache was twitching, and he leaned heavily on his cane, favoring his allegedly bum leg. Both men stared at me like I'd interrupted a secret Illuminati gathering.

"The Buick acting up?" Don finally asked. "Ya' know Skeeter, of course," he continued with a nod to Clovis.

"Gracie and I, we go way back," offered Clovis. He threw me a mean look. "I took her out to The Barn one evening, quite a memorable night that."

"Not the Buick, Don, my Mustang...again," I said, ignoring Clovis.

"That old thing," laughed Don. "It acting up?"

"No, someone knifed my tires," I said.

Don looked dumbfounded, like I'd just tried to pass him a suspect twenty. Clovis burst into laughter, guffawing so loud that he forgot to use his cane and stood straight and strong. I hid a grin when I saw the disdainful look Don threw Clovis's way. Don may have been something of a wild child when he and Papaw were younger, but now the man was as straight-laced as a preacher on a Sunday morn.

"Skeeter," boomed Don, cutting Clovis's laughter short. "I'll get to working on that oil change. You get on now and get settled in the waiting room, or you can come back in an hour or so. Gracie," he continued looking at me. "I'll give Tony a call and have him take a look. If they done it right, you'll need new tires."

Don needed the particulars, and once I gave him the details and the keys, he headed into the shop to make some calls before starting on Clovis' oil change. Much to my chagrin, Clovis just stood there watching until Don left. Eventually, I found myself alone with the man.

"So, someone got ya' tires," he said with satisfaction. "Couldn't happen to a nicer gal."

"Clovis, just leave me alone," I said. The man didn't act like he'd done the deed, but I found it suspicious that he'd been at Don's this morning, as if waiting. And I knew Clovis could act; his whole retirement plan financed by Hank had relied upon his acting skills.

"I was just telling Donny there, I got served on Monday, as in sued," he said ominously. "Apparently ol' Harry Waderich believes that the case I had against him wasn't fair. I got this bum leg that won't allow me to work no more and he thinks he paid too much for it," explained Clovis.

"Well, I'm sorry to hear that, Clovis," I said politely. I was happy to hear that Hank's case was progressing. That might relieve a bit of stress, but I certainly didn't want to be involved anymore at this stage.

"Yeah, according to the paperwork, they got video. Some trumped up thing that claims to show I have no injury. They just don't know how much pain I'm in. I told Donny there about taking pain killers. I gotta', just to hobble around some."

"Well, Clovis, I'd best be going. You take care," I said, extracting myself. I knew what video he was referencing. It was the one I'd obtained from the bartender at The Barn the morning after Clovis had blackmailed me into going there with him——security-camera footage showing Clovis walking easily without the cane.

"Hey, ya' 'member that barkeep, Liz, a real looker like you." continued Clovis as I walked away from him towards the Buick. "She got hers, she got fired, she did."

I stiffened and turned to the man. I felt sick, not like I'd felt after the Event-That-Changed-My-Life, but in the same neighborhood.

"Yep, I done her in good. Told the owner about how I was being sued and all with the video coming from The Barn. Told him how I was going to spill the beans to all my friends if he didn't do sumthin'. And by gosh, right then and there he called up Liz and fired her. Said he'd mail her last check. Told her not to show her face in his bar no more. I heard it," smirked Clovis, mustache twitching. "Eye for an eye, Gracie," he said.

I looked Clovis flat in the face, and I could see the barely restrained wrath there. He either knew of my involvement or suspected it. Since that night at The Barn, Clovis had been hostile towards me, inconsiderate at best and downright rude at times. I knew he was capable of more than just mischief. It had to have been Clovis who'd knifed my tires. I wondered what he was planning next, or if he'd already done it. I'd thought once before that Clovis had committed murder, but could he have attacked Tommy in Gracie's Grounds hoping it' would cause me no end of trouble, and accidently killed him?

Without another word, I turned back to the car. I glanced his way when I opened the car door and saw a satisfied smirk on Clovis's face. The man almost looked gleeful, like he'd won a match in a little contest between the two of us.

I put Clovis out of my mind as I drove back to town. There was little I could do at the moment, since he hadn't admitted anything. I needed to contact Liz and see if I could help. I hated being responsible for her being fired. Jobs were too scarce in these parts to have one pulled out from under you like that. I grabbed my cell and called Emily; she was on speed dial. Thankfully, she picked up on the second ring.

"Hi, Gracie," she began. "I'm as lucky as a cock in a henhouse hearing from you twice in one day."

"Hi, Emily," I laughed. "Listen, do you know a Liz something-or-another, used to work out at that seedy bar called The Barn. I think her real name was Sally Amanda." When we'd first met, Liz had told me how Sally Amanda had gotten shortened to 'salamander' in grade school. Shortly afterwards, she started going by Liz——short for lizard.

"Used to? She get fired or something?" asked Emily.

I told her about my run-in with Clovis, and how Liz had lost her job by Clovis's vengeance. Afterwards, Emily was ready to go have a few choice words with the man, but I was able to dissuade her. Emily didn't need the hassle of involving herself in this mess. She did make me promise to let her know if Clovis did anything remotely threatening. She also said she'd text me Liz's address. Apparently, Liz was a cousin of Henry——Emily's husband. In towns like Alpine, there was always some family connection or another.

I headed back to town towards Margaret's. When I drove through downtown, I glanced at the Mustang. The Beast looked forlorn, sitting askew with the driver's side lower than the passenger's side. Evan's truck was gone for some reason, maybe to get supplies. I hoped the work was progressing. I pulled into the lot at Margaret's and parked near the front. There were a few other vehicles in the lot, but it was still early for lunch, yet late for breakfast. I hoped I had timed it right so I could capture a few moments of Margaret's time.

I walked in the door, having tucked the projections and my hastily written proposal in a manila envelope under one arm. I looked for Margaret, and saw she was busy talking to the short-order cook. I had the time to wait, so I headed towards my favorite booth. I didn't realize until I was there that it was already occupied. Two women, both a bit younger than I, were drinking coffee and talking after having finished a late breakfast. It took me a moment to recognize the woman on the right—the last few days had not been particularly kind to Sandra. She looked like she'd endured more than a few sleepless nights. The woman on the left I didn't know well, but I recognized her pinched nose and perfectly coiffed hair from somewhere. I couldn't place her name, but I knew she was privileged, a bit spoiled, and as mean as a pit-bull facing a rabbit.

"Sandra," I stated. "I wanted to express my condolences on the loss of your father. Tommy was a good man, and a competitive bridge player," I continued. "I just hate that he was killed in the future home of Gracie's Grounds."

"And you are?" interrupted Sandra's companion in a snotty sort of voice.

"Sorry," I smiled. I could be polite, even if Snotty couldn't. "I'm Gracie, Gracie Thies."

"Sandra, don't you own a dress like that?" asked Snotty, eyeing me up and down.

"I donated it this past spring," replied Sandra quietly. "You hired my husband to renovate your building. I think I saw you, when..." I could see the tears in her eyes.

"Yes, I was there," I confirmed softly. I could feel the heat on my face from embarrassment. You weren't supposed to come across the previous owner when you bought something at Goodwill.

"Wait," interrupted Snotty. "She's the one? You mean Evan's having an affair with her!"

"I'm not having an affair with anyone," I firmly stated.

"It's written all over your face! You can't deny it," laughed Snotty. "Sandra, not only is she stealing your man, but also your look."

"Look, Evan is just my contractor. Nothing more," I said heatedly, frustrated by how the conversation had turned.

"Wait until I tell Brandi this——she'll have a hoot," added Snotty with a snort.

"Please stop," murmured Sandra to her snotty friend. "Thank you, Gracie, for your kind words," offered Sandra to me. I felt my heart go out to the woman; she looked shrunken, like an apple left out too long in the sun.

I nodded, ignoring the gleeful smirk on Snotty's face. I picked a nearby booth and sat facing away from the two women. I wouldn't let them chase me away. I couldn't make out any of Sandra's words as they continued talking, but Snotty wasn't quite so circumspect. She was arguing that I was the obvious candidate for Evan's indiscretions. I gathered that Sandra believed Evan was having an affair, but that she was uncertain with whom. From the conversation it was clear that Snotty had no hint Evan was gay.

Margaret gave the two their check before coming my way. She looked harried, and none too pleased to see me. She had her order pad ready and nodded to take my order.

"Do you have a minute to chat," I asked. "Can you sit?"

"Gracie, now is not a good time," replied Margaret. "I'm training a new short-order cook and I'm not sure he's up for the lunch crowd. I really need to get back to him. Now, what can I get ya?"

"It'll only take a minute," I said, gesturing to the seat across from me.

Margaret sat, and I could see the relief on her face from getting off her feet. "Look, I'm sorry I treated you poorly the other day," she said. "I reacted badly to the news of more competition for the lunch crowd in town."

"I know," I said. "But I don't want to talk to you about that. I want to talk business."

"I don't have time to give any advice," laughed Margaret. "I wish you the best of luck, but I'm not going to help."

"Not advice," I smiled. "Listen, Gracie's Grounds won't have a kitchen. It'll be a coffee bar and little else, but I want to serve a few food items. Maybe baked goods——bagels, croissants, that sort of thing. My original plan was to order them from a bakery in Gadsden and have them delivered each morning, but I haven't signed the contract yet. If I change up the menu, I was thinking I could get a local supplier. It would cut on transportation costs at least. I was wondering if you and Frank might be interested."

"In what exactly?" asked Margaret.

"We use the kitchen at the Piggly-Wiggly for some of it, the breads and such," I began. "And use the kitchen here for the pies," I continued. "You have the best pies this side of the Mississippi. I should know——I've eaten enough of them."

"You want to serve pies in a coffee house?"

"Why not?" I asked.

"Won't that just steal customers from here to there?" asked Margaret.

"Maybe, but I doubt that many," I said. "From what I've observed, most of the folks here have a meal before pie. Any lost business should be more than made up for in the profits from a steady customer in Gracie's Grounds, and you can even out the workflow a bit, have something for your employees to do during slow times," I explained. "Here, I wrote up a draft proposal for you and Frank to consider." I handed over the envelope.

"Ha, as if there's profit or a slow time in the restaurant game," laughed Margaret. "Let me talk to Frank about it," she continued as she stood. "I got to get back; you want anything to eat?"

I ordered an old favorite——a Rueben on rye with a side of potato salad and a slice of pecan pie. By the time I was finishing the pie, the place had gotten busy. Margaret looked pretty frantic trying to keep the short-order cook on track. I left a fat tip and earned a smile from Margaret as I left. Whether or not we went into business, Margaret and I were on better terms.

Before I started the Buick, my cell rang and I saw it was Emily. I smiled and answered wondering about the hat-trick of speaking to Emily three times in one morning. The conversation with Emily was short, but no less disconcerting for its brevity. Emily thought she had brought me good news, not realizing that, in fact, all she did was make my panic spike. Doeppers had just brought in Manny Gomez for questioning concerning the murder of Tommy Hilgeman.

I needed to talk to Evan. I knew he'd be devastated. This was almost as bad as if Evan had been arrested. I turned the key and anxiously drove the few blocks to Gracie's Grounds, parking next to the listing Mustang. No one was there—upstairs or down. All I found was a space in the midst of demolition, the chipped commode prominently positioned on the top of a pile of lathe and plaster, like a throne upon a pile of treasure.

I pulled my cell from a pocket and dialed Evan's number. Eventually he answered, and from his tone I knew he'd already heard.

"Evan, I'm so sorry," I said. "I know how this must hurt."

"He didn't do it," Evan pleaded, his voice shaking. "Manny didn't murder Tommy. He was with me that night."

"Why doesn't he just say so?" I asked.

"He can't. We didn't want people to wonder what we were doing together. It wasn't like we were playing charades. And now he's being questioned and there's no way to get our story straight. Whether right or wrong, we both lied and said we were alone that night."

"And you told the police this..."

"When we were interviewed, the morning Manny and I had discovered the body. We'd arrived together. I'd tried to call you, remember, after I'd phoned the police," Evan explained. "Anyhow, the police were on the way and we both looked at each other, trying to decide what to do. I suggested that we claim that we were both alone that night, just in case it came up. Manny agreed. How I wish I'd suggested a different story. This is all my fault."

"No, it isn't," I insisted. "This is the killer's fault."

"Well, Manny isn't going to jail for this. I'll go in and confess before that happens," Evan said.

"Calm down," I replied. "Don't do anything rash."

"Gracie, I think I love him," whispered Evan.

And that was when I knew I had to solve this murder, before an innocent man got convicted for a crime he didn't commit.

Chapter 9

I told Evan that I'd help, that Manny would be fine. I told him to worry about the renovations and let me take care of proving Manny innocent. I told him I'd done this once before, even as my heart thudded with the exaggeration. It wasn't as if I'd solved a murder before. I had more accurately blundered my way through it until the killer had sought me out as a way to end my inquiries. I was an avid mystery reader, though, and knew I could do this. As I was hanging up with Evan, I prayed I wasn't getting in over my head.

And the case against Manny was strong, or at least, strong enough. The man had a prior record and had been unable to give an alibi for the night of the murder. As for motive, Evan's business had suffered as a result of Tommy's refusal to issue permits, that I knew. The police could claim that Manny was afraid of losing his job, and so murdered Tommy when given the opportunity. Perhaps most troubling of all, Manny was Latino. Mexican, in fact. In a place like Alpine, you didn't need an air-tight case when your juror pool would include folks like Mamaw with their learned biases.

The simplest solution was for Evan to provide Manny's

alibi, but at this point about the only thing he could tell the police was the truth, and Evan was not ready for folks in this town to know he was gay. It wasn't as if the police could keep it a secret or would even want to. No, the only way to clear Manny of the murder was to find the killer. And that meant discovering what had happened the night Tommy died.

I thought of Hercule Poirot, and his "method of little grey cells." There were clues here, things I'd discovered over the past couple of days that could lead me to the killer. The trick was figuring out which strings to pull and which others would just make the knot tighter.

Although I'd just had a Rueben, I decided my first stop was Panda Garden for a light lunch. Tommy had eaten there the night of his murder and perhaps Mr. Wang, or someone else who was there that night, could add some insight on that evening. If nothing else, maybe I could narrow the time frame during which Tommy was killed.

I locked up and walked down the block past the Pole & Arms to the Chinese restaurant. The sun was shining, and I knew it would be another scorching day even this far into fall. The door to the Pole & Arms held a hastily scribbled note indicating they'd be open again in 30 minutes. I figured Ida was having trouble with staffing. Considering Cheryl's attitude earlier, I was not really all that surprised.

The lunch crowd at Panda Garden was heavy, but Mr. Wang seemed to have it under control. He gave me a booth and I ordered a Crab Rangoon appetizer with a glass of water. When I indicated I wanted to speak with him or someone else who had been working on the night of the murder, he gave me a skeptical look before nodding. I knew I'd have to wait, but at least I could enjoy the appetizer while I did so.

My order arrived and I ate with relish. I loved the light crab flavor smothered in the sweet red sauce. Afterwards, I saw Mr. Wang speak with a waitress, who looked young enough to be in high school although she clearly wasn't since she was working the lunch shift, and both glanced in my direction. The waitress scanned her area to make sure her customers were content, and then headed my way.

"My Dad said you wanted to talk to someone who was here on Monday night," she stated in a quick, clipped accent. The girl was a few inches shorter than I, with long black hair and Asian features. You could see a hint of her father in the eyes, but her face was much thinner than the older Wang. "I've already gone over this with the police. Why should I talk to you too?" she asked.

"I'm Gracie, and you are?" I prompted, indicating with a gesture she could sit across from me.

"You can call me Yan," she said, slipping into the seat. She crossed her arms over her chest and glanced to her father.

"Well, Yan, I need your help. I need to know what happened the night Tommy Hilgeman died."

"He ate, he left, and was murdered," Yan replied.

"I know that," I snapped. "I want to know what happened before he was killed."

She sighed reluctantly and recited, "He ate dinner here, had the Crispy Duck. His daughter had the Mongolian Beef. I was their waitress. He drank three or four bottles of beer, the daughter had water. He paid for both meals and left a meager tip." Her eyes shifted to her father, and he gave her a nod. Clearly Mr. Wang kept his daughter on a short leash.

"Did you overhear anything? What was Tommy's mood?" I asked, hoping to get something out of this.

"Look, I don't know anything," she said.

"What happened that night?" I persisted. "What you know

may save an innocent man from prison." I saw a crack then, a flicker of interest. I explained that a man I knew, who I also knew was innocent, had been targeted as a suspect. I didn't reveal any names or even hint about homosexuality, but I did shamelessly use the minority card. I could tell by the sudden interest in her eyes that Yan and her family had had some bad experiences on account of their Asian heritage in rural Alabama. As I continued, I could almost see the girl warm to me, uncrossing her arms and sitting in a more relaxed manner, slumped like a bag of potatoes. I hoped she would tell me what she knew, even if she hadn't told the police everything.

She stared for the longest time after I finished. I watched as she stole a glance to her father before continuing, "Mr. Hilgeman was a regular here," she whispered, leaning close. "He mostly ate alone or came with his daughter, but I've seen him once or twice with another woman. He never left a good tip and would pretend not to understand my dad when he talked, saying in his southern drawl that Dad's accent was too thick," she explained with a hint of anger, confirming my suspicions. "I usually got stuck taking his order and serving his food. No one else wanted to deal with him."

"And on Monday night?" I asked.

"I have class on Monday down in Gadsden at the community college, so I'd just started my shift when Mr. Hilgeman and his daughter came in. That would have been around 6:30. They sat over there," Yan said, indicating a table on the other side of the room. "He was upset about something, and I could tell his daughter was getting angry too, something about a construction project. They would stop talking though whenever I checked on them, so I don't know anything else. They left a little before 8:00, I think."

Nothing, or at least nothing very helpful. "Who was this

other woman Tommy sometimes ate with?"

"I don't know, some lady," Yan said, sitting back and relaxing. "Oh, and she was here as well on Monday night—came in for take-out. It was weird though, she didn't say anything to Mr. Hilgeman, didn't even wave."

"Can you describe this other woman?"

"Blond, petite. She dresses nice. Like she spent a lot of time on hair and make-up. Perfect——like the women you see on TV."

"And you don't know her name?" I confirmed, getting a head shake from Yan. It almost sounded like Brandi-With-An-I, but that didn't make any sense. She was the only petite blond I knew in Alpine. I wished I had a photo. "Anything else? How old was she?"

"Younger than Mr. Hilgeman," she snorted. "They would pretend to be just two people eating together if anyone was looking, but he would sit a little too close and would occasionally lean in like he wanted to smell her or something creepy. She, on the other hand, would only smile demurely, like she had to be polite while they talked. You know, encouraging without being too encouraging. You could tell she wasn't interested. You could see it in her eyes when he wasn't looking."

That definitely sounded like Brandi-With-An-I; it was her MO. Maybe Tommy was one of her sources. Had Tommy tired of the cat-and-mouse game Brandi played? "You think Tommy was pressuring her for something more?" I asked.

"I don't know," answered Yan. "Maybe."

"What time was she here?" I asked. "And did Tommy see her?"

"About 7:30ish, I guess. Maybe a bit earlier. I don't know if Mr. Hilgeman saw her or not." She looked around then, like she'd just remembered where she was. "Listen, I gotta' check on my tables," Yan continued as she stood.

"Can I talk to you again later?" I asked. "I may have more questions."

"That's up to my dad," she replied with another glance his way. "It was nice meeting you," Yan continued politely as she left.

I watched as the girl quickly checked her area, filling a few water cups and getting a pair of chop sticks for a portly young man who'd dropped his original pair. A young mom entered with a baby in hand, and I felt the maternal itch as they were seated. I'd always wanted a child of my own, and I had thought Pierre wanted that too, but that was before the accident and my discovery of his subterfuge. Now I was back home, unsure of my future, feeling like my life was on hold.

Once Yan had finished checking her tables, she spoke to her dad before retreating to a corner where a book bag and a scattering of papers cluttered the space. The girl picked up a crumpled paperback and began to read and make notes. I paid my bill and left, thinking about what I'd learned. Brandi had been here that night, shortly before Tommy had been murdered. She'd avoided greeting Tommy and Sandra. Was that because she didn't know how to act in front of them? Or maybe she was afraid of how Tommy would act in front of Sandra, revealing a more intimate relationship between Tommy and her than what was warranted? Sandra and Brandi knew each other, that was clear from this morning's encounter at Margaret's. And Brandi had been embarrassed when I'd caught her with Bert earlier. Maybe she didn't like witnesses to her flirting for information. What if Brandi had waited to talk to Tommy after Sandra left? What if they had stepped into the coffee house for privacy, and Tommy had persisted in his advances? Brandi could have used the hammer in self-defense and had been either too shocked or too embarrassed to admit it.

It was all speculation, but the theory fit the facts. I already knew from the bridge table that Tommy was an overbearing man, with a tendency towards tunnel vision. What if he behaved the same way at work and with his family? I knew Tommy was blocking the building permits for Evan's projects, and I'd learned at the courthouse that Tommy might have delayed the permits for the Carlyle. From what I'd heard, Sandra had been cowed by her father, let alone her life experiences. If Tommy had thought his relationship with Brandi was more than what Brandi had intended it to be, then I could imagine him trying something uncouth in private. It fit with who he was.

I headed to the Buick, and when I opened the door, I regretted not cracking a window. The heat from the interior billowed out like a sudden dust storm in the Sahara. I stood and waited, hoping it would dissipate enough that I wouldn't pass out from a heatstroke trying to drive the car to Mamaw's. Before I could brave the sauna, I saw Tony in his AAA truck head my way. I decided I might as well hear Tony's opinion straight from the horse's mouth as opposed to hearing it secondhand from Don.

The truck pulled into the spot on the other side of the Mustang, and Tony stepped out, hitching his belt over his ample belly while spitting to the side. Tony liked his chew. The only time I'd seen the man without a wad in his mouth was on Easter morning in church. I'd never cared for the habit. Personally, I found chewing tobacco disgusting, but I was polite enough not to show it. Besides, I had no business judging people on nicotine use after the trouble I had quitting smoking.

When I joined Tony by the Mustang, he gave me a mealy grin. I gave a polite one in return, barely keeping myself from flinching at the remnants of chewing tobacco in the cracks of his yellowing teeth. He hitched his belt again before kneeling and running a calloused hand over a deflated tire. You could see the gap where the knife had gone in.

"Yep, gonna' need a new one," Tony drawled. "Can't repair it when it's the sidewall like this," he continued with another spit. He glanced up my way, the chew making his lower lip bulge like a water balloon ready to burst.

"I was afraid of that," I said. "What's the best way to do this?"

"Well, Missy," replied Tony. "Could call a flatbed, I guess." He stood and paused, thinking. "You got a spare?"

"I think so," I said.

"Well, let's check then," he said. He hitched his belt after fishing for the set of keys I'd given to Don. Tony popped the trunk and grunted. "Yep," he confirmed. "I'll put the spare on the front, hitch it with Betsy there," he said with a thumb to his truck, "and take her on out to Don's. That'll save you a penny or two."

"Sounds like a plan," I said. "What do I owe you?"

"Don will take care of it," Tony said with a spit. I watched as he hefted the spare and began to roll it to the front tire. "He'll tack it on with the bill for setting you up with new tires."

"How hard is it to knife a tire?" I asked. Maybe I could make some progress on solving this little mystery.

"Well, Missy," Tony said, giving me a glance. "It doesn't take much force in a sidewall like this," he explained. "There's no steel in the sidewall, unlike the thread. You could do it with a pocketknife easily enough."

"So, anyone could have done it?" I asked deflated.

"'Fraid so," confirmed Tony.

I thanked him and left him to his business. He didn't need me there supervising his work. And besides, the stench from the chewing tobacco was beginning to make my stomach curl.

The temperature in the Buick was bearable, if just. I turned the key and immediately set the AC on high. I knew it wouldn't do much on the short ride to Mamaw's, but anything was better than nothing. As I pulled up to the Victorian, I saw Mamaw and Ada Mae sitting and talking on the front porch. I cracked a window, leaving the Buick on the street just behind Ada Mae's white sedan, and joined them. Mamaw wanted the car later and I'd learned my lesson.

"I invited Ada Mae for a light lunch; you want anything?" asked Mamaw. She'd set out a plate full of sandwiches and a pitcher of sweet tea, with three glasses. That was all the hint I needed to know I was expected at this powwow.

"I ate already," I replied, and then explained about my dual lunch. I did pour myself half a glass of tea. While in Paris my taste for the drink had waned, but I wanted to show my appreciation for the effort Mamaw had made.

"It's a shame what happened to your car," Ada Mae offered. "Any idea who did it?"

"I just saw Tony; he said about anyone could have knifed the tires. Said I'd need to get two new ones."

"Don will take care of that," insisted Mamaw. "I told Ada Mae about the misunderstanding. That you and Hank are going through a rough patch but that there was no truth to the rumors of you and that other man," Mamaw finished with a pinched nose.

"I'm sure you and Hank will work things out," offered Ada Mae, with a pat on my knee. I watched as she took a bite of her sandwich.

"I'm not sure how that rumor got started," I said, taking my cue. "There's certainly nothing between Evan Petrovich and me other than business. He's my contractor for Gracie's Grounds, nothing more."

"That's what I told her, dear," replied Mamaw with a smile. She was working hard to counteract the rumor mill.

"Well, I'm glad to hear it," said Ada Mae. "I knew you could never be involved with a married man. That's just not done in these parts."

"City ways," replied Mamaw sagely, as if infidelity were a plague restricted to the metropolitan areas.

"Can I ask you something?" I said. "Do you know if Tommy Hilgeman was seeing anyone before he died?"

"Tommy?" answered Mamaw. "There was this rumor a few months ago," she said, her face looked like she'd been cooking cabbage.

"I remember," added Ada Mae. "Tommy was seen out with a married woman. And the other circumstances there, unsettling."

"Now there's nothing wrong with a man Tommy's age dating," added Mamaw. "He just needs to keep to the single woman."

"True," said Ada Mae. "And she was so much younger than him."

"It's not unlike the rumors floating about you, Gracie," said Mamaw. "Dating and romance is fine among the single folk. But you don't mess with a union sanctioned by the Lord above."

"Amen," crowed Ada Mae.

"Who was the woman?" I asked, prepared to hear Brandi's name. I hadn't realized Brandi was married——maybe that was why she didn't like to be seen flirting for information.

"Well, I'm not sure we should say," smirked Mamaw.

"Wouldn't want to spread rumors," chimed Ada Mae.

I waited patiently, knowing it was only a matter of time.

"And I'm sure it was nothing, a misunderstanding," said Mamaw.

"No need to speak ill of the dead," offered Ada Mae.

"But you know with Tommy's murder, those rumors may start up again," said Mamaw thoughtfully.

"Only way to counter them is with the truth," said Ada Mae. "The Lord above knows that."

"Gracie knows all about rapacious rumors," said Mamaw. "And how hard it is to fight against them."

"You've gone through so much," said Ada Mae. "I've told Nora how proud I am of you, moving on so beautifully after all that you've endured. And to think, now you're starting your own business!"

"You probably do need to know the details," offered Mamaw in a voice I immediately recognized. It was the voice she used before revealing a secret——one that she only used to indicate a faux reluctance before revealing what she knew. I braced myself in preparation.

"It was Marion Vinner," said Mamaw and Ada Mae together as if rehearsed.

"Who?" I asked. I thought I knew the name from somewhere, but I was so shocked on not hearing Brandi's name that the connection escaped me.

"Marion Vinner," said Ada Mae. "She does something for the city. Works for the Health Department, I think."

"She does the health inspections for restaurants and such. Tommy was her boss," offered Mamaw. "And she's married to boot. Two good reasons for Tommy to keep clear."

I felt like I was back in high school, when Mr. Klink

announced a pop quiz over the War Between the States when I'd prepared for the War of 1812. "What does she look like?" I asked.

"Nice looking, a bit older than you. Maybe mid-forties," offered Mamaw.

"Younger than Tommy for sure," crowed Ada Mae.

"Small-boned, blonde hair," continued Mamaw. "Why, dear?"

"When I was at Panda Garden, one of the waitresses mentioned that Tommy had eaten there recently with a woman. I was just wondering who she was."

"Well, I guess that could have been Marion," said Mamaw. "Or maybe it was someone else, that rumor about them is a couple of months old now. He may have moved on."

"You know, Tommy had a type," said Ada Mae. "His late wife, Sandra's mother, was also blonde and small-boned."

"Did Tommy date many women since his wife died?" I asked.

"A few," murmured Mamaw thoughtfully. "He was pretty busy with Sandra and her sister early on, I think, and he was grieving, of course. Those two girls of his were quite the pair, gave him a run for his money. College must have been good for Sandra; she settled down with that husband of hers quite nicely when they moved back, at least until recently. Tommy so wanted grandchildren; I know he was hopeful before things went south."

I knew exactly why Sandra had 'settled down,' but I wasn't going to share that with Mamaw and Ada Mae. Sandra deserved her privacy and didn't need the gossip mill using her experience for grist. "So, what happened there anyhow?" I asked. "Between Evan and Sandra, I mean?" It would be interesting to hear what rumors were floating. I caught a stern look from Mamaw which was strange, but Ada Mae answered my question.

"Most folk believe Evan had found another woman, that or Sandra had found another man. That's usually the cause of a sudden split like that around these parts. After your argument with Tommy at the bridge club, that's why so many thought it was you, Gracie. I'm so glad that you were able to clarify that situation," said Ada Mae. I could see the glint in her eyes. The progress I'd made with my earlier denials had just been eroded by my ill-advised queries. That was probably the cause of Mamaw's look. I should have known better than to show interest in Evan's personal life.

"It must have been Sandra," I said confidently. I hated to throw Sandra under the bus, especially when I knew it was false, but I couldn't allow any hint of a romantic relationship between Evan and me to persist. Not with what I knew and if I hoped to have any chance with Hank. Besides, once Evan came out all would be explained away. "I saw how upset Evan had been about Tommy the morning his body was discovered, and how his heart ached for Sandra in her grief. He was devastated by how his marriage was falling apart. That was what we were talking about, you know, when we were seen together," I clarified.

I could see the delight in Ada Mae's eyes——she'd bought it hook, line and sinker. It was like I'd just given her an unexpected gift at Christmas.

"You know, consoling a man can lead to dangerous ground," said Mamaw ominously. She still looked a little miffed about where this conversation had gone.

"True," replied Ada Mae thoughtfully.

"I was just trying to be kind," I said to reinforce my denial. "I have no interest in Evan, other than as my contractor. I'm devoted to Hank."

"And what is the cause of this row between the two of you?" Ada Mae asked.

I explained then. How Hank was working two jobs to pay Harry's debts while still taking care of his crippled father. How there was no time remaining for the two of us to be together. I explained how it made me feel like I was not a priority in Hank's life, although I knew all the pressures he was under. I poured my heart out, knowing that Ada Mae needed to hear it if she was going to defend me to others. I laid it on a little thick, but better safe than sorry.

The conversation wandered, leading to people who hadn't lived in the area for years. Ada Mae had already committed to visiting her sister in Anniston on Sunday, so Mamaw and I agreed to partner for bridge that afternoon after church. Gladys had co-opted the regular game, making it into a memorial game for Tommy much like what she'd done for Edward Schultz a few months ago. As the two finished eating, we discussed logistics for the afternoon. Mamaw agreed to drop me off downtown at the courthouse while she ran her errands. I hoped to learn something about Tommy there, and I could use the excuse of getting a copy of the building permit to explain my visit. I promised to give Mamaw a call once I heard from Don, and she said she'd give me a ride to retrieve the Mustang. We said our goodbyes to Ada Mae, and it took just minutes to clear the dishes before Mamaw and I were back in her Buick.

"Why the sudden interest in Tommy?" asked Mamaw when she turned the key. "It's not like you to pry," she continued, pulling onto the street.

I stiffened. I didn't want to involve Mamaw in my quest. The fiasco with Edward Schultz had taught me that Mamaw could and would go her own way in a misguided effort to help if she discovered my interest. "I was just curious is all," I stalled. "He was murdered in Gracie's Grounds."

"The man is dead, and I hear they found the killer, some lowlife Mexican. I don't know why they let that kind in this country," said Mamaw. "Those migrants working on the Carlyle was why I had to purchase the revolver, and we both know how that turned out."

"His name is Manny," I said. "And how can you blame any Latino for the incident with Edward Schultz? The workers at the Carlyle had nothing to do with it." I paused, and then went for broke. "You've got to stop, Mamaw."

"Stop what?" she asked looking towards me while at the stop sign on Main. We were not far from the courthouse.

"Stop blaming an entire people for perceived wrongs," I said. "You're better than that, a better Christian."

"I don't do that," she argued in a huff.

"Mamaw," I said.

"Fine," she snapped. "Maybe I do a bit," she admitted sheepishly after a moment of silence. "I'm sorry. But in this case, I'm not wrong. This Manny is Mexican and he committed murder."

I sighed, in for a penny in for a pound. "He didn't do it," I said. "He has an alibi. The police just don't know that yet."

"How do you know?" asked Mamaw, pulling to a stop in front of the courthouse.

"I just do," I answered, feeling the heat on my face. My promise not to reveal Evan's secret was taking its toll on me.

"Gracie Amelia Thies," said Mamaw sternly. I was in for a lecture.

"I made a promise," I interrupted. "And I won't break my word. But I know the police have this wrong and there is a killer on the loose."

"Are you trying to solve this murder?" asked Mamaw with a gleam in her eye. I'd seen the look before, back when Edward Schultz had been killed.

I didn't answer; I didn't want Mamaw to get involved, not if I could help it. Instead, I ignored her, opened the car door, and walked away. I prayed Mamaw wouldn't do anything foolish, but I feared my prayers were in vain. Mamaw would do what she wished. Unfortunately, there was nothing I could do about it now.

Although the day was scorching, the interior of the courthouse was pleasant enough. The thick limestone blocks from which the structure was built provided a natural barrier resistant to the temperature fluctuations outside. The woman manning the metal detector gave me a quick nod as I passed through, my footsteps echoing upon the old-growth wood floors.

The door to the Department of Code Enforcement and Permits was ajar, and I knocked softly upon the doorframe as I entered. I found Tina perched in the small space wearing an off-white shift dress today, with only a tie-dye scarf to lend a little color to her outfit. Her eyes were puffy, and the lines on her face were more pronounced than what I'd remembered from Monday. The only other change to the space was the addition of a small wall hanging behind her desk——a poem for the dead, complete with a six-pointed star inscribed in a circle centered above the text.

"Hi, Tina," I said. "I was hoping you could help me."

"A servant of the White Lady strikes, and the flame yet seeks," intoned Tina. "By the blessing of the Goddess I have seen it. How may this one serve in her grief, and thus do Her will?"

"I'm so sorry about Tommy," I said after a moment. "I'm just sick he was killed in Gracie's Grounds. I hate to bother you, but

I came in to get a copy of the building permit. Somehow the original has gone missing."

"One of his last noble acts," she sighed. "I can make you a copy," she continued opening a file drawer to search for the document. "Who have you selected to administer the cleansing ritual?" she asked.

"What?"

"The cleansing ritual, to banish the remnants of the White Lady's touch from that place," Tina explained. "I have foreseen that ill-fortune will lurk until the space is rededicated to Brighid. There is no choice."

"I'm not so…"

"I have the book right here," she said. Tina closed the file drawer and instead opened the top drawer of her desk to pull out the same leather-bound book I'd seen earlier. There was an intricate Celtic knot embossed on the leather cover. It reminded me of some of the mass-produced occult texts I'd seen in bookstores, although this one looked older and of higher quality. Tina lovingly opened the tome and carefully flipped through the pages.

"Tina…" I tried.

"Here it is," she interrupted. "Let me see…ah…yes. It says so right here. The White Lady's presence has been felt, a murder. It has left a wound, a scar that must be healed. A ritual to cleanse, to relink the space to Brighid." She looked up from the book and I could see the pleading in her eyes. "I could do this for you. I must. It will allow me to regain the blessing of Cethlion."

"Ah…"

"You have been brushed by the White Lady. Ill-fortune clings to you, although Brighid has not left you in your time of need.," she said. "I have seen it. You will have no peace until the space is cleansed and Brighid is allowed full access to your spirit again. It is no accident that bodies are drawn to you."

I thought about the months since I'd returned to Alpine, and all that had happened. There was a bit of bad luck there. I didn't believe the same as Tina, but I saw no harm in it. "I haven't found anyone yet; I'd be honored if you would do the ritual for me," I said on a whim. "Maybe before the grand opening."

"The sooner the better," said Tina sagely, and then the smile broke upon her face. I knew I'd made her day, so at least some good had come from this mess. "And you and those closest to you must be there. It will link you to the space and form a bond that will help protect you from the White Lady and her disciples. I will make all of the arrangements. I know exactly who to ask for help."

"And what does this ritual entail?" I asked, hoping I hadn't agreed to flinging animal parts or something less savory within my newly remodeled coffee shop.

"A commune with the Goddesses Arnamentia and Brighid, nothing else will suffice," Tina replied as if that explained everything. "You must be careful until then," she warned. "Another disciple of the White Lady lurks in Alpine, and is drawn unwaveringly to you."

"Listen," I said, changing the subject before Tina unnerved me with talk of murderers stalking me. "Was Tommy dating anyone?" I asked. "I'd heard a rumor about him and...well..." I said waving vaguely towards Marion Vinner's office. It wasn't very subtle, but then again with Tina I figured it didn't matter.

"Alas, Tommy had sought comfort in Marion's embrace, but it was not to be. Her aura was tied to another by the Goddess. Tommy was a stubborn man, one who found rebuffs to his advancements as a personal affront. I cannot help but wonder if

Tommy's darkness drew the White Lady's disciple, but that thought is uncouth, unworthy of a follower of Cethlion. In any case, his pursuit of Marion upset the Balance and uprooted his tree. I have spent hours on spells to invoke blessings on this office, and now I must prepare a cleansing ritual. You will attend?"

"I'll be there," I laughed. "As long as I don't have to do anything unseemly. Now about that building permit."

"Oh, of course. Let me get that for you," she said, opening the file drawer again. As she was looking, she told me about the ritual. We would need some candles, and a few herbs and incense to burn. Nothing that sounded too outrageous, thank goodness.

When Tina turned to put the paperwork in the copy machine in the corner, I noticed the broken vase had been replaced with a small pot filled with morning glory. It looked nice, and I told Tina so.

"Oh, that," she said. "Clyde bought it as a kinda' apology. It was very sweet of him," she continued as her cheeks turned crimson. I wondered if there was more between the two than I'd realized.

"Did Clyde get the permits updated for the Carlyle?" I asked, remembering what he'd said on Monday.

"Oh, that," said Tina, handing the copy of the building permit to me. "With Tommy's demise, that task fell directly to Clyde. I suspect he will give a cursory review and approve."

So, with Tommy gone, the Carlyle project would move forward unhindered. That sure sounded like a motive for murder.

Chapter 10

With the building permit in hand, I had no excuse to linger, even as I wondered if I'd stumbled upon the true motive for Tommy's murder. I hesitated but figured I'd learned what I could from Tina. I said my goodbyes, reassured her that I'd be in touch on the timing of the cleansing ritual, and headed on my way.

Don called as I was leaving the courthouse, and the timing could not have been better. The heat promised earlier in the day had begun to bake Alpine, like a pound cake in an easy-bake oven. I found a spot of shade on the north side of the statue of Colonel Corbert and gave Mamaw a call. While I waited, I pondered what I'd learned.

Tommy had been a headstrong man set in his ways and not very observant. He tended to take the most obvious lines at the bridge table and scowled fiercely when things didn't fall in his favor. He'd pursued a relationship with Marion Vinner, only to be disappointed. It was still an open question on whether Brandi Yugler had used him as a source and had led him on by doing so. And he'd delayed the work on the Carlyle, either for some legitimate reason or out of pure mischief. Tommy had been fiercely devoted to his family, had wanted grandchildren, and had not been above using his position to put pressure on others to achieve his goals.

And that left with me several avenues I could pursue in my efforts to clear Manny's name. There was a very real possibility that Tommy had been removed to clear the way for some building project, either at the Carlyle or elsewhere. Maybe some crooked investor down Birmingham way had hired someone to pressure Tommy, and the result was murder. Yet the circumstances of the killing were inconsistent with that theory. No self-respecting thug would use a happened-upon-hammer to murder Tommy, not when he would have been armed. On the other hand, perhaps Tommy's floundering romantic life had led to his demise. Maybe he'd pressured Marion or Brandi one time too many, and they or someone close to one of them had taken matters into their own hands either in anger or self-defense. It fit the scene, at least from what I knew. Or was there yet another, undiscovered, target of Tommy's unwanted affections?

I shook my head, realizing I was spinning in circles like on the merry-go-round over at Mary Francis Woods Elementary. On every hand, bridge players have to make decisions based on partial information, and then take the most likely line of play. The same was true in life; make the best decision you can based on what you know at the time. I needed to approach the investigation in the same way, and that meant thinking of this murder as an act of passion. I'd ignore the building permit as motive for now and pursue the unrequited affection angle.

I saw the Buick, pulling me out of my ruminations, and waved to Mamaw as I hurried to the curb. Thankfully, she had the air going so the Buick felt quite pleasant as I hopped into the passenger side. I saw the determined look on Mamaw's face and knew that she had an agenda for the impending discussion. As she pulled away from the curb she began.

"You say this Mexican has an alibi," she said, "but that you made a promise not to reveal the details."

"Yes," I agreed. "Manny is innocent."

"And the police don't know the alibi," continued Mamaw.

"That's correct," I said.

"You aren't the alibi. You wouldn't have phrased it that way if you were the one with Manny that night," she mused. "And to want to keep it secret must mean there's something to keep secret."

"Mamaw…" I said, dread filling me.

"So," she interrupted. "Manny was with someone else, someone who'd have confided in you."

"Don't," I said.

"I'd guess Emily, but she's on the force and would've circumvented a problem like this herself. And it isn't as if you've made many friends in this town, not who'd confide in you so freely. And it must be someone with whom you'd spoken recently."

"No more speculation," I said sternly.

"I don't need to," she laughed. "Your face says it all. And it explains so much more as well——the marriage problems, lack of grandkids, Tommy's frustration."

"You can't say anything," I said. "I'm serious."

"Such a shame too," she snickered. "That man reminds me of your Papaw, back in the day. With that smile of his that could charm the pants off a virgin."

"Mamaw!" I blushed. "How…why…"

"Oh, don't be such a prude, Gracie," Mamaw said. "I had my day, even if now is yours. The question is what you are going to do about it?"

"There's nothing to do; Evan was born that way," I said. I so did not want to get into the discussion of nature versus nurture with Mamaw. That would be a nightmare without end.

"I know that, silly goose; I meant about proving this Mexican innocent," Mamaw said. "Excuse me, I meant proving Manny innocent."

"No," I said. "First we need to discuss Evan and his situation. You can't tell anyone, Mamaw. Not here, not in this town. It could ruin him. He has the right to his privacy, and I only know because of circumstances."

"Oh, I get it," she said. "My lips are sealed. You know your uncle Thom was gay."

"What?" I said. She explained then about Great Uncle Thom, Papaw's brother, who passed when I was little. I remembered him as a bear of a man, big and hairy. He'd always sported a shaggy beard, with longish hair on his head. The hair on his legs and arms had been like a carpet. On the drive to Don's, Mamaw mentioned several other Alpine residents from days past, who either were gay or were generally assumed to be so. There were the two elementary school teachers, both unmarried woman, who'd bought a little house together where they lived until retirement. There was the owner of the dime store, before it closed, who was a lifelong bachelor and had rebuffed all efforts at matchmaking. They were here all along——valued residents of Alpine, living a life of quiet existence in the shadows.

"And then there are the Strange sisters," Mamaw said as she pulled into Don's. "Neither of the two married, but then again…they are quite strange."

"Mamaw," I moaned. "Do you have any idea how many times I've heard that pun."

"Too many," she laughed. "I know, you can't get away from

it with those two."

"You really think they're gay, or at least one of them?" I asked.

"I'm not sure. Sometimes people just prefer to remain unmarried."

We'd arrived at Don's, and so we left the conversation there. As I got out of the car, I told Mamaw that I'd see her this evening and mentioned my plan to head to the farm to see Harry. I knew Hank was scheduled to work, and someone needed to check on the old coot. Hank and I might be in a rough patch, but I still cared for him and his father. Mamaw didn't look pleased; but didn't look unhappy either. If anything, she looked resigned.

Don had rotated the tires on the Beast and checked the alignment, putting the two new ones on the back. He gave me a good price for the work, too good of a price. When I objected, he waved me off, saying it was the least he could do, considering. I thanked him and started the Mustang, feeling a wave of satisfaction as it rumbled to life.

I took the road back towards town, but quickly turned onto an old county road to head north. It would put me out near the old round barn, a historic structure where Hank and I had spent a lazy afternoon back in high school. That day had been the end of the tentative exploration stage of our relationship, when neither of us knew if the attraction we felt was real and the beginning of something more, or if it was a chimera doomed to vanish. Hank had asked me to be his steady girl that day, the sun shining through the slats in the barn making golden bars across the hay covered floor. He had been my first love, our whirlwind romance only ending when marijuana was found in my car that spring, and then Hank distanced himself at the demand of his father.

The barn looked worn when I passed, more fragile than the structure in my mind's eye. I wondered for how many more years the place would stand, and if others would have the chance to find love exploring its depths, like Hank and I had.

I pulled my mind from woolgathering as I turned onto the drive that headed to the Waderich farmhouse. The single lane road was lined with pecan trees, the result of an ill-conceived plot by a Waderich ancestor to add an additional cash crop. The nuts had never been of a quality to be harvested and sold, and instead were left to litter the drive and lawn each fall. The last productive use of the crop was as an additive to the hog feed years ago.

The house at the end of the gravel was much like the trees that guarded the drive, a structure that never quite lived up to its potential and had seen better days. The white paint was peeling, and the covered front porch was settling a bit on the west side, making the house look like it was leaning towards the setting sun, not unlike a sunflower following the light. I could see a hint of curtains showing from the rightmost gable window on the second floor. The lace sheers were yellowing, I knew——that was the room that I shared with Hank when I was visiting. And the farmyard still held the choked flowerbeds and dead redbud trees that I'd noticed on my first visit after returning to Alpine. Hank didn't have the time or inclination to keep the place as it had been when he was a child.

I sighed and turned the key to the Beast, killing the engine. Katydids and songbirds filled the void, defying the otherwise obvious conclusion of a lifeless place in decay. So little had changed here since I'd reconnected with Hank, I wondered whether it could or if I had a future with the man. Could we build a life together, in this place and in this time, given what we had against us?

I planted a smile on my face and marched to the front door. I didn't bother knocking, having dispensed with that necessity weeks before. I called to Harry as I entered, hearing nothing, and worked my way past the front room and stairs towards the kitchen. I figured Harry was ensconced in the family room, a space tucked in the back part of the house.

A gasp escaped me at the sight of the kitchen. Food and a broken plate covered the linoleum, a glass of tea had been spilled on the red countertop, and the table sat askew with a chair overturned. I worriedly called for Harry, but heard nothing, and carefully picked my way past the mess. I saw the upturned wheelchair first, and found Harry huddled on the floor unmoving on the far side. I rushed to his aid, knelt, and saw his face was swollen and bruised. My heart was beating so loudly I swore it could be heard on the other side of the county. My pulse only settled when I saw that Harry was still breathing. The man was alive, although barely.

Blood leaked from Harry's ear, and I felt a moment of vertigo when I realized how near I was to that crimson liquid. Thankfully, it passed, and I stood and took a deep breath before pulling my cell from my pocket. I dialed 911 and quickly gave the address saying that Harry had been attacked and that I needed help. I said Harry was alive and looked stable, or at least there was nothing that I knew to do to help the man. The dispatcher urged me to leave the victim untouched so as not to make matters worse, and assured me that help was imminent. She said I needed to stay on the line until that help arrived.

I retreated to the kitchen and sat in one of the upright chairs. I knew my nerves would fail me if I stayed too long in a room with fresh blood. I answered the inane questions the dispatcher barked, grunting personal details as my mind wandered. I felt the urge to clean, make pristine the kitchen that Mildred had spent a lifetime using to care for Hank and Harry. I knew I couldn't. The Waderich farmhouse was now a crime scene, and there might be evidence hidden in the mess somehow. I needed to call Hank; I had to tell him about his father, but I was stuck on the phone with the dispatcher, unable to do anything until help arrived. Who could have done this to poor Harry, a cripple in a wheelchair?

It had to be Clovis. I suddenly knew it in my bones. And that meant he'd also been the culprit who'd knifed my tires. I told the dispatcher my revelation, that Clovis Jones had attacked Harry. She asked if the man was here with me, and if I'd witnessed the attack. I told her that I was alone, that I hadn't seen Clovis since this morning when he'd threatened me. She asked if Clovis had threatened Harry too, and I had to say no, that Harry wasn't there this morning. And then I insisted that Clovis had attacked Harry, and that he was a cripple. She thought I meant that Clovis was a cripple, and then I had to explain Harry was the one who'd lost his legs after the accident, not Clovis. I told her Clovis only had a limp, but that it was fake, and that Hank was suing him. I said I needed to call Hank to let him know, and she reminded me to stay on the line until help arrived. I insisted that I really needed to call Hank, and that he had knifed my tires. She asked why Hank had knifed my tires, and I told her Clovis had done it. Eventually she asked me to calm down, and to tell the story from the beginning. I knew then I'd made a muddled mess of things, and that was when I heard the sirens.

I hung up, disgusted with myself, and quickly checked on Harry again before heading out front to meet the EMTs. The ambulance was led by two police cars, with lights flashing. I saw Emily at the wheel of the front cruiser. She slammed the car into park next to the Mustang, making gravel fly, and I felt a tension I didn't know I held loosen as she headed my way. I motioned to the paramedics that were moments behind, indicating that Harry was in the back of the house, and then my vision blurred as the tears came. Before I knew what was happening, Emily was there, holding me gently and murmuring that all would be well while I tried to collect myself.

I lost track of the number of people who entered the house. Doeppers was there, managing the commotion, yet thankfully leaving me alone, his firm presence driving home the reality of what I'd seen. And then I saw Harry rolled out on a gurney. I rushed to his side, but the paramedics didn't slow as they quickly rolled him to the ambulance. As I watched the ambulance streak down the pecan-lined lane, I knew I had to break the news to Hank. I didn't know what I'd say, but I knew I had to say it.

"Have you called Hank?" asked Emily.

"Not yet," I wavered. "I called 911 first and the dispatcher kept me on the phone."

"That's protocol," answered Emily. "Are you ready to make a statement?"

"No," I said, taking a big breath. "But let's do it anyhow." It would at least give me some time to figure out how to tell Hank about the attack on his father.

Emily called to Doeppers, and we retreated to the porch swing, well away from the front door. It was not an ideal location for an interview, but at least it was out of the way. I perched on the edge of the swing, and Emily sat next to me, both of us trying to keep the swing still. Doeppers remained standing, hovering over us like the old weeping willow by Cacanaw Creek. The man pulled a notepad from his back pocket and gave me an expectant look, while the katydids continued chirping in the background filling the silence.

Having been in this position before, I knew what to expect and took a deep breath before I began.

I told Doeppers that Hank and I were in a relationship, and that I routinely checked on Harry on those days that Hank was working in Gadsden. I told him this was just a normal trip, and that I'd last been to the farm on Monday afternoon. I explained which roads I took today, what I saw when I arrived, and how I'd found Harry. I told him I immediately called 911, and that I stayed on the line until I heard the sirens, disturbing nothing. And then I told him that Clovis Jones had done it.

Doeppers threw me a skeptical look, the corners of his mouth turning downward even as an eyebrow rose. I felt a slight thrill, having for once surprised the man. I knew he needed my reasoning, and so I continued.

I told Doeppers that Clovis was enraged by a lawsuit, Hank's attempt to recoup some of the money that Clovis had won as an award in the case Clovis had filed against Harry. The auto accident that had cost Harry his legs had also injured Clovis, I explained, but the charlatan had exaggerated his injuries to get a much larger award than what was warranted. I said that Hank just wanted a fair settlement, enough that he could pay off the lien on the farm they had been forced to take to make the payments to Clovis.

I explained that Clovis had threatened me this morning at Don's service station, because he'd correctly identified my involvement in obtaining the video evidence. I told Doeppers how Clovis had already gotten revenge on another woman, the bartender who'd given me the video footage, and that Clovis was so enraged by the threat to his comfortable life that he was lashing out at everybody, including Harry.

I was not surprised when Doeppers ignored my conclusions, and instead concentrated his questions on the scene at Don's. It was his method. I spent the next fifteen minutes recounting every detail that I could remember of that conversation, and I swear he even elicited a few details I had forgotten. After a time, he seemed satisfied, closing the notebook and shoving it back into his rear pocket.

"You should send out an APB for Clovis Jones. Get him before he does something else," I explained. "The man is a menace."

"We'll question Mr. Jones," Doeppers replied. "But tell me, in what way does attacking Mr. Waderich help Mr. Jones?"

"It doesn't," I said after a moment of thought. "He did it out of pure thorniness. An act of revenge."

"Now, who gains from the removal of Mr. Waderich?" pondered Doeppers. "Any thoughts?" he asked, watching closely.

I took a moment to think, and then felt the heat on my face. Just days ago, Hank and I had fought over Harry and how Hank's life had been upturned by the actions of his father. It would be simpler if Harry just vanished, leaving the space for Hank and me to move forward, but I'd never harm the old coot. "I don't appreciate the tone of your questions," I said sternly.

"Then let me ask another," posited Doeppers. "Why is it, Miss Thies, that whenever there's a body or a violent assault, I find you at the center of it?"

"Look," I said, my Irish heritage getting the better of me. "I had nothing to do with what happened to Harry, or Tommy, or whoever. I was just unlucky enough to find them, or whatever," I continued vaguely waving an arm.

"Ah, a real body magnet then," smirked Doeppers.

I stood, rocking the swing, causing Emily to tumble to the porch floor with a thud. I pushed my way past the annoying man, ignoring Emily's squawk, and marched to the front yard trying to regain control of my anger. I couldn't believe that arrogant, spiteful, deceitful man. I prayed the remaining scattering of hair on his head would fall out. I wished to shove his fat face into the old well on the north side of the house yard. I wanted...it didn't matter. I grabbed hold of my anger and shoved it to the back of my mind. Harry had been attacked; Hank still didn't know his father was injured. I wouldn't let this man sidetrack me from what needed to be done.

I pulled my cell from my pocket, but before I could dial, Emily was beside me. She took the phone from my hand and shook her head negatively. I told her I needed to call Hank, and she replied that she'd have to do it. For the time being, Chief Doeppers didn't want any communication between the two of us, not until the chief had had a chance to question Hank first. Not until the chief confirmed that neither Hank nor I had anything to do with the incident in the farmhouse.

It was a body blow, like when I finally accepted that Hank and I were finished in high school, like when I'd first heard of the plane crash, like when I discovered Pierre's secret after his death. It felt like a pillar of my life had been taken from me, forcing me to balance on what remained.

I had to accept it. Harry was alive and once he regained consciousness, he could tell the police what had happened. In time, all would return to normal, or at least a facsimile of normal. For the time being I had to endure. I nodded to Emily and saw the look of relief in her eyes. She knew how hard this had to be for me, and somehow her concern gave me strength. I would survive, yet again.

I turned and walked back to Doeppers. I saw the weariness in the corners of his eyes, and the fatigue. The man had a murder to solve, and now an assault as well. The sleepy town of Alpine, not unlike the fabled Brigadoon of Irish lore, had a sudden rash of violence, or as Tina would probably say, the White Lady had been roaming the streets. It mustn't be easy to be a police chief in a town Alpine's size, with the expectation that he keep folks safe.

"I did not assault Harry Waderich," I said firmly.

He nodded——it was not agreement I knew, but only an acknowledgment of my claim of innocence.

"You should know that Hank and I had a fight, a misunderstanding over something he thought he saw that's unrelated," I explained. "It grew into a row over Harry, and how we were going to move our relationship forward while still meeting Harry's needs. Hank and I are still working on that," I admitted. "I tell you this so you know I had motive, but I didn't harm Harry," I said, feeling the steel in my voice.

"I understand," said Doeppers quietly.

"And you arrested the wrong man for Tommy's murder," I finished as I spun and walked away.

Chapter 11

Surprisingly, Doeppers let me go, well at least didn't try and detain me for further questioning. Instead, he sent Emily my way and headed into the farmhouse. By the time I got to the Mustang, Emily was by my side. She silently handed me my cell phone, and then a smile broke on her face like the sun breaking through the clouds.

"Bull's balls, girl, I've never seen Jon cowed that way," she snickered. "And I was married to that man."

"I don't believe you," I laughed. I couldn't help it. My Irish heritage may come upon me like a sudden summer storm, but it dissipated as quickly.

"I think he likes you," Emily said.

I was appalled. Jon high-and-mighty Doeppers liked me? Impossible.

"Oh, not that way," laughed Emily. "Ya' should see the look on your face, like I just claimed the swill served at The Barn is better than one of your fancy Merlots. I'm only saying that Jon is not surprised by most folks, and yet ya' seem to throw him curve balls. He finds ya' a tough nut to crack."

I looked back to the front porch, seeing Doeppers in a deep

conversation with Bert Lancaster. I hadn't even been aware that Bert was here. I wondered if I'd be reading about the assault at the Waderich place in tomorrow's Tribune.

I found nothing about Doeppers attractive. He tried to hide his impending baldness with a buzz cut, keeping his thinning hair short like he was in the military. His once muscular frame was sagging, but you could still see that some power remained. And he was a smart man, something he usually kept hidden behind a façade of southern mannerisms and a drawl. There were worse men in Alpine, that I knew.

"I called the Gadsden police," Emily said. "We got the address for Hank's work from a paystub inside. They're sending an officer over to inform Hank, and to see his reaction," she admitted. "Doeppers will want to talk to Hank when he gets back into town, but I 'spect that won't be 'til tomorrow. They took Harry down to Gadsden for treatment, and Hank will probably go straight to the hospital."

"Will Harry be all right?" I asked.

"I talked to one of the paramedics, only briefly now, and he said it looked like a concussion, maybe bleeding in the brain. Too early to tell."

"Emily, what am I going to do?" I asked. I didn't like hearing the whine in my voice, but I couldn't stop it.

"Hogs tits, girl, buck up now. Everything will be fine. Now tell me why you think Manny Gomez is innocent."

I knew it was coming. I knew it as soon as I'd opened my mouth. I didn't know if my temper was to blame or if it had been inevitable as soon as Evan had told me. I'd hoped it wouldn't come this soon, but I should've known I wouldn't be that lucky. Maybe I could still finesse this. "Listen, I just know Manny couldn't have done it. I have no idea who committed the murder."

"And how do you know this?" asked Emily.

"I can't tell you that. I made a promise," I said, fingers crossed that it would be enough.

"Jon isn't going to accept that," replied Emily. She chuckled as she continued, "Man, you really stepped in a big ol' stinking pile. You think Jon will stand by after a statement like that, ya' got another thing comin'."

"I know," I said. "I'm stuck, Emily, like I'm being pulled between a bucking stallion and a fence post."

"I take it Jon's the stallion?" Emily laughed. "Quite an image that. Well, let's see if we can calm that horse some. Give me something."

I gave Emily a flat stare. Jon Doeppers was in no way a bucking stallion. If anything, the man was a stubborn donkey, or more likely, the fence post. Yet I needed to say something, or I might be spending an uncomfortable night or two on the city's dime, in a jail cell. "I know for a fact, well, from a reliable source, that Manny was with someone that night. And that's all that I'll say."

I watched as Emily's eyes grew large, and then a huge smile broke on her face. "Oh my," she cackled. "Jon is going to be so pissed," she said with glee. "He thought that case was all wrapped up and now this."

"Emily," I said. "I don't know what you think you know, but there are good reasons for secrecy." She was almost dancing a jig; the woman was so pleased with what she'd discovered.

"There were only two people Jon interviewed who couldn't provide adequate detail on how they spent that evening," she explained. "With the rumors floating around and the facts we already knew, we figured one had a good reason to be circumspect about how he spent that night, and with whom. The other was obviously the murderer. Jon didn't think to match them up," she laughed.

"Emily, this is serious," I said. "You could ruin them."

"Oh, it's serious all right," she agreed. "Funny as hell, but also serious. Jon will have a conniption fit."

"Emily!" I cried.

"Hold your horses, girl," she replied. "Don't get your panties in a wad. It'll all work out."

Evan was doomed. Somehow, I'd revealed his secret to the two worst gossips in Alpine. All that was left was sneaking into the boys locker-room in the High School and scrawling Evan's number on a wall with the message, "For a good time call." Within a week everyone in town would know that Evan was gay. "Emily," I said. I had to try. "If you say anything to anyone, word will get out. Evan's business will suffer. You can't tell." Emily gave me a level look, her face settling into a more composed form. Oh, I could still see the laughter in the corner of her eyes, but at least she was beginning to think of the repercussions. "You remember in high school when the rumors started about you and Greice? How people treated you afterwards?"

"Those were more than just rumors," Emily snorted.

"Regardless, you remember how it was?" Emily had been labeled, and our classmates treated her differently afterwards. I was ashamed to admit that I'd been one of them, not as bad as most, but I still treated Emily a bit differently once the rumors got started. It all paled, of course, with how I'd been shunned after the marijuana had been found in my car. Then only Emily had remained my friend. "Don't do that to Evan. It would be worse, much worse."

"You really think so?" she asked.

"In rural Alabama? In Alpine? You know how it is," I said.

"I'm not sure you give us enough credit," Emily replied.

"It's not like we're Monroe. Those folks are the true rednecks."

"Do you remember the Truscott twins?" I asked laughing. They were a year ahead of us in school, both of them central to the high school sports teams in the neighboring county.

"Harold and Harvey," she said. "Big, chiseled, with a mop of red hair that was to die for."

"And both dumber than ganders," I replied.

"I would have said more randy than ganders, but that's me."

"Emily!" I said shocked. "You didn't...together?"

"I plead the fifth," she replied, blushing.

"But they were so stupid; I swear neither could complete a sentence."

"Well, that happens when their father and mother are cousins," Emily offered.

"Really?" I said.

"I don't know," laughed Emily. "It's Monroe!"

"Listen," I said. "Keep what you know quiet, hear?" I hoped Emily understood; she knew how rumors could cause irreparable harm.

"I'll have to tell Jon," Emily replied. "He needs to know if he's to catch the real killer."

"I understand that," I said. "He may even want to confront both Evan and Manny to verify their alibis, but don't let this get out."

"I'll try," said Emily. "And about Harold and Harvey."

"Mum's the word," I smiled, seeing a bit of worry flee from around Emily's eyes.

We said our goodbyes and I got into the Mustang. I promised not to talk to Hank until tomorrow afternoon, giving Doeppers ample time to question him. I wanted to check on Harry, but Emily said I should wait on that until tomorrow as well. She did promise to text me the details on Harry once she knew. That left me with little I could do with the Waderichs.

As I drove away, I wondered what had happened to my sleepy little hometown. Could it be as Tina Thompson thought, and the White Lady stalked the fields, turning otherwise innocent residents into murderers? And Doeppers was right that I was connected to all of it? It really did feel like I was cursed, that I was somehow drawing the violence to me. Could it just be happenstance, or were all three incidences related? And then there were the less malignant mysteries. Who had cleaned Gracie's Grounds between the times when I'd pounded on the walls and when Tommy was murdered? Surely not pixies or elves or whatever. Had this mystery person seen anything? How had Tommy gained access to Gracie's Grounds in the first place? And where was the original building permit? It felt like cracking any one of those mysteries would provide clues to everything else, like in bridge when learning the distribution of one suit hinted at the holdings of the others.

I took the eastern route to town, turning onto Main near the Piggly Wiggly. I stopped by the Pig and got a bottle of Merlot. I felt I deserved it after the day I'd had. It was late enough that Frank had already left, his station at the butcher counter dark and lonely. My hope to talk to him about providing the food stuffs for Gracie's Grounds was dashed for tonight. I was in and out in less than ten minutes and then headed to Mamaw's house.

Mamaw was home when I arrived, the Buick parked in the carport behind the house. I pulled the Mustang in beside the sedan and made my way to the kitchen via the back door. Mamaw had dinner started, a skillet of fried chicken on the stove top with a mess of beans and fried green tomatoes. I greeted her as I pulled the corkscrew from the drawer beside the stove. In moments I had a glass poured, the deep maroon soothing my shattered nerves. I then told Mamaw about Harry.

Mamaw started off shocked, then went to concerned, followed quickly by angry and then back to concerned. The emotions on her face fluttered quicker than a hummingbird. When I got to the part about Doeppers implying that I might've had something to do with the attack, she finally settled into a deep anger. The woman wouldn't countenance any threat to her only grandchild.

"So," she uttered finally. "Well…" she continued.

"That's a deep subject," I interjected quickly. It was an old pun of Papaw's. It earned me a shallow grin before the anger returned.

"So that man has put you at the center of things," Mamaw said. "Doeppers, I mean."

"He's right," I interjected. "I'm connected to everything that has happened around here."

"As if you were to blame," Mamaw said derisively.

"He didn't say that," I said, wondering how I got to the place of defending Jon Doeppers.

"Well, we'll just have to clear up this mess," Mama said, decision made. "We'll have to solve this murder and figure out who assaulted Harry. Simple as pie."

"I can solve one of those already," I said. "It was Clovis who attacked Harry." I told her my theory then, about Hank and the court case and how Clovis had threatened me at Don's this morning. "The man is out for revenge."

"Skeeter," Mamaw seethed. "I suppose he has it in him."

"The man is a menace," I said.

"Well, we'll just have to catch him then, won't we?"

"I suspect he'll be at the game on Sunday," I offered.

"We'll have to lay a little trap for him," Mamaw said. We discussed possibilities over dinner but didn't settle upon a firm plan. We had to coax Clovis into saying something incriminating and be overheard doing so. The trick was in not admitting anything too leading ourselves; once Clovis knew we suspected him, the rascal would be alerted and not utter one word. We had to trick him without revealing our intentions.

With little resolved, but the day dying, I headed upstairs to bed. I felt a little tipsy after the two glasses of wine and wondered how my tolerance for alcohol, established in Paris, had dissipated so completely in the months since my return to Alpine.

My sleep was uneasy, either on account of the wine or the stress of the previous days. I awoke disoriented, the room dark, and when I glanced out the window, saw the heavy cloud cover. It was a day that screamed to me to stay in bed. I somehow found the strength to resist, reasoning that at least the storm would be followed by some cooler temperatures. I took a long shower, trying to wash away my fatigue and unease. Afterwards, I wiped away the condensation on the mirror to contemplate my image. The crow's feet near my eyes were deeper. Time had passed. I'd wasted too many years on Pierre, and now I was treading water with Hank, or at least it felt that way. Maybe Mamaw was right and I should move on.

I put on slacks and a maroon silk blouse; I knew the colors contrasted nicely with the green in my eyes. I headed downstairs and greeted Mamaw in the kitchen. She was still in her housedress, on the phone, of course. The gossip always started early. I poured a cup of coffee in an aluminum travel mug and waved as I left the house.

I planned to head to Gadsden to see Harry at the hospital this afternoon, which meant that I needed to check on the progress at Gracie's Grounds this morning, and also drop off the copy of the building permit. Being a Saturday, I didn't know if Evan and his crew would be working, but I had a key to the place. And that reminded me I hadn't changed the locks to the building since getting the lease from Ida. Whoever had had a key to the Cobbler's Corner would still be able to enter the building. Maybe Ida had claimed a set of keys from the Strange sisters, but considering that the Cobbler's Corner had been in the space for over eighty years, I imagined that the sisters had a key or perhaps a number of keys squirreled away somewhere.

I pulled the Mustang into the parking space next to Evan's truck, in front of the building. As I opened the car door, the screech of a ripsaw assaulted my ears and I quickly covered them with my hands until the noise vanished. As I walked to the door, I could hear two people talking inside between the thuds of a hammer. I pulled the glass door open and entered.

The space had changed. The pile of debris remained, but it had grown like a corn stalk in July. Next to the debris sat a neat stack of lumber and PVC pipes, while a collection of copper plumbing pipes leaned against the west wall. The biggest change was the framing for the new restrooms that needed to be installed to bring the building up to code. They protruded a bit further into the space than I'd hoped, but I knew there was no real choice. Douglas and another employee near his age were working on the framing. Evan and an older man I didn't recognize were talking closer to me. I waved as they turned my way, earning a brittle smile from Evan in return for my efforts. He looked worn and wary. I knew the situation with Manny had taken a toll.

"This is Fred Petersen," Evan said, introducing me to the man with a wave. "He'll be doing the plumbing here and upstairs. We were just finalizing the details. It'll probably be next week before he can start because we still have to finish the framing."

"Nice to meet you Miss…"

"Thies, Gracie Thies," I said, holding my hand out for a shake. "Are you related to Clyde Petersen? He works in the courthouse."

"Yeah," Fred said. "A cousin of mine," he clarified. Fred was an inch or two shorter than Evan, a bit heavier, and stocky. His smile was crooked, like the right side of his face worked better than the left. He kept glancing between Evan and me, expectantly.

"Evan, it looks like you've made quite a bit of progress," I offered.

"It always looks this way at first," he admitted sheepishly. "Demolition is quick; putting it all back together takes longer." He explained the timeline, keeping a flow of words going like a river in flood. The plumbing and new wiring would happen early next week. After that, came the drywall and spackle on the new walls. The following week, if all went well, would be the installation of the equipment. In between would come the inspections, and that was the biggest question on whether the space would be ready for Oktoberfest. With Tommy's murder, it was not clear how the city would handle signing off on the work. He said he'd certainly get the space up to code, but without the paperwork signed, I couldn't open.

It was another worry, yet somehow with all that had happened I wasn't as concerned as I probably should have been. I asked about the studio, and Evan took me upstairs. He seemed hesitant on the steps, like he was preparing himself. I whispered that all was well, that Manny would be fine. I hated to give false hope, but the look of relief on Evan's face and the genuine smile he gave was worth it. I just had to find a way to meet my promise. Once we reached the second floor, we discussed the flow of the space and moved one wall a few inches to give a little more space for the bathroom. It would make the kitchen nook smaller, but I thought it would make the studio more livable.

Before I left, I made sure to give Evan the copy of the building permit. He mentioned he wanted to stop by the cottage on Elm tomorrow, as there would be no work here on Sunday. I just gave him the key, no need to risk being seen together there again. I'd completed the sorting regardless, and this way Evan could begin to make his own plans. We didn't discuss Manny further, and Evan seemed to want it that way. There were too many ears in the place to talk about something that personal. I didn't know how Evan was keeping it all together. I knew I'd have been a mess in his shoes.

When I started the Mustang, my stomach growled louder than the engine. I decided breakfast at Margaret's was in order as my mug of coffee clearly hadn't been adequate. I drove the short distance to the diner, found the lot was bursting, so I parked on the street. When I entered the diner, Margaret gave me a knowing smile before waving me to one of the few empty tables. The murmuring of voices grew, like a crescendo at the apex of Mozart's fifth, and I swore people were staring at me. An acquaintance of Mamaw's, one of her Sunday school members, hid a smile behind her hands as I walked by. I itched for a mirror, wondering if I had dirt on my face or perhaps toilet paper stuck to the heel of my shoe.

When I sat, I used the menu as a shield while I scanned the place. I saw Brandi-With-An-I in a booth, with Snotty sitting across from her. They were smiling knowingly while looking my way. Those two were in cahoots about something. And there were other customers staring too, not everyone, as it was clear some were busy with their own affairs, but enough.

Margaret appeared and with an emphatic look handed me a copy of the Alpine Tribune, already opened to an interior section. She said she'd return shortly with my regular——two eggs over easy with grits and toast. I set the menu aside and picked up the paper; it was an article updating the investigation into Tommy's murder. With dread I began reading, and then I saw my name. I never should have gotten out of bed this morning.

At that moment, the storm broke, punishing the earth with a downpour.

Chapter 12

I stayed for my breakfast, the rain drumming the windows like the performers in Stomp. I wouldn't let Brandi and her posse chase me away, regardless of what she wrote about me. The woman had crossed a line, and I was certain Snotty had been involved as well. I should've guessed that something like this would happen after the encounter with Sandra and Snotty yesterday.

The article didn't outright say that Evan and I were having an affair, but it suggested it. It described Evan as the "estranged son-in-law" of Tommy, and me as a "single woman of marriageable age" who was currently "unattached." The article stated that Evan and I were witnessed having "intimate conversations," and openly wondered if they were connected to the "marital problems" between Evan and Sandra that "so upset" Tommy, and whether all this "was instrumental" to his murder. Anyone who read the article couldn't help but draw a line between Evan and me, and a carnal one at that. Somehow, Brandi had even obtained a quote from Evan. He hadn't said that we were romantically involved, but he hadn't denied it either.

I figured I had just discovered the true reason for Evan's unease only minutes ago. Sure, he was worried about Manny, but he'd also expected me to blast him for his role in Brandi's article. While he certainly had earned my wrath, Evan's quote was not the real problem——Brandi was. Besides, Evan was accustomed to hiding who he was and doing so behind a woman. Now that Sandra was no longer a suitable option, I had inadvertently been drafted to fill the void.

About the only positive I could see was that Manny's name hadn't been mentioned. Either Brandi didn't know that the foreman had been arrested for the murder or she hadn't learned that fact soon enough to make the deadline. I suppose she could be saving that little tidbit, preferring to soil my name instead. At least there was no hint of some three-way orgy. Maybe Brandi was saving that angle for a future piece.

I ate slowly, giving a cold glare to anyone who smirked in my direction. I wouldn't give them the satisfaction of seeing me visibly upset, despite how the acid in my stomach churned. Brandi's little prank would put a serious dent in my denials of anything untoward between Evan and me. The gossip mill would be a-turnin'. Oh, I knew that time was on my side, that eventually Brandi would find herself made a fool by her implications once it was known that Evan was gay. But until that day, I had to bear the repercussions, like Jesus with the cross, or perhaps more accurately——Hester and the Scarlet Letter.

By the time I'd finished, so had the storm. I left enough cash on the table to cover the cost of the meal with tip, not worrying about the change. The air was fresh when I stepped outside, the temperature almost chilly, and the ground was washed clean. If only my reputation could be salvaged so easily. I pulled my cell from my pocket and dialed Mamaw's number, but I didn't get through. By now Mamaw would've seen the article, or she would've heard about it. She was probably busy trying to limit the damage. Brandi would pay for this little treachery. I didn't even need to get involved; Mamaw would savage her with or without my help.

I considered returning to the worksite to have a little chat with Evan, but the harm was already done. I prayed the people I cared about, and who cared about me, would know better to than to believe in Brandi's slander. Well, implied slander. I didn't think there was enough there to sue the woman; Brandi had been too careful for that. No, I had to trust in my circle of friends and acquaintances, that the article would cause no lasting harm with anyone. That was, anyone except for possibly Hank. He needed to be my priority now.

The Mustang roared as I headed out of town, following the Old Gadsden Highway south. I had the windows cracked, and occasionally moisture from the road made its way to me. The windshield wipers were a blur, providing visibility while simultaneous giving a steady swish-swish to my thudding heart. As I drove, my anger calmed; there was little I could do about the rumors now. That was Mamaw's realm, and she was more suited to it than I'd ever been. The miles flew by, and I found myself lost in thought.

My 'to do' list was getting out of hand, with so many irons in the fire that I was afraid that some would melt. I needed to solve Tommy's murder, or at least prove Manny innocent. In some ways that deed was started with my inadvertent revealing of Evan's nature to Emily. It was possible that little problem would resolve itself, but I couldn't count on that. I also needed to trap Clovis before he could accomplish more mischief. If the man were willing to beat someone in a wheelchair, what would he not be willing to do? No, the sooner that Clovis was behind bars, the better. And that reminded me of Liz, the bartender whom Clovis had maligned, costing her the gig at The Barn. I needed to find her and see if there was anything I could do to help. And my last problem, written in bold, was Brandi-With-An-I Yugler. My revenge would be sweet indeed, once I figured out what it would be.

I shook my head ruefully. I was avoiding thinking about my real problem——Hank. I loved the man; that I knew. I had first loved him in high school, remembering those heady days when the whole world was before us. Even afterwards, when we'd split after the marijuana had been found in my car, I still had my heart on my sleeve for Hank. After high school, I'd gone to college up north, mostly as a way to flee the tatters of my life in Alpine. There I met Pierre, so different from my first love. I'd married Pierre straight out of college, moving to Paris and building a life there. I'd spent a decade married to the man, a decade away from Alpine, a decade of lies as it turned out.

I needed to confide in Hank, tell him what had happened between Pierre and me. If I had any chance of a future with Hank, then that future needed to be built upon mutual trust. Hank must have sensed my inability to speak of those years, to speak of that hurt. It explained his reluctance to move our relationship forward. Either that or I was reading too much into things. It was possible that the love was one-sided, that Hank viewed our relationship as something more of a convenience than something to be cherished.

I wiped the tears from my eyes, making my decision. It didn't matter. I would tell Hank what had happened between Pierre and me not for his sake, but for my own. I needed to take back ownership of those years; I needed to reclaim my life. It was an act of healing, a way of finding closure. The Event-That-Changed-My-Life would be banned from my psyche.

I slowed as I entered the outskirts of Gadsden. When I saw a Starbucks, I pulled in and parked. Stretching after the drive felt better than it should have——I could feel knots in my back and thighs caused by Brandi's shenanigans. I ordered a mocha latte, treating myself, and pulled the address from the text message Emily had sent. The hospital was only about 15 minutes away.

I got back into the Mustang and followed the directions from my cell. After fighting a bit of traffic, I found a space in a parking garage and headed inside. A volunteer gave me the directions I needed to Harry's room.

I saw Hank before he saw me. There were new lines on his face, his eyes held unreleased pain, and his shirt looked like a topographical map of Alabama it was so crumpled and wrinkled. And then he held me in his arms, crossing the distance between us faster than a dog after a squirrel. He just held me, unrelenting, like a warm blanket on a cold day, while the seconds passed. Eventually, he'd had enough, releasing me and pulling away, yet keeping his hands on my shoulders to look into my eyes. The pain was still there, that I could tell, but it had softened somewhat.

"You saved him," he whispered. "You saved Pop," he continued, pulling me back into a fierce embrace. This time he was quicker to release me, not quick, but a few moments quicker. When he had his fill of me, his arms fell. My heart ached with the lack of physical contact between us; I hadn't known I'd been affected so.

"Harry is okay, then?" I asked, following Hank to a collection of plastic chairs in the waiting room. He sat first, almost collapsing into a chair. I sat next to him, pulling his hand to mine to hold.

"He hasn't woken yet," Hank answered. "But the doctors think he will." He gave my hand a squeeze, and I returned it.

"What happened?" I asked.

"That's what I wanted to ask you," he laughed.

I smiled and told him my story. I explained how I knew he was working and had decided to check on Harry while he was in Gadsden. I described the farmhouse, how there must have been a scuffle in the kitchen, and how I'd found Harry collapsed on the floor of the back room. Hank asked why I'd not called him immediately, and I explained how I'd needed to call for help first, and that afterwards I'd been forbidden to speak to him until after the police had done so.

That promoted Hank's story, and I learned how the Gadsden police had arrived at CrankWorks and pulled him aside. They'd told him that his father had been assaulted and asked if he knew who could have done it. Only after they were satisfied that he knew nothing, did they tell him where Harry had been taken. Hank said that he'd come directly here and hadn't left since. He said he'd slept in the recliner in Harry's room last night. He glanced at his watch and sighed, saying that enough time had passed.

Hank stood then, pulling me up and led me down the hall to Harry's room. He explained the nurse had been giving Harry a sponge bath earlier, but that she should be done by now. I entered behind Hank and saw Harry unconscious on a bed connected to a series of monitoring equipment. The bruises on his face had deepened, going from an initial reddish brown into a deeper purple. There were a few small bandages on his face, and a small section of hair had been shaved above his right ear with a bandage covering it. Hank pointed at it and said that was where the doctors had drilled to relieve the pressure.

"If you hadn't gotten help when you did, I don't think he would've made it," Hank said.

"I had no idea it was that bad," I replied.

Hank smiled, and I knew we were better. "It's not now," he said. Then he turned to me and continued, "Listen, the doctors said Pop's so doped up on pain meds that he won't wake until late afternoon at the earliest. So, let's get out of here." He looked down at his shirt, as if he were just noticing how soiled it was. "I need a shower, and a change of clothes."

"You do stink," I teased.

Hank laughed. "I know a little motel just out of town, not too far. I don't want to be too far away in case something happens with Pop. They have good rates. We could get a room and I could grab a shower. I think I have a change of clothes in the truck."

"And then we could talk," I said.

Hank blushed, and I knew he was thinking of something other than talk. "I don't want to fight, Gracie."

"Neither do I," I said warmly. "We can talk without fighting," I assured him. "We need to talk," I said grabbing his hand and giving it a squeeze. "But we don't have to spend all our time talking."

Hank nodded and we were on our way, well almost. Hank stopped by at the nurse's station first, letting the attending nurse know that he was heading out for a spell but would be back by late afternoon. I could see the sympathy in her eyes, and she said that some time away was probably a good thing. She offered to call if Harry's status changed and took Hank's number. The turn of her lips said she wanted his number for something other than to update Hank in case of an emergency with Harry. She was dark haired, about our age, and not unattractive. No wedding ring donned the finger of this minx. I could feel the sparks she sent his way even if Hank seemed not to. Hank smiled his thanks to her after writing his cell number on the pad she provided, and I smiled to myself. I ought to be jealous, but I had no strength for it.

I offered to drive, and Hank agreed after taking a moment to retrieve the change of clothes from his truck. Hank gave the directions, and I teased him about the nurse. His reaction was like the five stages of grief in fast forward. He started with disbelief, moved to outrage, and made a stop at uncertainty on the way to wariness. Eventually, he admitted that perhaps the nurse was interested, reaching acceptance, and commented that she'd been particularly helpful and supportive. After a moment, he quipped that perhaps he should pursue "a little kiss and tickle"——his words. I laughed and retorted that if he really thought so, he could walk back to the hospital.

With the motel in sight, I pulled into the parking lot and stopped under the portico. Hank jumped out and went inside to get a room while I stayed in the car. It felt a little sordid to be getting a motel room in the middle of the day with a man, even if we were in a relationship, especially in as seedy a place as the Gadsden Getaway. I promised myself that we would talk first, even as my pulse quickened in anticipation.

Hank returned with keycard in hand and jumped back into the Beast. I pulled around back, Hank pointing to the room numbers plastered on the doors until we came to ours. He yanked open his car door almost before I got the car into park and hurried to my side opening the door for me. I knew then that talk before the "kiss and tickle" was going to be about impossible, but I vowed that Hank would at least have a shower first.

The room was like all cheap motel rooms, but worse. There were the two double beds along one wall with the bath towards the back. Dusty abstract art hung on the walls and dappled Berber in blues and purples covered the floor. I stepped into the space and could almost feel the bodily fluids of previous patrons. It made me shiver. The room smelled musty.

"This will do," Hank said, stepping past me and stripping his shirt away as he headed to the bath. He dropped the garment on the far bed and stepped into the closet-sized protrusion that held the commode and shower. I sat on the bed nearest the door, feeling the comforter for any unpleasantness beneath my fingers. Thankfully, I found none. I heard the water running and Hank stepped back out towards me. "It'll take a bit for the water to warm," he explained heading my way.

"So," I said. "You take all your girls to such romantic getaways?" I asked with laugh.

"Be nice," he snorted. "At least there isn't red velvet and hearts."

"No mirror on the ceiling," I noted.

"Exactly," he said. "It could be worse." He sat beside me and pulled me into an embrace, capping it with his probing lips upon mine.

After indulging him, I pulled back and wrinkled my nose. "You still stink," I said. "And now I think you soiled my outfit as well."

"Well then," he said. "You will just have to get out of those dirty things."

I laughed, telling him to go shower as I pushed him away. He growled but consented, and when he was preoccupied in the shower, I spent a little time checking the sheets, making sure they were adequate. I closed the blinds on the window and turned on the light on the tipsy nightstand that sat between the two beds. It was not an ideal setting for a romantic interlude, but I could withstand it. My preparations done, I sat mentally rehearsing what I needed to say, thinking through Hank's possible reactions and my counters. Essentially brooding.

I knew my time was up when the noise from the shower

ceased. I stood and waited, looking towards the bathroom door. Hank came out like Adonis, a towel wrapped around his beefy frame covering the most intimate parts. His smile lit something deep in me, and as he stalked towards me, I felt a weakness in my knees. He clutched me in desperation, and I could feel his need. We fell as one upon the bed. The talk could wait.

Afterwards, I lay comfortably on my side, held gently by Hank's right arm while I used my left hand to stroke the hair on his chest. Nothing separated us, our clothes flung around the room like a tornado had hit. Our time together had been energetic, intense, and at other moments playful. We knew each other's bodies so well. It was time to talk, and I thought I knew where to start.

"Hank," I said. "I want to talk about what you saw the other night." I could feel him stiffen, like the cooling meringue on a coconut cream pie fresh from the oven. I snuggled a little closer, continuing to run my fingers through the silky hair on his chest until I felt him relax again. "His name is Evan, and he's my contractor," I said. "He's also gay."

"What?" Hank asked.

"Evan, my contractor, is gay." I said. "But you have to keep it a secret. No one can know. What you saw really was innocent. I was sneezing so fiercely from the dust that I had lost control and started to fall. Evan was just trying to help."

"I saw the look in your eyes, Gracie," he said. "That was more than a simple rescue."

"Yes," I said. "The man is beautiful, drop-dead gorgeous, in fact," I said with a giggle. "But there's nothing between us. There can be nothing," I insisted. "And I'm here, with you, now, like this."

That seemed to stick, and it was a time before Hank found a way to answer. "It's hard, Gracie," Hank admitted. "Look at me—just a country hick about to lose his family's farm. And then there is you – refined, worldly, simply lovely. Who could believe we could be together?"

I sat up to see his eyes, leaning on an elbow to gain the height I needed while not abandoning my comforting nest. "Hank, what nonsense is this?" I asked.

"You're too good for me, Gracie," he said, softly meeting my eyes.

I could tell he meant it, that he really believed. I was so shocked by the absurdity that I didn't know how to react. That claptrap was nowhere present in any of my rehearsed mental conversations. Nothing even close to such a farce. I snuggled down in his arms again, gaining comfort from his presence. "Hank Waderich," I temporized. "I don't ever want to hear such foolishness from you again."

"Gracie…" he said.

"I mean it, Hank," I interrupted angrily. I felt him flinch and released the handful of hair I'd inadvertently grabbed on his chest. I smoothed the ruffled lengths and slowly continued, "Listen," I said, shedding a tear. "There are rumors going around about Evan and me. And there was this newspaper article."

"Gracie," he said. "You can't just ignore…"

"I said listen, Hank." My voice broke, and there was a tightness in my chest. I could feel more tears forming, the grief tied to such an idiotic belief from one I loved. "There are these rumors, about Evan and me, and then there's that article too, in the Tribune. There is nothing to them. You have to believe me on that."

"Okay, I do," Hank said softly.

I chose to believe him. My plan for our conversation shattered by his insanity. "Now, about the cottage on Elm," I continued, wiping a tear from my eye. "I'm moving. I'll be staying at Mamaw's until the new place is ready, a studio apartment above Gracie's Grounds. Evan is subleasing the cottage. That was why I was packing the other day, to get out of Evan's way."

"Your Mamaw told me something like that," admitted Hank in a flat tone.

I took a deep breath. I had to face what he'd said. "Now about this foolishness of yours. It is not true, Hank."

"Gracie," Hank said.

"It. Is. Not. True," I said sternly.

"I have nothing, Gracie," he whispered.

"You have me," I said, shifting to meet his eyes once again.

"I have you," he said with a warmth in his voice I hadn't heard since high school. Our lips met, and we held each other to confirm the bond. We whispered our love for each other; and said we'd find a way. After a while, Hank shuffled, and I knew our time was short.

"I want to tell you about Paris, about Pierre and me," I said. "I will tell you about Pierre," I promised. "But not today, we need to head back."

I rolled away from him then, and we silently made ourselves presentable. Oh, he flashed a lewd grin my way, and I gave him the required stony one in return, but it didn't take long for us to both get ready. It was funny though; we'd spent enough time in bed that Hank's hair had dried. He looked like a porcupine, one that had encountered an electric fence.

We talked about small things as we headed back to the hospital, and then Hank began to voice his worry about Harry. I commiserated, knowing how hard it must be. When Hank wondered who could have done such a thing, I told him my theory. I explained how Clovis had been served, and that he'd already sought vengeance against the bartender who'd supplied the video evidence. I told him how someone had knifed my tires, and how Clovis had threatened me at Don's. When I pulled my eyes from the road to glance his way, I saw steel in his frame. Hank looked like he was ready to pound someone.

"Hank," I said a bit worried. "Are you all right?"

"He threatened you?" Hank asked coldly. "I'll kill him."

"Ah, no, you won't," I said firmly. "You will stay away from Clovis Jones and let the police handle it."

"You can't expect me to do that," Hank raged.

"Yes, I can, and I do," I said. "I don't need you to play all shining knight to my damsel in distress."

"He hurt Pop."

"Maybe," I replied. "But, let the police handle it. Please." I felt a warmth——Hank had prioritized Clovis's threat to me over the harm to his father.

Hank nodded. I could tell he didn't like it, but he'd keep his word, at least for a while.

We had reached the hospital, and I parked in the same garage as I had earlier in the day. On the walk to Harry's room, I told Hank that I'd be heading back to Alpine later. Hank was disappointed, saying he'd stay at the Gadsden Getaway tonight, and had hoped I'd stay with him. I told him I wanted to, and I truly did, but that I hadn't brought anything for an overnight. Besides there was too much happening in Alpine for me to stay away.

When we neared Harry's room, Hank checked in with the attending nurse. The minx's eyes darted between Hank and me, clearly noting Hank's change of clothes and my soiled ones. It didn't take a genius to deduce something between us, and the attending nurse was smart enough. She explained there was no change in Harry's status, but that he should wake at any time.

Just to reinforce things a little, I put my hand on Hank's upper arm, like a momma bear with her cub. It earned me a gentle nod, acknowledging my claim.

I laughed as we turned to head into Harry's room. Hank asked what I found funny, but I told him nothing. Perhaps I wasn't precisely above a bit of jealousy, or maybe I just was protecting what was mine.

Harry looked the same, so awful. He seemed to stir a bit as we watched; yet remained with eyes closed. Hank sat in a chair near his father, holding the old coot's hand with unshed tears in his eyes. The minutes passed and the silence stretched. I couldn't watch it any longer and told Hank that I was leaving. He saw me out, walking me to the car, saying how he wished that I could stay. I lied, told him I would if I could, and got in the car. I said I'd call him later. As I was driving north out of town, I felt moisture on my cheeks.

The rain had stopped hours ago.

Chapter 13

It was dark by the time I arrived at Mamaw's house, the lights from the windows making patches of yellow on the lawn. I pulled into the carport next to the Buick and headed inside. Tomato soup sat simmering on the stovetop, and the makings of turkey sandwiches were laid out nearby. I set my purse down on the kitchen table and Mamaw appeared in the hall, dressed ready for bed in a nightgown with a pattern of little chickadees.

"I thought I heard you come in," she said. "I left out a little something," she continued, pointing to the food. "Soup sounded good on such a rainy day."

"Thanks, Mamaw," I said with a sigh. I collapsed into a chair by the kitchen table, my head in my hands.

"I take it you saw the paper then," she said. The woman crossed the floor, and before I realized it had a sandwich made with a cup of soup on a plate in front of me.

"I saw it," I said, taking a spoonful of soup. The tang revived me, the warmth of the pungent brew seeping down my throat. "At Margaret's," I continued, seeing Mamaw flinch. I told her about my day, how I started by getting an update on the work at Gracie's Grounds, and then heading to the diner for breakfast. I told her how eating there was like swimming in a lake of pike fish, you just didn't know from where the next bite would come. I explained that afterwards I went to Gadsden and spent the day with Hank and Harry. I skipped over the diversion to the Gadsden Getaway. Mamaw didn't need to hear about that little tryst.

"And how is Harry?" she asked.

"Apparently, they drilled a hole in his skull to relieve the pressure," I answered. "Hank seems to think he'll wake sooner rather than later; and be better eventually. I didn't talk to any of the doctors though," I admitted.

"After all that time?" asked Mamaw. "Not one doctor checked on him?"

"I didn't say that," I said. "I just didn't talk to any of them." I could feel the heat on my face and prayed Mamaw wouldn't pry. I took another sip of soup and said, "This is still pretty hot."

That distracted her, and Mamaw went to check for herself. She turned the heat down on the stovetop, and quickly put the remaining foodstuff away. She then returned to the chair across from me and began telling of her day. As I suspected, it centered around me and the article in the Tribune. I ate what was prepared quietly, letting Mamaw say her fill.

"I knew the truth, of course," Mamaw explained, after describing a rather involved series of telephone calls between her, Ada Mae, Gladys Chisholm, and Ida Bea. "So, I kept on denying and the other three came around. It would be so much easier if that man would come clean with his nature," Mamaw admonished.

"Not our decision," I said.

"I know that," she complained. "Just saying is all. And then we got to speculating on that Brandi. You know she spells it with an 'i'?" she said as if offended.

"I knew that," I said, trying to cover a smile.

"That woman——she lives over in The Pines, not that far from poor Sandra. Anyhow, that woman has quite the reputation. She's known for wrapping menfolk around those manicured fingers of hers——the fools, all of them."

"I'd heard that," I said, thinking of Bert, and maybe even Tommy.

"Single a 'course. Been a reporter for the Tribune for about three years now, and you know how she has pestered poor Ida Bea. Wouldn't leave the poor woman alone after the unpleasantness with Wilhelm."

"You mean when he broke into my house and tried to kill me?" I said stiffy.

"Oh, poo," Mamaw said. "Enough of that now. Ida had nothing to do with it. Anyhow, we all agree that reporter is a menace."

"So, what are you going to do about it?" I asked.

"You know, the thing about rumors, it's like playing with fire. If you're not careful, you can get burned," Mamaw said mysteriously.

"What are you planning?" I asked.

"Oh, nothing, dear. Nothing for you to worry about."

I asked again, but Mamaw refused to say anything further. She changed the subject to less consequential things, and I continued my respite. I even got a second cup of soup before Mamaw put the remainder away. Mamaw mentioned that she was heading to church in the morning, and would meet me at Margaret's for a quick lunch before bridge in the afternoon. I told her my plans as well, sleeping late and checking on the progress at Gracie's Grounds before lunch.

I headed upstairs shortly afterwards, the day having drained me like an old battery plopped into a new toy. I decided on a shower before bed, wanting the water to wash away the strain. I felt a little better afterwards, more like myself, and curled up in the bed I'd slept in since I was eight. I missed Hank——his smell, the sound of him, and especially the warmth of his body against mine.

At least Hank and I were back together, a tentative restart to a relationship that seemed to have too many such beginnings. I was still flabbergasted by his words today. How could he belittle himself so, and put me on such a pedestal? This was not the Hank I knew, not the football star from high school who'd earned a scholarship to play for Georgia Tech. Sure, he'd endured a string of bad luck, but that was mostly caused by his father, not him. Something must have prompted that reaction, some negative feedback loop that discouraged him while uplifting me. And then I knew——Mamaw.

It had to have been Mamaw all along, for months now, using her ways to discourage Hank and put a wedge between us. It had been only a few nights ago when Mamaw and I had discussed my relationship with Hank, and finally put to rest her meddling. But Hank didn't know that. Hank was still under the delusion that Mamaw disapproved of him. And here I was, taking Hank to task for his relationship with his father while he must think mine with Mamaw was equally toxic. Oh, the webs we weave.

I should have been angry, but instead I felt happier by the minute. It explained so much. Hank hadn't asked me to move to the farm, even after he'd learned how the cottage on Elm haunted me. That was not his lack of faith in us, it was because he knew Mamaw would disapprove. In fact, she'd said those very words to him when she learned I was packing. The grief I saw on his face that day was not caused by the loyalty he had for his father; it was caused by his fear of the connection I had with Mamaw. He was afraid that I'd choose Mamaw over him.

Now that I saw the lay of the cards, I knew what to do. Hank would have his day of reckoning. How dare that man not trust me enough to voice his doubts before now? How could he have kept secret the tension between him and Mamaw? We could have been together; we'd wasted months!

And then there was Mamaw. Oh, we'd had our heart to heart, and Mamaw knew how I felt. But she'd repair the damage she'd done. She would approve of Hank, treating him like blood. I'd put up with nothing less. She'd treat Hank right. At least she would if she ever wanted to see those great grandbabies!

That thought hit me like a brick between the eyes. It was a tentative thing, fragile, as I examined it from all angles. I'd spent so many years believing that I couldn't have a child, convincing myself that it was impossible, that I hadn't completely internalized reality. Maybe it was possible. Maybe Hank and I could have a child together. I knew I wanted one, had always wanted one. Coming at it from another direction, I knew that Hank had wanted children as well, had planned to have them with his first wife before their dreams of different futures pulled them apart. Hank had wanted kids, as did I—— why shouldn't we have one together?

I pulled the blanket over my head and huddled in the middle of the bed with knees drawn up and arms around them. It was too new; we were too new. Such a thought, if voiced, could ruin us. Hank and I both had too much on our plates to think of such a thing——me with Gracie's Grounds and Hank with the farm and Harry. The timing was rotten, yet the mirror also said that time was short.

And then it hit me. The blood drained from my face as the

realization struck. I shivered, knowing that my subconscious had already answered the question my conscious mind had just found the courage to ask. Hank and I had been like two bunnies, or two high school idiots, we'd often been close in the past months, and neither of us had taken precautions. It hadn't even dawned on me; I'd thought of myself as barren for so long. After the years of trying with Pierre and failing, it wasn't something I'd considered relevant. I figured Hank thought that I was taking care of that little detail, men always seemed to, if they thought at all at such times. I should have realized that by now.

It left me terrified; yet thrilled. The risk——well, the reward really——was something I was willing to take. I felt a grin split my face——imagine telling Mamaw I was pregnant with Hank's baby when we weren't even engaged. I wiped that silly grin off my face; this was serious. I needed to take precautions, at least for now. If Hank was unwilling to take measures, then I needed to be the responsible one. I'd see a doctor down in Gadsden—— it had to be someone outside of Alpine. I'd get a prescription and that would be that. Unless it was too late already, but if that was the case, so be it. I made this bed, and I'd sleep in it.

I dreamt of babies that night——a boy and a girl. I dreamed that Hank and I had made the most beautiful of children, with my red hair and his smile. We were happy, living in a house that was sometimes Mamaw's and at other times the farmhouse. The sun was always shining, the children laughing. It was a dream, I knew, just a fantasy of my imagination. I woke with a smile regardless. I decided there would be no trips to a doctor in Gadsden.

Mamaw had left the pot of coffee brewing, and I poured a cup as I contemplated the day. The sun shining through the kitchen window revealed little specks of dust floating in the air like precious gems, and in the light, I realized I'd made a few leaps in logic last night. In my nighttime fancy, I'd laid the blame for my on-again off-again relationship at Mamaw's door. There was some truth there, that I believed, but the blame included all of us, not just Mamaw. Hank and I had as much, if not more, to do with the troubles in our relationship as Mamaw.

After a second cup, I headed back upstairs to get ready. I chose a snug pair of jeans with a black flowing top. A few minutes putting on some light make-up and I was ready. I skipped down the steps and headed to the car. I felt unreasonably happy. With everything that had happened in the past week, I should've been anxious, even fearful. Instead, I felt hopeful, like after picking up a moderate hand in bridge only to have partner open Two No-Trump. Even the most pedestrian of hands would look promising then.

On the way downtown, I detoured to pass by Grace Lutheran. Mamaw's Buick was parked in the usual space, and the lot was surprisingly full. After a decade in Paris, where some of the world's most impressive churches remained barren on a Sunday morn, it still amazed me that a place like Grace would fill to capacity. I felt a momentary pang of guilt; I knew Mamaw wanted me beside her. I'd been a faithful churchgoer as a child, losing the habit only during my college years. While in Paris with Pierre, church was not something we did as a couple. Now that I'd returned to Alpine, I hadn't begun again. Mamaw had offered, welcoming me back to the fold, but I had demurred. I was unsure if I'd ever be interested again.

I continued my way downtown, pulling the Mustang in beside a rusty green sedan in front of Gracie's Grounds——the only two cars on the street. I pulled the rabbit-foot keychain from my pocket and selected the one to open the glass door. As I walked in, I heard a crash, and saw motion towards the back of the space, near where the new bathrooms would be. I felt a moment of unease, realizing that someone or something was in the building with me. No one should be here; Evan had said there would be no work done today. The unease gradually built to something closer to panic——it could be the killer.

I pulled my cell from my pocket, ready to dial 911. Before I entered the digits, I caught a better glimpse of the form hiding in the rear of the building. It was a crumpled individual, shorter than I was and a bit stocky, and it looked to be trembling. I kept the phone in hand, digits entered, call button ready. I called out to the mysterious individual, asking who they were.

"Sorry," called the form back to me. "We're closed."

"What? Closed?" I asked confused.

"Of course, I'm clothed!" snapped the person. "Daddy wouldn't tolerate any daughter of his walking around naked."

"Is that you, Mary Sue?" I asked. It couldn't be, yet my eyes were not fibbing. And apparently, the woman's earpieces were acting up again.

"Gracie?" called the voice, shuffling to retrieve a push broom from the floor. The handle falling must have been what I'd heard earlier. "You scared me half to death coming in like that," she continued, beginning to sweep. "I remember you had those lovely suede flats. Sorry we couldn't help with that; now that Junior has passed and all." The dust started to fill the air.

I stepped closer, remembering how I'd ruined those shoes in a sudden rainstorm this summer, and what had happened afterwards. The dust obscured my vision, and the fine particles threatened to make me sneeze. "What are you doing here?" I asked.

"Bah, I'm not telling you my fears," scoffed the woman. "I'm certainly not scared of you. And what kind of question is that anyway?"

"Mary Sue," I said, and then I sneezed. "Can you stop?"

"I'm not going to hop. I gotta get this place cleaned up. Daddy always said that was one of my jobs. Keep the place clean."

I stepped forward and took the broom from her hand. I saw the fear there, regardless of what she'd said earlier. And something else too——confusion? defiance? I made sure to speak clearly, not a yell but something close. "What are you doing here?"

"What does it look like?" she huffed. "I'm sweeping."

It clicked then, one of the little mysteries falling into place. "You've been doing this all along," I said. Not a question, a conclusion.

"I still got a key," she replied defiantly. "Daddy said it was my job. I've been cleaning this place since I was sixteen. I'm sure not going to stop now."

"Were you here on Monday night? The night Tommy died?" I asked as clearly as I could.

Mary Sue met my eyes, her watery blues staring deep into mine. There was something there——confusion beside the defiance. And then she nodded.

I called Emily. This was not an emergency, but it was relevant to the murder investigation. The call went straight to voicemail. I'd forgotten that it was Sunday, and Emily taught the Sunday school class taken by her little girl, one of the vast contradictions in the life of my friend. I left a message, saying that I needed to talk to her as soon as possible, that I had discovered a witness to the happenings Monday night. I didn't have Chief Doeppers' number, or I would've called him directly. And that left me with the emergency number.

I looked into Mary Sue's frightened face and then imagined Bert Lancaster or some other yahoo arriving, emergency lights flashing and sirens blaring, making a scene. Mary Sue looked too fragile for that. Instead, I texted Emily, asking her to have the chief call me immediately. It was the best I could do.

My time was short, but I needed to know. "What do you remember of that night?" I asked Mary Sue softly. It was a mistake; I knew that by the confused look on her face. I'd forgotten about the hearing aid.

"No, I don't want to fight," she replied, backing up looking even more frightened. "Why would you ask such a thing? Unless…I won't tell, really I won't."

I laughed and squatted to the floor, trying to look as unthreatening as possible. I smiled up at her and then lost my balance and plopped onto my bottom, laughing even harder. "What happened that night?" I asked clearly and loudly, sitting in the dust on the floor.

Mary Sue laughed, eyeing me as if I were daft, but she began to talk. "I came in the back door. I usually do, leaving the spaces in front for customers, that was what Daddy wanted. I found you pounding on the walls, making an awful mess of things. Still not sure what you were trying to do, but you looked determined. I waited," she said, blushing a bit. "I know we lost the lease and all, but I still had a key, and Daddy said I needed to keep the place clean. And it was a good thing I did too. You just up and left, leaving the place like some pigsty. You should know better than that, Gracie Thies!"

I nodded, conceding the rebuke. I had left in a tizzy that night after the row with Hank. "What happened then?" I asked, again clearly and loudly.

"After you left, I began to sweep. You and that other one just don't know how to keep a place clean," she complained. "It's been a mess in here. Daily. Anyhow, I propped open the front door, for the dust you know, and began to sweep." My cell phone rang, an unlisted number, and I held up a finger to pause Mary Sue in her rendition. I answered and as expected it was Doeppers. When I told him where I was, and who and what I had found, he cursed. He told me to stay put and stay out of his investigation, that he'd be there shortly, and then he hung up. I ignored his instructions and asked Mary Sue to continue. I wasn't going to miss the story now.

"So, I cleaned the place, taking the mess to the dumpster out back. You really need to call and get that emptied. It's starting to get full," she admonished.

I nodded, indicating I understood. This was becoming something of a sermon, church or no church.

"I'd just finished the last trip to the dumpster when the screaming started. I couldn't tell what they were saying, something about fishing or cars or whatnot. Anyhow, I was afraid I'd be discovered," admitted Mary Sue sheepishly. "So, I just left. Daddy would have been mortified, me leaving the place open like that, who knows what could have happened, and then poor Tommy," she said, taking a big breath. "I didn't know," she said, her voice cracking with emotion.

"There was nothing you could have done," I said clearly from the floor. I hoped Mary Sue didn't believe she was responsible, that she could've prevented it. I gave her a moment to collect herself, and then I had to ask. "Did you see them?" I whispered.

"What? Yah they were seething all right," she said, confused. "I said they were yelling."

"See them?" I asked again, a little more clearly.

"Oh no," she replied shaking her head. "I didn't go back inside."

The front door opened, and I turned to see Chief Doeppers, marching our way. He wasn't in uniform, wearing an old pair of jeans and a plaid shirt so worn that it must have been new last century. He glared as his gaze toggled between us, using a hand to smooth the nonexistent hair on his head, a habit the balding man hadn't yet broken. When he arrived, he reached out a hand for me. When I took it, his pull almost launched me from the floor into orbit as I stood. He handed me a card, and said it was his personal number. He said I should use this next time and sighed like he expected there to be a next time. And then he told me to "scat."

I snorted, took the card, and thought about saying that I wasn't some dog at his feet he could shoo away with a word. But I saw the look in his eyes; and knew him well enough to know that his irritation was already aroused. No need for me to add to the man's problems, well, not at the moment at least.

I asked about locking up, getting a flinch from Doeppers at the volume I used. Mary Sue offered that she had a key. The woman was eyeing Doeppers skeptically, and I knew Doeppers' demeanor would compound the problems he faced with this witness. I thought about warning him about the hearing aids, but with the scowl on his face decided not to. The chief would learn that himself soon enough, and I didn't need to be shot as the messenger.

I walked away, leaving the two behind me. I heard Doeppers ask a question; and snorted as I heard Mary Sue give an answer to something unasked. That prompted a follow up from Doeppers and an irrelevant answer from Mary Sue. When I passed through the glass door, Doeppers had raised his voice to the volume needed.

I was late for lunch, and so hurried to Margaret's in the Mustang. Mamaw's Buick was in the lot already and I parked on the street outside. Mamaw waved when I entered, and I hurried to join her.

"I ordered for you already," she said. "A Rueben, fries, and a slice of pecan pie. I didn't want to be late to the game."

"Thanks, Mamaw," I said, and then I told her what had delayed me. Mamaw was as shocked as I'd been that Mary Sue Strange had been sneaking into Gracie's Grounds to clean the place.

"You say she didn't see anything?" asked Mamaw.

"She only said that she'd heard shouting; but couldn't make out the details."

"As if you could trust anything that woman heard," scoffed Mamaw.

Margaret appeared, dropping off our lunch. "I got your back," she said to me sternly before scurrying away.

Mamaw gave me a satisfied nod, and I had to ask, "Mamaw, what was that all about?"

"Margaret went to the early service today," she said.

"And?" I asked.

"I may have asked Reverend Carmichael whether he could use John 8:7 for the gossip lesson," she said. "He also used it to base his sermon——it was quite the hit," she continued smugly.

My memory failed me; all I could do was look at her questioningly.

"Tsk, tsk, dear," Mamaw said. "You've been gone too long. John 8:7——'Let he who is without sin cast the first stone.' You should have seen Rev. Carmichael lay into those who accuse others of the deeds they themselves commit."

"Brandi?" I asked with a grin. "The Tribune article?"

"There may have been an example along those lines. I think Hawthorne's Hester was invoked."

"But who has Brandi been with? Wouldn't he have needed to be married?" I asked. I knew about Bert, and maybe Tommy. Neither of them was married, however. Was there another I didn't know of?

"Well," Mamaw blushed. "We couldn't just put that shame onto anyone."

"You didn't," I said. From the look in her eyes, I knew she had. "Mamaw, really? Evan?"

"Nice symmetry that," Mamaw said smugly. "It does Evan no harm and now Brandi has to deal with what you've been going through."

"But it's a lie," I said. "How did you do it?"

"She lied about you too, indirectly at least," Mamaw justified. "As for how? You don't think I can't plant a rumor? Easier than that pie before you."

I laughed; there was a kind of justice to it. An eye for an eye. We ate then, before our meals got colder. Margaret stopped by to top off our water, giving me a reassuring pat on the shoulder. I finished before Mamaw and looked around meeting the gaze of those around me. There were still a few judgmental looks, folks who hadn't gotten the message or didn't care, but there were more friendly gazes than not. Of course, most didn't notice me, being too involved in their own lives to worry about the drama in mine.

Game time was approaching, and so we left soon afterwards. Mamaw drove her Buick, of course, and I followed in the Mustang. When Mamaw pulled onto a side street to park in the lot in back, I headed straight as I preferred parking on the street in front of the club. My usual spot held a dark SUV, but I found a bit of shade further down the road.

The old Carlyle hotel looked lonely, with the construction fences surrounding the place beginning to show a layer of rust. I wondered how soon the investors in Birmingham would restart the work. Had Tommy held up the progress out of spite, or were there legitimate concerns about the project? The renovation of the Carlyle was key to the revitalization effort instrumental to turning the sleepy town into a tourist attraction. There was history in Alpine, and some of the architecture in the homes was unmatched this side of the Mason Dixon line. I could imagine some of the empty spaces downtown transformed into antique galleries and knickknack stores. It would certainly help Gracie's Grounds, although my business model didn't depend upon much of an uptick in tourism. I sighed and headed into the club.

I would have expected it if I'd given it any thought, but too much had happened in the past few days for me to put those pieces together. Sandra, Brandi, Snotty, and a woman who could only be Sandra's sister sat together at a table talking.

Chapter 14

I stood frozen, unsure if I should greet the foursome or not. I decided there was no purpose in poking that bear and moved to an empty table on the far side of the room. I looked around as more people entered and took seats. Gladys was busy at the computer, getting the game set up, the boards for the game ready beside her. The walls were covered in advertisements for bridge events around the southeast. There was a sectional in Chattanooga next month, and the regional down in Birmingham in the spring. I noticed Clovis at a table with his partner Samantha, and only then remembered that Mamaw and I hadn't settled on a strategy to trap the man. Too late now. Mamaw entered from the back door and made her way to join me.

"So, they came after all," said Mamaw with a glare to the group.

"You knew about this?" I asked. "And didn't warn me?" The tables were filling up, with most players examining the newcomers and talking softly. At least those whose hearing aids were working were talking softly. There were a few stealing glances from the foursome to look my way.

"Of course not," huffed Mamaw. "I knew that Gladys had invited Sandra and Cindy. And she called the paper, of course, free advertising and all. I don't think even Gladys believed they'd show." Ida Bea came in the back door, saw the foursome, and bleached whiter than an albino. When she saw us, she scurried our way taking a seat at our table. Mamaw smiled in greeting and asked, "I'm so happy you made it, Ida. Who are you playing with?"

"Ada Mae," Ida replied. "She called to ask yesterday, and I thought why not. It's been a while," she admitted scanning the place. "Since Wilhelm..." she continued, but then she turned to me and wilted. She bleached even whiter than she had upon entering, if possible, and opened and closed her mouth like a fish, sputtering.

"I understand," replied Mamaw, coming to her rescue. "It was difficult for me too, when Ned passed."

"Wilhelm was a part of your life for a long time," I said reassuringly. "Regardless of how it ended," I continued, unable to stop a small shiver. "You can talk about him if you need to."

"Thanks, Gracie," she said with a smile. "That means a lot, especially after, well, you know." She swallowed and gave a little shake. "I'd been married to Wilhelm for thirty-two years——most of those were good ones." She wandered a bit, talking of Wilhelm and how strange it was to be without him. I did my best to ignore the chatter; thinking of Wilhelm Bea was not a favorite pastime of mine. "You don't think..." Ida said, changing the subject, with a wave towards the group of newcomers.

"I'm sure that Brandi Yugler will leave you in peace," replied Mamaw firmly. "She isn't here for you."

"You have nothing to worry about there," I agreed.

"I just hope I can remember how to play," offered Ida

breathlessly. "Edward had taught me so much, and now I just don't know if I can remember it all."

"Ada plays a pretty simple card," Mamaw said. "Speak of the devil."

I turned, looking behind me to the front door and Ada Mae standing nearby. She saw us then and hurried our way. As she approached the table, she discretely nodded to the foursome that had attracted so much attention. I smiled, as did Mamaw, Ida seeming to have lost herself looking through the heavily altered bridge convention sheet she'd pulled from her purse. Ada sat with a glare for the newcomers, giving me a reassuring pat on the shoulder. The four of us exchanged pleasantries and when I asked about Ada Mae's change of plans, learned that her sister had caught a cold and they'd decided to delay the visit. She then explained that since Nora had already committed to me, that she'd asked Ida if she was interested.

The mention of her name brought Ida out of her contemplations. Ida and Ada quickly got into the weeds, talking about what agreements and conventions they planned to play that day. It mostly consisted of Ida suggesting something, and Ada saying no. There were even a few I didn't recognize, and I'd made it a point to learn the most common conventions. While I'd heard of Roth-Stone Astro as a defense to a One No-Trump opening, I couldn't recall the details. Thankfully, Mamaw and I had played often enough that we had no need to review. Besides, our system was basic.

The noise in the room grew and the newcomers slowed to a trickle. Most of the tables were full——it would be a large game. I saw the club president, Otis Greer, was playing with a young girl who had to be his granddaughter. She'd just turned fifteen last week. Otis had made sure the whole club knew to be careful on the roads now that his granddaughter had her learner's permit. It was nice not to be the youngest in the room for a change.

Like a flock of birds leaving a telephone wire, some unseen moment came when the majority of players stood and made their way to the one empty table left in the center of the room. Mamaw and I joined, of course, and contributed our purses to the other purses, raincoats, and sundry items stacked there that no one would need until after the game. It was a peculiar ritual, having one table informally designated as something akin to a communal locker, but a familiar one by this point. All close-knit communities had idiosyncrasies, including bridge clubs, especially in Alpine.

Gladys knew her cue, and as the players returned to their chairs, took a position in the front of the room, just beside the table that held the four guests. When everyone sat, she clapped her hands to gain the attention of the crowd before the chatter could begin again. When most players looked in her direction, she began to speak. "Thanks to everyone for making it out to today's special game. I especially want to thank Otis and his granddaughter, Jillian, for bringing a plate of cookies to share." Gladys paused for the dutiful clapping, and I could see the girl blush even as Otis smiled politely. "As you know, we lost a longtime member of the club this week——Tommy Hilgeman. Today's game is in honor of his memory, and I'm pleased to welcome his family and friends who've joined us today as we remember our friend." Gladys paused again, and the crowd clapped, although it seemed to me that the room had been more enthusiastic for the cookies than for Tommy's memory. "It's a club tradition," continued Gladys, "for members to say a few words at times like these. I thought we might share before the game, so that Tommy's loved ones could leave if they so desired."

There was a shuffling then, as players scanned the room to see who would speak. Otis stood first, reluctantly followed by Howard Ellis when it appeared Otis was the lone speaker. And then I felt Mamaw's kick under the table. I met her gaze, and she indicated with a head shake that I should stand as well. I must have given her a confused look, because then she mouthed, "Go on now."

"I don't know what to say," I whispered back, drawing looks from a table nearby.

"You have to say something," Mamaw replied just as quietly. "It happened on your grounds."

I looked to Ada, and she nodded her agreement. Ida hadn't noticed, or at least was more interested in the happenings at the front of the room than the conversation at the table. I took a big breath and stood, thinking quickly, and slowly walked forward to arrive after the two men. I nodded to our guests, earning a small smile from Sandra and her sister, a mocking snort from Snotty, and a look so cold from Brandi that it would have ruined the peach crop if it had happened in Chilton County. Otis began, and I thanked my lucky stars that the men hadn't tried some chivalrous nonsense with ladies going first; it gave me a few more minutes to think.

Otis spoke of Tommy's length of membership, and his dedication to playing bridge. He mentioned Tommy's love for the game and for his family. Oh, Otis used all the right words, but there was little substance and nothing on the type of bridge player Tommy had been. None of the glowing praise Otis had used for Edward this summer. The truth was Tommy had been an average player with a poor disposition, who'd never done anything substantive for the club. Otis finished by saying that Tommy would be missed; and expressed his condolences to his family.

Howard nodded, indicating that I could go next, but I demurred. I saw a look of terror in his eyes, and he swallowed as he turned to the crowd. Howard cleared his throat, and then did so again. I was beginning to wonder if he'd speak at all when he began. "Tommy and I had been partners at the bridge table for a while now," he said. "Tommy always liked to play; and loved to be Declarer." That earned him a chuckle or two, it was a common conceit for some players, those who thought they were better than what they were. "Anyhow, I'll miss him," Howard said abruptly, gave the crowd a salute, and headed to his seat.

All eyes turned to me, and I felt a shadow of the fear Howard must have felt. It reminded me of the spelling bee in eighth grade, when I was given 'chrysanthemum' and the faces in the crowd unnerved me enough that I flubbed it. I smiled nervously, not knowing precisely what I was going to say. "Tommy and I didn't always get along," I began. That generated a laugh. "But we respected each other. He was a fierce competitor, a demanding bridge player, and loyal to his friends and family." I paused, seeing the nods of confirmation in the audience. I stole a quick glance to the table of guests, seeing impassive or even bored expressions. I took a big breath and continued, "Many of you know that Tommy met his fate in Gracie's Grounds, a coffee shop that will open soon. I cannot express how sorrowful I feel. No one wants harm to befall any one of us, especially in a place I hope many of you will soon regard as another home, as much so as the Alpine Duplicate Bridge Club."

I saw several players shift, casting quick glances at each other. I had stumbled, phrasing things in a way that felt like an advertisement for my business, and at Tommy's expense. I needed to refocus on Tommy, distract from my inadvertent self-serving message. I wracked my brain, thinking of what more I could say——something meaningful and truthful that I could add. It must have been my dreams of the night before, or maybe the look of affection I saw Otis give his granddaughter. Whatever it was, inspiration struck. "But what cuts me to the bone, what really hurts, is that Tommy will be unable to greet a grandchild to this Earth."

Silence reigned, and as I watched, the color in the faces of several players bleached like chestnuts in boiling water, getting paler by the second. Several looked to the table of guests, and then I realized I'd jumped feet first into a cow pie, a fresh cow pie.

"How dare you!" seethed a voice——Sandra's as she stood. She wasn't the only one, all four at the table stood now. "How dare you say such a thing!" she continued.

"If you hadn't stolen Sandra's husband, maybe he could have," added Snotty.

"That wasn't Gracie," interjected Ada Mae, also standing. "It was that one," she continued, pointing a finger at Brandi, shaking in rage.

"What?" asked Brandi, her perfectly coiffed hair shaking.

"Stop this!" tried Gladys, stepping forward and holding her hands out in a peaceful appeal.

"I'm not sleeping with Evan," Brandi interjected. "Gracie is the cheat."

"Tommy wouldn't want this!" cried Gladys, trying again.

"I am not," I said. "That's your game," I sneered, thinking of Bert.

That was the last clear utterance, as all four guests started speaking at once. In moments, voices erupted throughout the room, with accusations flying like the food in the cafeteria scene in Animal House. Everyone was trying to get a word in.

Snotty, nose wrinkled, flung drivel my way. Sandra and her sister were discussing Evan——apparently Sandra had hidden her marriage troubles from her sister. I heard Ida Bea, a voice so shrill it cut through the crowd, calling Brandi "a snake" and accusing her of hounding her "like a dog in heat." A few picked up that refrain, using language a little more colorful than that to describe the reporter. I heard bits of bible versus——"cast the first stone" and "don't judge lest ye be judged." Even Clovis's voice reached my ears, with some nonsense containing the words——women, catfight, and Jell-O. By this time, Gladys had retreated to the chair by the computer, head in hands, either crying or laughing. It was pure pandemonium.

Somehow Mamaw made it to me; and pulled me aside from the mayhem. "What were you thinking?" she asked.

"I wasn't," I said. "I was caught off guard. I didn't know what to say."

"Well," she laughed. "This is the most excitement this place has seen in years." We waited and watched, trying to stay out of the center of things, and the crowd began to calm. The endurance of a bunch of senior citizens was limited after all. In a few minutes, Sandra, her sister, Snotty and Brandi all left, strutting out of the building with heads held high and looking down their noses with an arrogance that was palpable. They took the energy of the room with them, its disappearance so sudden that it left some gasping.

Gladys stood and took a position at the front of the room, not even trying to hide her grin. She asked if we were ready to play, and then we did.

It would probably seem strange to the non-bridge player that the game would go on, but I wasn't surprised in the slightest. The dedication to bridge was so encompassing for some players that nothing short of an unexpected death would stop them, and possibly then only delay the game slightly. A little scene like we'd just witnessed was nothing. A few players left, having lost the will to play, but the majority remained.

We combined some tables since it was a smaller group than just a few minutes ago, but Gladys had us organized in short order. Mamaw and I started against Ida and Ada Mae, playing four hands relatively quickly. Ida's defense had never been particularly good, and her sabbatical from bridge had only made it worse. I was able to steal an extra trick on the first hand, making a contract I shouldn't have. They got a good board in the second, a fluke based on a bidding mistake. It looked like we split the last two, it was hard to tell without examining the hands more closely. Since we finished early, we had a few minutes to chat.

"I just can't believe that reporter stood there and denied the affair, and after trying to shift the blame to you too, Gracie," said Ada Mae. "Using that so-called newspaper for her own purposes. I'm just about ready to cancel my subscription."

"I did already," offered Ida Bea. "A month ago, when they were printing all those awful things about Edward, and Wilhelm too," she added.

I looked to Mamaw but couldn't tell if she looked embarrassed or satisfied. "I'm wondering if there isn't some other reason. Marriages fail all the time," I said. I then explained, talking about life goals or maybe money problems. I shied away from the true reason, not wanting to plant that seed.

Gladys called the round, and Ida and Ada Mae left our table to go to the next. We got our new boards and our new opponents——Otis and his granddaughter. The fifteen-year-old was skinny——unlike her portly grandfather——with long dark hair and a cherub face. She wore a simple A-frame dress, and flats, with a touch of makeup that helped define her features.

She smiled when she arrived, and that was where the resemblance shone; she had the same mischievous grin as her grandfather.

"Welcome Otis, Jill," I said. "I'm Gracie, and this is Nora," I continued pointing to Mamaw.

"I prefer Jillian, ma'am," replied the girl, taking a seat. "And thank you."

"I hear that you just got your learner's permit," I said, recalling the sense of freedom that little slip of paper had allowed.

"Yes," enthused Jillian. "Last week. Papa Otis has promised to let me drive home."

"Ya'll beware," laughed Otis, his belly jiggling like Santa.

"I'm so happy to see young people playing bridge," offered Mamaw. "How long have you been playing?"

Jillian sighed, rolling her eyes so dramatically you would've thought she was after an Oscar. She shared a put-upon grin with her grandfather and explained in a rehearsed sort of way how she'd been drafted into playing a couple of years ago to complete a foursome with her Papa Otis and some other relatives. She said she'd liked it and had continued playing mostly at home.

I had to stifle a snort, covering my smile with a hand, and pulled my cards from the little plastic container. I wondered how often the girl had answered that question already today, and how many more times she'd be asked it again. I examined my hand, seeing seven spades and little else noteworthy.

Otis was up first and opened the bidding with One Club. I jumped to Three Spades, a preempt, to try and get in the way of the opponents. Jillian bit her lower lip in thought, and then brought out the green card to Pass. Mamaw passed too, a bit quickly. Otis paused, and then Doubled to reopen for their side, which just meant he wanted Jillian to bid something. I passed, having achieved my purpose, and waited to see what Jillian would do.

A small grin appeared on her face, and then Jillian passed. My pulse quickened; Jillian had converted Otis's Double to penalty. I looked to Mamaw and I could tell it almost pained her to use the green card ending the auction.

Jillian led a small club, and when Mamaw put down the dummy, I almost groaned. Mamaw had a singleton spade, the only feature being a string of diamonds headed by the queen. There were tricks there if I could promote them. It didn't work. I never got to the dummy——a true dead dummy. Jillian was behind me with four of my missing spades, and I ended up down four——a disaster.

The second hand was better, Otis and Jillian stopped short of game and we held them. On the third, Mamaw made a partial in Diamonds, although it looked like it made game in No-Trump. On the final hand, I tried to make up a little ground. I knew better and shouldn't have. A risky game in Hearts went down one.

I congratulated Jillian on her excellent play, and Gladys called the round soon after. Otis and a grinning Jillian followed Ida and Ada Mae, while Mamaw and I awaited our next opponents.

I learned little over the next couple of rounds. Almost by an unspoken agreement, folks avoided talking about the scene earlier. A few asked politely about Gracie's Grounds, and promised to stop by when it opened. I tried to learn something more of Tommy, but if anyone knew anything relevant, they kept that to themselves. Oh, folks shared stories, but of years gone by or anecdotes that were harmless enough. It did confirm that Tommy had been the man I thought he was, a figure stuck in a 1950s fantasy who railed against the so-called excesses of the common day. After a pleasant round with Sam and Debbie Klauss, I groaned when I saw that our opponents for the penultimate round were Clovis and Samantha.

Clovis grimaced as he headed our way, leaning on his cane like his 'bum' leg was made of cooked spaghetti. Samantha hovered near, ready to pounce like a she-cat to rescue the man at the first sign of trouble. Clovis settled into his seat with a sigh, turned to Mamaw and said, "Nora" with a little head nod and a twitch of his bushy mustache. Me, he ignored. I suppose I should've been insulted, but it almost felt like a relief.

"Skeeter, Samantha," mumbled Mamaw in acknowledgement.

"Skeeter was telling me that you had a little trouble the other day," offered Samantha. She flipped her long greying locks over a shoulder and continued with a faux sympathetic smile, "You had to get new tires?"

"Yes," I said, purposefully allowing my eyes to widen in surprise. "Someone knifed my tires when I was parked downtown."

"Probably some teenagers playing a prank," sneered Samantha. "That younger generation; the whole lot just isn't any good."

"Oh, I don't know," offered Mamaw. "That Jillian of Otis's sure gave us a run for our money. A good player there, and sweet."

"Well, of course, there are exceptions," said Samantha in a tone that suggested Mamaw was suffering from dementia.

We all grabbed our hands then, taking a moment to sort the cards. I had a nice collection, not outstanding, but five decent hearts with some strength in clubs. Clovis was dealer, and he started the bidding with One No-Trump. Samantha remained quiet, and Mamaw passed. I asked Samantha the range and she blushed, apologized for not saying earlier, and gave 11-14 as her answer. Mamaw's eyes widened a bit, and I knew that she hadn't known that Clovis and Samantha were playing a weak No-Trump. Samantha then bid two Hearts, which Clovis announced as a transfer.

I huddled, not sure if I should double to ask for a heart lead or just bid my suit. I glanced to Clovis, and my decision was made. The man would outbid me anyhow so I might as well make him go high. I jumped to four Hearts.

Clovis glared my way, and almost defiantly tossed the Four Spades bid card on the table. That was passed around to me and I shrugged and then Doubled. If Mamaw had anything, odds were we could set the contract. That was passed out leaving Mamaw on lead.

She led a low heart, and when the Dummy went down, I knew Clovis was in trouble, at least if his 11-14 count was accurate. I won the first trick with the ace, cashed the king of clubs to show Mamaw I held the ace, and tried another heart. Clovis covered and Mamaw trumped. She returned a club to my ace and I gave her another heart ruff. We'd taken the first five tricks and got another later to set Clovis by three.

"I shoulda' doubled your heart bid," growled Clovis.

"Yeah, poor luck, that," offered Samantha.

The second board was uncontested, with Samantha getting to four hearts and making an over trick. On the third, I picked up a nice hand, a 6-5-2 distribution with enough high cards to be interested in slam if Mamaw had anything to help. Samantha was dealer and used the green card to pass. I opened Two Clubs to show my strength, and Clovis glared my way before studying his cards intently. Eventually, he produced a Two Spades overall and I smelled blood in the water. Mamaw passed, as did Samantha. We weren't vulnerable against vulnerable, and Clovis had hit my five-card suit, so I doubled which after three passes ended the auction.

Mamaw hit my void on the opening lead, playing a low card in the suit. Clovis tried to win in the Dummy, but I trumped, ending that plan. I studied the Dummy and led the ace of my six-card suit, followed by another, which Clovis trumped in hand. I had just the right cover cards to keep Clovis from getting to Dummy, so he was never able to finesse my trumps. He ended up down three, giving us a top.

The man almost growled, shoving the cards back into the board, sputtering about bad breaks. We pulled the cards for the last board and I twisted the knife. "That was pretty aggressive, Clovis," I said. "Competing after I bid Two Clubs."

"Ya' gotta bid to win," Clovis muttered angrily.

I studied my hand, an unimpressive lot of cards. I competed anyhow, knowing that in Clovis's current state of mind, he'd probably outbid me. I was right; Clovis competed to four diamonds, making five with a nice line of play. Our boards done, I looked around seeing that several tables were still playing. Samantha excused herself for a restroom break, and Mamaw joined her, leaving me alone with Clovis.

"Heard you been messin' with that Petrovich fella. You give up on dat Waderich guy?" asked Clovis, raising an eyebrow.

"No," I said. "Hank and I are just fine."

"Heard the older un took a tumble or something. Out on da farm. Dangerous that, so isolated and all," he sneered.

"How did you hear that?" I asked. Was Clovis admitting to being there?

"Heard it somewheres," Clovis snorted. "Don't 'member where. Ya' know ya' still owe me that drink. If yer gettin' tired of yer man, I'd show ya' a good time," he continued.

"That's quite…generous of you, Clovis," I said. "But I think I'll pass."

"Shame, dat," he said. "A woman like you, needs a real man. Sum' one willin' to take what he wants."

"Do you ever actually listen to yourself, Clovis?" I asked, my anger rising. "Truly listen to the crap that comes out of your mouth?"

His jaw dropped, shocked that I'd said such a thing, his Adams apple bobbing like a bungee jumper. Before he could utter a reply, Gladys called the round. I looked and saw Samantha and Mamaw chatting as they headed our way. Once they arrived, Samantha helped Clovis stand, with him scowling and simpering about his bum leg.

Mamaw sat and when the two were out of ear shot but before our last opponents arrived, whispered, "Skeeter didn't do it. Someone else must have attacked Harry."

Chapter 15

The last round was a blur. Thankfully, the hands were straight-forward, and I was Dummy for two of the four, which meant my mind could wander. I'd been so sure that Clovis was the culprit; it had made so much sense. He had reason to wish Harry harm and was certainly capable of it. But Mamaw had seemed certain. I wanted to ask how she knew but couldn't, not while our opponents were at the table. It was a relief when we finished the last board, and the session was over.

Mamaw and I were able to have a hurried conversation before we left. She told me that Samantha had gone on and on about Clovis in the restroom, saying how they'd been spending so much time together. Apparently, Samantha believed that Clovis "had a thing" for me, and Mamaw thought she was warning me away through her. The she-cat was effectively marking her territory. The relevant bit was that Samantha had spent most of the day with Clovis on Friday, picking him up from Don's while his truck was in the shop and staying together all day. Hence, he couldn't have been the one to attack Harry. Oh, he could still be involved. He could have arranged for someone else to attack Harry while he had an alibi. But it wasn't in his personality. Clovis would want to be there in person.

And why in the world did everyone think I was on the prowl for a new man?

Mamaw headed out back to the Buick and I left by the front door. I pulled my cell from my pocket and turned on the ringer, seeing I'd missed a call from Hank. I returned the call as I opened the door to the Mustang and got in. After a few moments of greeting, and both of us saying how much we missed each other, I asked about Harry.

"Pop woke up last night," Hank said. "The doctors want to keep him for a couple more days, and there's been talk of sending him to rehab after that. Pop wants to go home."

"That's going to be tough," I said, wondering if I should try and drive back to the Victorian while talking on the phone. I decided it was best to just stay put. I wasn't in a hurry.

"You know how Pop is," Hank replied.

"Does he remember anything?" I asked, thinking of Clovis.

"Well, about that," he said. "It might be best to talk about that later."

"Hank," I said sternly.

"The cops have been by already," Hank said. "Pop didn't tell them anything, said he didn't remember."

"Hank," I tried again. "Spill it."

"Later, Gracie, in person."

"And when is that going to be?" I asked.

"Well, I was hoping that could be about now," he said. When he knocked on my car window, I jumped so high I hit my head on the roof. Then he was opening the car door and I was in his arms. The embrace and kissing lasted until we heard a car horn. I looked, seeing Ada Mae driving slowly by shaking her head and laughing. I blushed, not used to such a public display, but part of me just didn't care about that anymore.

"When did you get back into town?" I asked, taking his hand into mine.

"About a half hour ago," he said. "I tried calling, but you didn't answer."

"I just got done playing bridge," I said.

"I figured that out," he laughed, looking deep into my eyes. "I love you."

I melted. I just melted, standing there on the street. Oh, he'd said the words before, but not with that confidence, not like he was stating a simple fact, like the sky was blue. "I love you too, Hank." I said softly. My eyes felt puffy with unshed tears and I took a deep breath. "Now tell me about Harry," I continued, trying to keep the emotion from my voice.

"I will," said Hank. He lifted his gaze and looked around, like he was stepping back from some unseen precipice. "But not here."

We spent a few minutes debating where to go. The cottage was out, the space unsuitable with the moving preparations. I suggested Mamaw's, but Hank's eyes shadowed then, and I suspected he was hoping for something a bit more intimate. We settled on the farm, although both of us regretted the need to drive so far. I said that I wanted to stop by Mamaw's first to pick up a few things. Hank perked up a bit at that and said that he'd stop at the Pig and get a bottle of wine and something to eat. We parted with a kiss, and I got back into the Mustang to run my errand.

Mamaw had beat me home, not really a surprise. I parked on the street and went in the front door, dashing up the stairs. I sorted through the suitcase, tossing a few things into an overnight bag. Hank had seen most of my intimates. I needed another shopping trip in Gadsden, not that he was interested in the lacy things. He seemed to be more interested in me out of them. I tossed in a white teddy regardless, with a change of clothes for the morning. I made a quick stop in the bathroom and I had what I needed. I came downstairs to find Mamaw waiting in the foyer.

"I'm heading to the farm tonight," I said.

"I can see that," replied Mamaw neutrally. "I take it Hank's back in town. How's Harry?"

"He's awake, and I suspect as ornery as ever. Hank says he's itching to get back home, but that it'll be a few more days yet."

"I'd think so, on both accounts," she said. "I take it you and Hank have worked things out?"

"Yes'um," I said in a drawl. It annoyed her, but then again, we'd already had this discussion.

"Well, I guess there's nothing else to say," she said, deflated.

I went to Mamaw then, hugging her and promising that everything was going to be fine. She mumbled about her worries, but I could tell that she felt better afterwards. I said my goodbyes and promised I'd see her tomorrow.

It was dark by the time I pulled into the tree-lined drive at the Waderich place. I slowly drove up the gravel lane, pecan nuts cracking beneath the tires, and parked next to Hank's F150. Night noises filled the air——crickets, tree frogs, and the occasional hoot of an owl. Something scurried in the undergrowth as I walked up the lane and entered the house from the front porch. I called to Hank, and he replied that he was in the kitchen. I crossed the front room and headed down the hall to join him.

Hank had noodles boiling on the stove and was browning some meat in a saucepan with a bottle of generic pasta sauce open nearby. Two wine glasses perched on the kitchen table, an open bottle of Merlot between. I crossed to Hank and put my arms around him from behind, squeezing him close. That earned me a growl, with some nonsense about needing to get dinner done and watching the splatter from the stovetop. I released him and went to sit at the table.

"Who cleaned up in here?" I asked. It had been a mess the last time I was here——the day I'd found Harry injured and had called the police.

"Tammy," Hank answered. "I called the family to let them know about Pop, and she offered to check on the place."

"That was nice of her," I said.

"Tammy has always been helpful; she's my favorite cousin."

"Yeah, well, some of those other cousins of yours are bit of hard to take." It had been Hank's cousin John who'd planted the marijuana in my car back in high school. While that was in the past, it had led to Hank and I splitting up.

"About that," said Hank. He drained the grease from the meat and added the pasta sauce to simmer. He then turned to me and continued, "I told you that Pop woke yesterday. Well, he told me what happened."

"I thought you said he didn't tell the police anything?" I asked. I could feel my brow furrow, something was not adding up.

"He didn't, or couldn't, but he told me."

"What happened, Hank?"

Hank came over and sat in the chair opposite mine. He poured a glass of wine for both of us and took a sip before continuing. "John stopped by on Friday afternoon, looking for me."

"Your cousin, John Waderich, attacked Harry?" I asked shocked.

"Not exactly," Hank said. "Pop attacked John."

"What?" I asked.

"Pop attacked John," he repeated. "John came around hoping to convince me to grow for him again," Hank explained. "He didn't know that Pop had learned what really had happened back in high school. He just came in thinking he could talk to Pop for a while and leave a message. Well, Pop attacked him. They scuffled a bit and then, well, you know."

"Why did Harry do that?" I asked. "That's ancient history now."

"You know Pop," Hank said meaningfully.

"Wait, how do you know what John wanted?"

"I talked to him on the phone," Hank answered. "I already said that I'd called the family, that included John. He told me then what had happened, his version at least."

"So, Harry attacked John, and in the scuffle, Harry got hurt," I summarized.

"That's what John says. John claims that Pop hit his head on the coffee table."

"I saw those injuries," I said. "I saw the bruises on Harry's face. That was no accident."

"I know," said Hank softly. His grey eyes turned cold; I wouldn't want to be John the next time Hank caught up with him.

"Why didn't Harry tell the police what happened?" I asked. "They're out looking for the culprit."

"I told him not to," Hank admitted. "I told him to keep it in the family. Told him to tell the police he couldn't remember. The doctors backed him up, with a head injury it's not unusual to lose those memories."

"Why the devil did you do that?" I asked, taking a long drink of wine.

"Gracie," Hank said. "I can't have the police poking into John's business. Not with having grown for him this summer."

"So, he's going to get away with it," I said annoyed.

"I don't know if I'd say that," replied Hank.

"Hank, don't do anything foolish," I said. I looked him in the eyes and tried to read what I saw there. Hank seemed calm, more calm than what I would've been if someone had attacked Mamaw and sent her into the hospital. Maybe he'd just had more time to adjust to the idea.

Hank stood, saying that dinner was ready. He made plates for both of us, and I poured more wine. When we settled again, I had a few bites of spaghetti, thinking about what I'd learned. Something was still not adding up. "I still don't understand why Harry attacked John," I said.

"You know Pop," Hank said. "He holds grudges, and it's gotten worse since Mom died."

"Oh, I know that," I said. "I'll never forget the way he came after me this summer when he still believed that I'd been the one responsible for the marijuana in my car back in high school. But that had more to do with protecting you, or his memory of you, than it had to do with me."

"Exactly," said Hank.

"But I still don't understand," I said. "How did John threaten you? Harry doesn't know that you were growing for John this summer, does he?"

"No, of course not. You're thinking about this wrong," laughed Hank. "Pop holds grudges against folks who harm, or could harm, those he cares about."

"But John wasn't threatening or harming you," I said. "At least not that Harry knew."

"I'm talking about you, Gracie," Hank said.

"Me!" I said shocked. "That old coot cares about me?"

"Gracie," laughed Hank, shaking his head. "You've spent the past six weeks visiting him multiple times, baked him I don't know how many pies, and listened to all of his old stories. At this point he likes you better than me."

"But I was doing that for you," I said.

"Pop knows that," Hank said. "He's been calling me a fool, saying I should man up and make you an honest woman. You should hear him, badgering me like a kid after candy."

I couldn't believe it. Harry had been a secret ally all along. I finished my wine, and then held my glass up indicating that Hank could refill it. When he finished that little chore, I spoke again. "Harry does have a point."

"Gracie," Hank said. "I can't burden you with how things are now."

"Don't you think that should be my decision?" I said.

"Give me some time," Hank replied slowly.

"Just don't take too long," I said, breaking into a smile. I leaned across the table to give him a kiss. I misjudged something, or maybe I'd drunk too much wine. In any case, I ended up knocking over the bottle. Hank made a grab for it but missed, and instead caused the glass he'd just filled to spill my way. The short of it, both of us ended up with wine in our laps.

"Well," I laughed. "I guess dinner is over."

"You know," Hank snorted. "If you want to get it on, there are easier ways to get me to take off my clothes. Like just asking."

"Hank Waderich," I said. "Take me," I sighed with a hand to my forehead like a damsel in distress.

Hank laughed, stood, and cleared the dishes. He then took my hand and guided me upstairs, both of us stripping off clothes as we went.

Later that night, afterwards, I pulled an old sweatshirt of Hank's over my head and tiptoed to the bath. I loved the smell of him——inhaling the scent was like cuddling with a warm blanket. After the necessities, I ran a comb through my hair and examined my image in the mirror. It was time.

I returned to the bedroom, finding that Hank had gone downstairs. I tracked him down in the family room, sitting on the couch and drinking a beer while watching the sports scores roll past on the TV. He smiled and scooted over to make space for me, but I sat across the room. I pulled an old afghan of Mildred's from the back of the chair and wrapped it around me as I tucked my legs up underneath. I then said that I wanted to talk about Pierre.

Hank nodded, turned off the television, and gave me his full attention. "You haven't said much of those years," he said. "You don't have to."

"I want to," I said. "You deserve to know."

"I know that he hurt you, or that you were hurt somehow," Hank said, standing and coming across the room to sit at my feet. "I don't need to know more than that."

"Hank," I said. "Let me say this. I need to tell someone." He nodded then, and I continued. "We had good years, many good years. It wasn't as if Pierre was cruel or anything. It was only afterwards, when I learned the truth, that I realized how much of my life had been a lie." I took a deep breath and continued, "You know how I'd always wanted kids." I waited for Hank to nod. "Well, I believed that Pierre wanted that too. We talked about it, made plans, and we certainly tried, but I never did conceive a child. We went to the best specialist, at least that's what Pierre claimed," I said still amazed at the lengths Pierre had gone to. "All evidence suggested that I was barren."

"I'm so sorry, Gracie," Hank said. "I figured it was something like that. It doesn't matter to me."

"Oh, stop that. Let me finish," I said. "Pierre died in a plane crash; you know that. Well, anyhow, afterwards I was looking through some papers, trying to settle the estate, and found some medical records." I took a deep breath and forced out the rest. "Pierre had had a vasectomy." I had said it, I had revealed the secret that had driven me home again. I expected to feel relief, but instead I felt almost numb. That deep dark secret didn't seem so terrible in the light of day.

"But," Hank said. "I'm confused."

"Yeah," I laughed. "So was I."

"But if you're barren, why would he bother to get a vasectomy?"

"Hank," I said. How could he be so dense? "Pierre had the procedure the first year we were married. I don't know why, but he kept it secret. He lied to me for most of our relationship. Elaborate lies that made me believe I was barren."

"But then, are you?" he asked.

"I don't know," I admitted. "I believed I couldn't have children for so long, and now I just don't know." I slipped out of the chair and joined Hank on the floor, allowing him to hold me. "It was the lies, Hank," I said, feeling the hurt, the betrayal again. "Instead of telling me how he felt about kids, he lied. Made me doubt myself." I shivered and felt the tears begin. "Don't ever lie to me."

He muttered assurances, saying how he'd be true and faithful. How he would always tell me the truth, that I could trust him. It didn't really matter what he said, what mattered was what I'd said. I'd told somebody what had happened to me. All those wasted years. Well, not wasted——living with Pierre in Paris hadn't been a waste, just living under false premises. Now I knew better. Now I could live my life free from the lies, the deceit. Pierre had no hold over me anymore. I turned in Hank's arms and gave him a kiss, stopping his flow of meaningless words. Oh, I was sure Hank believed them, but he would tell a fib when he needed, that I knew. I just hoped I'd healed enough to handle it, and that Hank's falsehoods wouldn't be at the same level as Pierre's. When we paused for breath, Hank began again.

"So, this means that we can try?" he asked. "I mean, once things settle a bit and if we're still, you know, we can try and have a child?"

"Oh, you silly, silly man," I said laughing. "if we're still, you know," I mocked.

"Gracie," he said. "I was just wondering is all."

"Hank Waderich," I said. "What do you think we've been doing for the past months?"

"But, I thought, I mean usually," he muttered.

"Men," I scoffed. "I spent almost a decade thinking I was barren, that I couldn't have a child. When I moved back to Alpine to be near Mamaw, I didn't plan on being intimate, with anyone, and I certainly didn't take any precautions. It didn't really even occur to me until recently."

"So, you mean?" Hank said with a silly grin on his face.

"Nothing has happened yet," I said. "But there's no harm in trying."

We did that night, several times.

Chapter 16

I woke the next morning to find Hank's side of the bed empty, still warm, but he was gone. I did my necessities and then went to look for him. There was coffee brewing in the kitchen, but otherwise no sign of my Hank. I headed out the front door and found him. He was waiting by the Mustang as a newer model GMC Outback drove down the lane. I waited and watched by the porch swing. If Hank had wanted me for this, he would have wakened me.

The Outback pulled to a stop behind Hank's 150, and out stepped a man from the driver's seat that I hadn't seen in years. Some people change as they age, while others remain remarkably unaffected by time. John was the latter; I'd have recognized him anywhere. His hair was still a dark, greasy, unruly jumble upon his head, his frame skinny, with skin pale like the underside of a catfish. John ran his left hand through the greasy mop, and tentatively stepped to Hank, a paper bag in his right hand.

Hank stood with arms crossed, the look on his stony face unfriendly. John tried a smile, but it vanished like beer at a Crimson Tide game. John said something and offered the bag to Hank. Hank grunted, took the bag, and glanced inside. John said something else, and Hank shook his head negatively. Then Hank cold cocked him. He moved so swiftly that if I hadn't been watching, I would've missed it. Hank just pulled back a hand and hit John across the face like he was swatting a fly.

John's entire body twisted from the blow, his shoulders and waist following his head in rotation. He fell to the ground groaning, and Hank gave a couple of kicks with John screaming bloody murder before heading back to the house. John was still rolling on the ground when Hank reached the steps and saw me. He shook his hand and said, "Damn, that hurt."

"What's in the bag, Hank?" I asked softly. I was conflicted, unsure if I should be proud of what Hank had done or appalled.

"Cash," Hank said. "Enough to handle the hospital bills along with a little extra. I'll be quitting the job in Gadsden."

"Drug money?" I asked.

"Probably, not that it matters. I'm done with John."

"For good?" I asked.

"For good," he said.

"About time," I said, going to Hank and giving him a kiss. I wasn't happy with how things had ended, but at least John paid a little for what he'd done to Harry. I glanced back to the cars, seeing that the moron had made it to his knees. I then followed Hank inside.

Hank stuffed the bag into a drawer in the kitchen and poured himself a cup of coffee. I got one for myself and sat across from him at the kitchen table. We discussed our plans for the day, by unspoken agreement ignoring the scene in the drive. Hank was heading back to Gadsden to the hospital. I told him to beware the nursing staff, and he laughed, saying that I was welcome to escort him if I thought there was any danger. I told him I wished I could, but there was too much for me to do in Alpine. I needed to check on the work downtown, and I knew Mamaw would want to talk.

John was long gone by the time we headed out, Hank in his pickup and me in the Mustang. I followed him for a while, until he turned onto the Old Gadsden Highway and I went the other way into town. I stopped by the Victorian first, catching Mamaw in the midst of making cheesy eggs and grits. She asked if I wanted some and, of course, I agreed. I never passed up cheesy eggs and grits. Once the food was on the table, we talked.

"Rumor is, you let that Tina Thompson talk you into some ritual at that shop of yours," Mamaw began.

"She wants to do a 'cleansing ritual,'" I said, using air quotes. "Something about banishing the evil committed there and rededicating it to 'my Goddess'."

"Not sure that's such a good idea," Mamaw replied. "That girl is touched."

"What harm can it do?" I asked. "And it'll make her happy."

"Child, how many times do I have to tell you? Reputations matter in this town, especially if your livelihood depends on the goodwill of folks."

"Who would care?" I asked shocked.

"Plenty, enough," Mamaw said, a bit of color rising in her cheeks. "Have you seen the paper this mornin'?"

"No," I admitted.

Mamaw got up and retrieved it. She almost threw the Tribune on the table, the headline read Spat at the Bridge Club, written by Brandi Yugler.

I quickly read the article, appalled by what I saw. "This isn't right; this blames me for everything."

"I read it," intoned Mamaw.

"But," I said, "factually, this is wrong. I never accused her of anything."

"Bah, as if that matters," Mamaw scoffed. "With the shouting going on, no one could tell who said what. Truth is, she has the bullhorn. And with you trying to start a business, you gotta make peace."

"How am I supposed to do that?" I asked. Even the notion of finding peace with Brandi-With-An-I Yugler made my stomach curl.

"Give her what she wants," Mamaw said. "You can't fight this, not every day."

"You know what you're asking?" I scowled.

"Do you have any choice?" asked Mamaw.

I knew Mamaw was right, and I knew why she was so concerned about the cleansing ritual. Once Brandi heard about that——and she would eventually——no telling how she'd twist it into something nefarious. She could make out Gracie's Grounds into some kind of Wiccan worship site, complete with goat skulls and chicken innards, or was that Voodoo? It didn't matter if Brandi got the details right, not in Bible-thumping Alpine. Oh, I might gain a few gawkers, but I'd lose more customers than I'd gain. With the paper behind her, Brandi could generate too much headwind for my business to survive. "I'll do it," I said, but I wasn't happy about it. "I'll call her later today and take care of it."

We ate silently for a few minutes, and then talked about small things. We discussed the bridge boards from the day before, and where we made good calls and bad. You had to give yourself credit when things went right or all you did was chase the ice-cream truck with changes to your bidding system. No system was perfect; they all contained trade-offs.

My stomach was full, and after my third cup of coffee I

headed back to the Mustang. Before I got into the Beast, my cell rang——a number I didn't recognize. I answered, giving a tentative hello.

"Jon Doeppers here. Ms. Thies, at your earliest convenience, could you stop by the police station?" said a voice briskly.

"I'll be right in," I said confused.

"See you soon then," replied Doeppers, and then he hung up.

I spent a second gawking at my cellphone like it was a copperhead ready to strike. Why would Doeppers want to see me? He must have more questions, although I didn't think there was any detail left unsaid after the interviews earlier in the week. I guessed I'd find out when I got there, my errand to Gracie's Grounds to check the status of the renovations delayed.

The Beast started right up, the smoke and rumble from the tailpipe like Smaug in the Hobbit movies. I drove straight to the station and found a legal spot to park. I knew from experience that a ticket was inevitable if you parked illegally this close to the station, no matter how quick you were. The sun was shining, reflections from the windshields on squad cars parked out front twinkling like lights on a Christmas tree. The white building looked peaceful enough, and empty. I saw no one as I walked up.

I went through the double doors, seeing the now familiar raised counter at the far end of the space, guarding the doors that led to the rest of the building. Chairs were scattered on either side, all empty, and old placards coated the walls—— wanted posters and such. Bert Lancaster was manning the desk today. He looked woeful, almost pitiful, sitting there with head propped on his right hand. I approached to talk to him.

"What's wrong Bert?" I asked.

"I got chewed out by the chief," he said remorsefully. "Said I wasn't authorized to reveal details of an ongoing investigation. I never said anything, I swear. But now I'm stuck on desk duty for a month."

"I'm sorry, Bert," I said. At least the man still had a job. That Brandi was a menace, and now I had to play nice with her. "That's a tough break. The chief asked me to stop by."

"I'll buzz 'im," he sighed. In moments, he was escorting me back. I was surprised when we stopped short at Doeppers' office instead of heading to the interrogation room further down the hall. The man rose when we stepped into the cramped quarters, acknowledging me with a nod and gesturing to one of a pair of chairs in front of his desk. Bert offered to go on patrol, but Doeppers just growled for him to return to his post. As Bert left, Doeppers and I sat.

A large oak desk dominated the space, although on the positive side, an impressive window offered some much-needed natural light. Papers were stacked neatly into piles beside an old computer that had seen better days. I crossed my legs, and my foot hit the front panel of the desk that separated me from Doeppers. I scooted the chair back to make some more room and looked to the man. He'd been studying me even as I'd studied his office.

"These belong to you, Ms. Thies," offered Doeppers, sliding a ring of keys towards me. He grabbed a form from one of the piles by the computer and placed it in front of him. Meeting my eyes, he asked, "Are you pressing charges?"

"What?" I asked confused. I didn't recognize the keyring.

"Against a Ms. Mary Sue Strange," he answered. "For unlawful entry."

"Ah," I said; the keys must have belonged to Mary Sue. I

took the offering and shoved the keyring into a pocket, even as I wondered how many other sets Mary Sue had squirreled away. "I don't think so."

"I see," said Doeppers, returning the form to the pile from where he'd taken it. "Manny Gomez will be released this morning," he offered. "An anonymous source indicated he has an alibi, and it checked out."

"About that alibi," I temporized.

"No need," Doeppers replied, holding a hand up. "Those details are confidential. At least that won't be leaked to the press," he grimaced.

"I'm sure those involved will be grateful," I said carefully. If the man wanted to talk obscurely, so be it.

"On another matter, the main suspect in the Waderich case also has a firm alibi."

"I've heard that," I said. Doeppers meant Clovis, I knew, as I was the one who'd suggested the name.

"Good," Doeppers replied. "That was something you needed to know. Do you have any other thoughts on that matter?"

"Not at the moment," I said nervously, thinking of what I'd witnessed this morning.

"Are you aware that Mr. Waderich claims not to remember what happened that day?" he asked.

"I am," I said. "Apparently an after-effect of his head injury." My heart rate increased as my foot began to bob; I had to mentally force myself to stop moving my leg after I bumped the oak panel a second time.

"And you have nothing to add?" he asked, drawing the words out as he pierced me with his eyes.

"Perhaps it was a passerby," I suggested weakly. I uncrossed my legs and tried to sit still. My heart was thudding in my chest worse than when Mamaw grilled me.

"There?" he barked in disbelief. "In that isolated locale with no signs of robbery," he continued. He just stared then, and I nodded, feeling guilty. I don't know how long we sat, Doeppers waiting patiently while I squirmed before him. My face felt hot, and I couldn't stop myself as I crossed my legs again, the opposite way this time. The seconds ticked by, and my leg began to bob in time with my thudding heart, gently tapping the oak panel of the desk. Eventually, a small smile appeared on Doeppers' face, like he'd decided something. "That may remain an unsolved case then," continued Doeppers.

"It may," I said, relief flooding me. I was able to get my nerves under control and stopped the fidgeting. I hated being in this position——lying was not my forte, and it was all Hank's fault. Him wanting to keep it in the family. Oh, I understood his reasons, but he'd pay regardless. I didn't know how, but I'd make him pay for today.

"I see," Doeppers said with a forced smile. The man knew I was holding back on him, and he wasn't pleased.

"Any more vandalism?" he asked abruptly.

"What?"

"Any other incidents like the tires on your car?" he questioned.

"Oh, no, none," I replied.

"And your thoughts on that?"

"Haven't changed," I replied sternly.

Doeppers leaned back in his chair, studying me again. After a moment, he said, "Your name has appeared frequently in the paper recently, and not always in a positive light."

"I'm aware," I said with a snort.

"Is that connected to any of this?" he asked vaguely.

"Not that I know of," I answered truthfully. "In fact, I plan to defuse that situation today."

"I see," Doeppers replied thoughtfully. His eyes clouded then, like he was deep in thought. After a time, he came back to the present. "Well, then, that's enough for now, Ms. Thies," he continued, standing. I took my cue and stood as well. As I turned to the door, he continued, "I trust you'll contact me if anything occurs to you."

"I will," I said, looking back to the man. I watched as he sat and began leafing through some papers, his mind onto other business. I slowly picked my way through the station and to the freedom beyond. Doeppers knew I was lying about Harry, that I knew something that would assist in his investigation of the assault. I didn't know why he was letting me go, why he hadn't sweated it out of me. Oh, I was grateful, but wondered what deeper game Doeppers was playing. Would he truly let the assault remain unsolved?

And Doeppers had revealed nothing concerning the murder, other than that Manny was being released. In fact, Manny was being released because of the alibi, presumably not because Doeppers had another suspect in mind. It was like in bridge, you may not know what suit to lead, but you knew what suit not to lead. And from his question about Brandi at the end, it seemed like Doeppers was reduced to grabbing at straws.

Which meant he was making no progress on the murder investigation, and at the same time was releasing the one person the town had wrongfully pinned for the murder. There would be an uproar; that was certain once word got out, and despite what Doeppers had said, the truth would be revealed. Evan's secret would not be safe. It would come out connected to a murder——not the way to find acceptance, if that were even possible, in a place like Alpine. No, the murderer must be found, and quickly.

Doeppers was careful, methodical. If there was anything to

be found connected to Tommy's work for the town, then Doeppers would have found it. The murder had looked like one of opportunity, not a planned attack, so there may have been nothing to be found in the paperwork. All we really knew was that someone had been there that night, someone in a rage at Tommy, and that someone had attacked and killed him.

I passed through the door behind the raised counter and saw Bert slumped before me. A sudden thought occurred, and I decided to act upon it. "Do you have a picture of Brandi on your cell phone?" I asked.

"Yes," he said with a smile. The poor silly man. "Why?" he asked.

"I like her hairdo," I lied. "I was thinking of showing it to my hairdresser in Gadsden."

"What's your number?" he asked. "I'll forward one to you."

I gave him the number and he texted me the photo. Yan had said that someone had picked up take-out the night of the murder, someone who was connected to Tommy. All I had was her description——one that matched both Brandi Yugler and Marion Vinner. It was time to figure out which of the two it was.

I got into the Mustang and drove downtown, parking in one of the slots in front of the Pole & Arms as the spots in front of Gracie's Grounds were full. I detoured to Panda Garden first, but when I talked to Mr. Wang, I discovered that Yan wouldn't be in until late afternoon. I should have realized; the girl was probably in class. On a whim I showed the cellphone picture to Mr. Wang. He confirmed that Brandi was a regular customer but couldn't say if she was in the night of the murder. I'd have to return later.

I walked into Gracie's Grounds and saw a changed world. Douglas and presumably Shane were using a power drill to connect conduit high on the walls. Every few feet a runner hung down, where eventually a plug would be located. The bathrooms in back had been framed, and Fred Petersen was using a welder to solder the copper pipes in place with sparks flying. Evan was on a ladder in the center of the room. He'd pulled the decorative ring from the ceiling for one of the chandeliers. From what I could hear, he was describing the state of the wiring to the man holding the ladder below. The pile of debris was long gone, and the pile of supplies had dwindled.

I waited and when Evan saw me, he flashed that nuclear smile and stepped down from the ladder. He gave some directions to the man who'd been holding it, before heading my way. "The work is progressing," he said. "I still don't know about the inspections."

"I'll stop by the courthouse and check on that today," I said. "I just spoke with Chief Doeppers, and he said that Manny will be released this morning."

"Thank God," said Evan, the relief almost palpable on his face.

"Just so you know," I said. "The chief knows about Manny and——you know. But I think he'll keep it quiet. At least as long as he can. It was the only way."

"Better that than the alternative," replied Evan grimly. The relief had been replaced with alarm, but not panic.

"Maybe if we can solve this murder, it won't have to come out," I said. "But as long as the murder remains unsolved, people will talk."

"I feel so helpless," replied Evan. "First with Sandra, now with Manny."

"Have you and Sandra spoken?" I asked.

"Not since Tommy died," he said. "I've called, but with all

that's happened," he explained. "No, the truth——she's not speaking to me anymore. We haven't talked since I moved out."

"I don't think she mentioned anything to her sister," I temporized.

"Sandra's in denial; she's always been a little that way, and I think it's gotten worse. Maybe she thinks things will go back to the way they were, even after all of this. Those friends of hers just make things worse. And she always kept things from Cindy. Tried to protect her, I think. Listen, I've moved one pile of your stuff upstairs yesterday. And the pile that was going to Goodwill is gone. We still got the pile that needs to be stored at your grandmother's house; we need to make arrangements for that. For now, I moved that into the smaller bedroom. I slept at the house last night," he admitted.

"That's fine," I said. "As far as I'm concerned, the cottage on Elm is now yours."

"Thanks, Gracie," he said. "I'll get the studio upstairs fixed up in a jiffy."

"Just get Gracie's Grounds done first," I laughed. "I can wait a couple of weeks for the studio."

"Deal," Evan said. "Hey, I better get back. The electrician is due this afternoon to run the wires. We need to get the conduit in place and make sure the wiring to the chandeliers will work. I hope we won't have to run new wiring through the ceiling."

"Go get at it then," I said. He flashed that nuclear smile of his and turned to give directions to Douglas and Shane. The two had stopped working and were busy trading punches in the shoulder to see who could bruise whom the worst——idiots.

I headed upstairs, but the progress here was minimal. Chalk marks on the floor showed where the walls would be. There was a hole in the wall near where the sink for the kitchen would eventually reside. A section of floor in the bath area was missing, the wood pulled up and stacked in a pile nearby. By the front of the space under the windows that overlooked the street sat my pile of belongings. The couch had boxes stacked on top, the bed still in pieces on the floor with the mattress and box springs leaning against a side wall. I wouldn't be sleeping here for quite some time.

I headed back down and waved to Evan as I went outside. The sun was still shining, and the air was brisk after the rain overnight. I decided to walk to the courthouse. It was one of those perfect fall days, warm enough that a coat wasn't needed, yet not so warm that you broke a sweat. As I passed the Pole & Arms, I noticed a 'Help Wanted' poster in the window. Not a surprise; Ida needed someone reliable to run the place.

I wasn't looking forward to giving Brandi an interview. Oh, Mamaw was right; it had to be done. I had to make peace with the woman and that meant giving her what she wanted—an interview centered around that night with Wilhelm. I just wished I could get something in exchange, some sort of recompense for the trauma that reliving that time would entail. The trouble was not only the interview itself, but also that she'd publish it. For days afterwards, all that I'd hear would be sympathy for what I'd endured, and thus the need to relive it over and over again. And it would drag Ida Bea through the mud as well, not a good way to please my landlord. I needed to endplay her, but I didn't know how. At least I could try and protect myself, make sure that nothing I said could be taken out of context. I found an appropriate app on my cell and downloaded it. I was as prepared as I could be.

I reached the square in front of the courthouse and started across. Colonel Corbert looked the same, a grim bearded face with sword raised in defiance. If only I could do the same against Brandi——strike a rebellious pose and give her nothing. I sighed and stopped to read the plaque at the base of the statue, something I hadn't done since I was a little girl. I remembered that the Colonel had worked for the governor of Alabama before the War Between the States broke out, but I'd forgotten the details on how Wilber Corbert had earned his rank. Apparently, the man had been captured by a Union patrol, and had ended up leading them on a useless chase until his southern compatriots had ambushed the patrol and freed him.

I left the statue behind, crossing to the imposing limestone structure that held the Department of Code Enforcement and Permits. After passing through the metal detector, which naturally was set off by the ring of keys in my pocket that I'd forgotten about, I headed down the wide halls. Today the door to the office was propped open, so I knocked lightly on the doorframe to attract Tina's attention. She was wearing an off-white dress with a dark purple overcoat laced up in front. A pentagram necklace rested between her breasts with a trifle more cleavage showing than was proper for a workplace. And she had on the largest earrings I'd seen since Paris——a pair of crescent moons with stars that hung almost to her shoulders. "Hi, Tina," I said.

"The flame returns," she said. "And I foresee that the White Lady has marked you for her disciples to see. You must cleanse yourself, and the places where that harm was done, or you'll be stalked forevermore. Here," she said, flinging a bit of twine with beads of multi-colored stones tied along it in elaborate knots. "Put that on as a bracelet, the charm will give some protection."

"Thanks," I said, taking the bit of twine. It looked akin to what Emily and I used to make and trade at Mary Francis Wood Elementary. I dutifully tied it about my left wrist, and I could almost see the relief in Tina's eyes as I did so.

"We must cleanse the wound in that shop of yours. Until that time, the White Lady has too much power in this place. The arrangements are almost complete."

"About that," I said. "I was hoping to do the cleansing shortly before opening, you know, so that it has maximum effect," I said. The more time before word gets out, the better, I figured.

"Delay just strengthens the White Lady and her servants," Tina replied. "The sooner we heal the wound, the safer all will be."

"Wait," I said, thinking furiously. "With the construction happening, there are a lot of materials going in and out. What I meant was, I'd hate for something harboring her touch to come into the space after the cleansing and ruin all your work."

"Perhaps," said Tina, thinking. "That could happen. Unlikely, but possible."

"And that's why," I said, "we need to get the inspections done quickly."

"Of course," replied Tina, a hint of a blush. "Clyde has taken on that responsibility for building permits. The man works so hard, with such little recognition."

"He seems like a nice enough fellow," I said. "And if we could get those inspections done, then we could complete the ritual, and all would be safe."

"My uncle said they're going to hold a special election to fill Tommy's role on the city council," said Tina in a huff. "Marion plans to run for the position; I have her flyer here somewhere. And all that work Clyde has done will go for naught. He sacrifices and gains so little."

"Can I see that flyer?" I asked. As I'd hoped, it was standard election fair, with a picture of Marion in a business suit with a small smile and twinkling eyes. When I asked, Tina indicated that I could keep it. I folded the flyer and stuck it into my back pocket. Now I had a picture of both Brandi and Marion to show to Yan. "About that inspection," I said.

"I'll speak with Clyde," replied Tina. She sat forward and whispered, "I fear for him. The Trickster, Dwynn, has struck."

I gave her a puzzled look, and asked, "What do you mean?"

"They found asbestos in the Carlyle. The previous contractor had been blinded by greed, precautions were not taken, and now the future is unknown. Even my sight has failed me, although I do what I can to comfort Clyde in his time of need."

My jaw dropped. This could be the motive I'd been searching for. "When was this discovered? Did Tommy know?"

"Tommy's role is unknown. My uncle has declared a wall of silence, so that shame does not befall him. Clyde confided in me," she said, blushing further. "He needed someone to talk to, and I offered my assistance as an agent of the Goddess. I've been teaching him on how to gain Her favor," she continued.

I suspected that Tommy did know about the problems, but there was no point in pursuing that line of questioning with Tina as she clearly knew nothing further. Instead, I asked if Clyde was running in the special election, and Tina admitted not knowing that either, but with the blessing of the Goddess, she was encouraging him to do so. The more Tina spoke of him, the more certain I became that she was interested in him more than just spiritually. I just hoped that Clyde felt the same way about her.

We said our goodbyes and I promised again to call her about the cleansing ritual as soon as the construction was finished. If she could get Clyde to sign off on the work, I'd let her dance naked at midnight during a full moon if that was her desire.

Having the permitting done wouldn't solve all of my problems, but it would be a start.

As I walked back along Main, I wondered if Doeppers knew about the asbestos at the Carlyle, and if it, in fact, had anything to do with Tommy's murder. Had Tommy perhaps planned on meeting with Brandi to expose the problem, and gotten killed before he could say anything? What if Brandi had killed Tommy? No, that didn't make any sense; it was just wishful thinking. I so did not want to meet with that woman.

I sighed and pulled out my cell phone. It was time; I'd delayed the inevitable long enough. I had her number; she'd pestered me enough over the previous weeks that I'd blocked her calls, but I still had the number. I called and when she answered said, "This is Gracie Thies. I offer a truce. I'll tell you about the murder, about that night, if you lay off the Tribune articles."

She gave me a time and place. My fate was sealed.

Chapter 17

Brandi had given me a half hour, but it didn't take that long to arrive at Bauer Park on the far side of town. I pulled the Mustang into the gravel lot and parked next to a dark SUV. I prepared my cellphone before I got out, stretched, and looked around. There were young children laughing and playing in the distance, taking advantage of the warm weather while it lasted. I sighed wistfully and headed to the covered pavilion Brandi had mentioned. It felt a little weird meeting here amongst the picnic tables, but at least it was neutral ground. As I neared, I noticed someone in the shadows underneath the remnant of the old growth forest that used to cover these parts. I stopped when I saw who it was. "Sandra?" I asked.

"Gracie," she replied, walking swiftly to me. "Thank God I intercepted your call," she continued. "Brandi was at my house, and I answered her cell while she was out of the room. You must have a guardian angel." She grabbed my arm and pulled me into the shelter of the pavilion, among the shadows. "I think Brandi killed my father, and I'm afraid you're next."

"What?" I said shocked.

"I think Brandi plans on killing you," she said. "She's gone insane, killing Daddy, thinking everyone's against her."

"But why?" I said, still trying to regain my wits.

"Daddy? Well, there was trouble at that old Carlyle hotel. A cover up. Daddy had told me about it, and I'd told Brandi. Anyhow, she wanted to break the story, make a name for herself that would launch her career, get her out of this town. She was desperate and wanted Daddy to corroborate so that she could publish. When Daddy refused, she killed him."

It was plausible. I knew that Brandi would stop at nothing to get a story. And she needed two sources to publish——the Tribune demanded that. She may have had one but was lacking the other. Yet why meet in Gracie's Grounds? "I still don't understand," I said.

"She was there that night," Sandra said. "I saw her but hadn't remembered until today. She must have waited until after dinner to try and convince Daddy, you know, after I had left. And when he refused, she flew into a rage and killed him," Sandra wailed.

"But why me?" I asked.

"Brandi hates you with a passion. Ever since you refused to talk about that other murder. She thinks you cost her a chance already to get out of this town," Sandra explained.

It didn't make any sense. Oh, sure I could believe in Brandi's animosity, but I'd agreed to give her an interview now. Killing me would solve nothing. I examined Sandra, seeing the puffy eyes from days of little sleep, and the quivering mouth. Sandra believed she spoke the truth. "Why haven't you told the police?" I asked.

"I have no proof," she replied with a slight smile. "I need your help, to trap her somehow. I can just see her, standing over Daddy with a bloody hammer in hand, raging over his stubbornness."

And that was when I knew. When I was sure Sandra was lying. I wrapped my fingers around my thumb to get ready. And then I swung, just like Hank had done to John.

I must have telegraphed it, or Sandra had been wary——in any case, she ducked. I missed her face and hit her in the shoulder instead. She stumbled backwards, the blow was effective, but my thumb exploded in pain. A snarl appeared on her face and then she was on me. I collapsed beneath the assault, but not for long. When Sandra fell on top, I squirmed and found myself perched atop of her. My right hand was useless, or at least the thumb was, but my left was still good. I grabbed her hair and pulled. She screamed and tried to scratch my eyes out. I used my right arm to fend off her efforts but lost my grip as I fell to the ground beside her. Sandra scrabbled away and we both rose warily staring at the other.

"You bitch," she said. "Why did you attack me?"

"Why did you lure me here?" I replied.

"You just couldn't leave him alone," she growled. "Even after I slit your tires, you still had to romance him. Evan is mine!"

"Evan isn't yours. He's not some possession to fight over," I replied.

Sandra screamed and charged, and I danced away. I didn't want to get too close to her, not with my right thumb throbbing unmercifully. I needed to take lessons from Hank, or maybe Douglas and Shane. I'd never actually tried to hit anyone before, not in my entire life. There had to be a trick to it. Somehow, I kept my distance, and Sandra slowed as her rage was spent.

"How did you know?" she asked, breathing hard.

"That you killed your father?" I replied, circling to keep my distance.

"Yes," she snarled. "How did you know?"

"The hammer," I said. "Only the murderer, or those who found the body, knew that Tommy had been killed with a hammer. You couldn't have known unless you were the killer."

"Evan could have told me," she snarled.

"You haven't spoken to him since he moved out."

"Bitch, if you hadn't stolen him away, none of this would have happened."

"Evan is gay," I said in disbelief.

"Liar!" she screamed, charging again. She caught me this time and landed a good blow to my ribs before I scrambled away. I did get a hit in too, but she was winning, and at this rate I wouldn't last long.

"Listen," I gasped, the pain in my ribs mirroring that in my hand. "There's nothing between Evan and me. You have it all wrong."

"I don't believe you. Did you know he said he wouldn't sleep with me, even to have kids?" she exclaimed. "He found me disgusting, used and dirty. And then you came into his life. Acting so pure. Well, I could see the rot, you slut," she said, charging.

I peddled backwards, out into the light and away from the pavilion. The woman was mad, utterly insane. She had so many things wrong, had seen a different world than what was real. Sandra followed, chasing me like a hound dog after a coon. I kept my distance, countering her feints with moves of my own. I had no idea what I was doing, and almost collapsed in relief when I heard the sirens. Sandra backed away slowly, and I let her go. When she was at a safe distance, I looked about me, seeing the concerned expression of a woman with a cell in one hand, while holding a crying child in the other, with yet another clutching her knees and sobbing.

When a squad car screeched to a halt in the gravel lot, Sandra scrambled towards it screaming for help. I stayed where I was, crumpling to the ground in the dirt and holding my right hand in my left while rocking silently. The hand hurt so much, worse than when I fell out of the oak tree when I was five and broke my arm, before my parents had died and I'd moved in with Mamaw and Papaw. I tried moving the thumb, and almost swooned from the pain. I had to take several breaths until my vision cleared, enduring the pain in the ribs. No more of that nonsense.

I heard steps and looked up to Emily's grim face. Sandra was chattering behind her, a steady stream of wrongs I'd supposedly committed. I ignored her as did Emily, sitting on the ground and meeting my friend's eyes.

"Aren't you going to arrest her?" demanded Sandra imperiously.

"Don't get your panties in a wad," intoned Emily. "Looks like you'll have quite the shiner there, Gracie."

I touched my left eye and felt the puffiness. I hadn't even known I'd been hit; the pain a mere trickle to that in my hand and ribs. Sandra was jabbering again, giving Emily grief for her irreverent response and demanded that she cuff me before I could cause any more harm. I grunted at the latter claim——I could harm no one. I looked down, realized I was sitting like a chicken in the dirt, and moved to stand. Emily offered a hand and I gratefully took advantage. I only groaned a little from the pain in my ribs as I gained my feet. My vision narrowed but snapped back as I took a shallow breath. There would be no deep ones.

"This one," said Emily with a thumb to Sandra. "Claims that you attacked her."

I looked to Emily and snorted, or tried to, but the pain in my middle cut it short. Eventually, I spoke, "You better call Doeppers."

"You want the chief involved?" asked Emily, clearly surprised.

"He'll want to hear this," I said weakly.

"Whatever she says is a lie," interrupted Sandra. "I demand that you arrest her. She started this fight. And she'll slander me to try and get out of it."

"I think the chief will have to settle this," replied Emily. "Why don't ya'll just settle down now," she continued, herding us like a shepherd back to the pavilion. I picked up my cell phone on the way. It had fallen out of my pocket during the scuffle. I glanced at it and was relieved that it still looked to be working. Emily sat Sandra at a picnic table on one end, and me at another, the distance between us as large as possible. Once we were settled, she raised Doeppers on the radio. Emily gave us a stern look, told us to stay put, and then waved over the mom with the kids. Once they arrived at the pavilion, Emily began talking with them quietly, occasionally looking our way to make sure we were behaving as instructed.

I looked over to Sandra and she glared at me but seemed content enough. She must think she could lie her way out of this mess, either that or muddy the waters enough that she didn't have to worry. I figured she thought it would be her word against mine, and God knows my word had taken a beating in recent days. But she didn't know what I knew.

I couldn't believe how this had gone down——the deranged things Sandra had said. How could she think that Evan and I were together, and what in the world had set her off to murder Tommy, her own father? What was she thinking meeting me here with that nonsense about Brandi, a friend of hers? Was she seriously trying to frame Brandi for the murder? Maybe she was, if she viewed Brandi as a threat to Evan's affections. It would make sense in her contorted reality to want to remove the woman. It was all a mess regardless.

Doeppers arrived in his own squad car, pulling in without making the gravel fly like Emily had. He marched our way with a purpose, stopping to speak first to the witness and Emily. They were too far away for me hear anything, but whatever was said didn't take long. I watched as the mother took her children and quickly left the scene. I felt a bit guilty that children so young had witnessed such violence, but knew it was not all my fault. Sandra owned as much blame as I did, even if technically I'd started it. I really did need to have Hank show me how to throw a sucker punch.

Sandra called for Doeppers' attention when he entered the pavilion; apparently she was ever the eager beaver. He sent an appraising look my way, and I gave a nonchalant one in return. I was happy enough to wait even if my right hand throbbed as I held it gingerly in my left. He called for Emily to join him, spoke briefly to her, and then headed Sandra's way. Emily plastered a grim smile on her face and came to sit next to me with a sigh. We both watched as Doeppers interviewed Sandra, the seconds passing, him writing in his little notebook while Sandra became more animated describing the fight.

"Sorry, Gracie," Emily eventually said, keeping a blank expression on her face and speaking softly.

"For what?" I asked just as quietly. No need to attract the attention of Doeppers and Sandra. "I did this to myself."

"She got away. You never should have been put in this situation."

"What?" I said.

"Doeppers had me watching Sandra, something like a stakeout, but she gave me the slip. I figured he'd pegged her for the murder although he hadn't said anything."

"You mean Doeppers suspected Sandra and did nothing?" I asked, appalled.

"Probably didn't have the proof. I shouldn't even be speculatin'; he'd have my hide if he knew."

"I can't believe it," I said. "He said nothing to me this morning, just that Manny Gomez was being released."

"Yeah," sighed Emily. "That was part of it, knowin' Jon."

"What do you mean?" I asked.

"He let the word out, quiet like. My guess is he figured it would make the murderer panic now that the case was wide open again."

"So, he was expecting something like this?" I asked, my Irish nature beginning to take hold.

"Now don't you get all in a huff," Emily said in a whisper. "And be quiet-like now. Jon just told me to watch ya', not chat."

"Then why are you telling me all of this?" I whispered back intently. Emily shot me an annoyed look, and I regretted my outburst. "Sorry," I said more softly.

"I figured ya' needed to know the lay of the land," she whispered. "And ya been through enough lately. Look, I'm sorry about Brandi. I really am. I don't know what's gotten into that girl. Bull's balls, I wish I could just shake her."

"Emily, it's not your fault," I said. "I'm to blame there as well."

"I just don't want nothing to come between us," she said softly.

"Nothing ever will," I said.

We sat in silence for a while, both of us affirming a bond that would last beyond this latest trouble. Eventually, Emily spoke, "Did you start it?" I could hear the smile.

"Yes," I admitted, sheepishly, a grin appearing unwanted on my face. "I tried to cold cock her and missed. And I swear I almost broke my thumb doing it."

"You mean you wrapped it," Emily laughed. "Girl, has no one taught you how to make a fist?"

"It's not as if I needed that knowledge," I said.

"Well, I'll be as useless as a nipple on a boar, let me see," she said. I pulled my pitiful right hand from my left and held it out for her. The thumb had swollen to twice its normal size, the swelling extending into the hand, and it had turned an ugly red. "You need to get some ice on that," she intoned seriously.

"I need to see a doctor," I snorted, causing a piercing pain in my middle. "And not just about the hand, she got me in the ribs too."

"Life threatening?" Emily asked worried. "You're not light-headed, are ya'? Or spittin' blood or anything."

"No. It just hurts if I breathe deeply."

"Could be cracked ribs," Emily said.

I left it there——time would tell——and looked to Doeppers and Sandra on the far side of the pavilion. She was pointing to her shoulder and rolling it, Doeppers writing down details in his pad. I still couldn't believe she'd killed her father. "Why did she do it?" I asked. "Why did she kill her father?"

"Don't know. Sandra has always been a bit...fragile. Sumthin' snapped, I guess."

"She said some peculiar things."

"Jon will get it sorted," Emily said. "Well, speak of the devil," she continued as Doeppers stood and looked our way. He called to Emily and they quickly exchanged places. Emily now guarded Sandra as Doeppers interviewed me. I wondered if she'd have a similar whispered conversation.

"Ms. Thies," he began, taking a seat across from me at the

picnic table and tapping his pad with a pen. "Would you please tell me your side of this…incident?"

I met the man's gaze, glared at him, and slowly pulled my cell from my pocket using my left hand. I had imagined it as a smooth arrogant gesture, but I flubbed the execution and dropped the thing. I cursed and picked it up, relieved that it had survived without breaking. That would've been a disaster, and all for my silly showmanship. When I met Doeppers' gaze again, he'd lifted an eyebrow and I swear he was covering a grin. I pulled my tattered pride back around me and said, "you set me up."

"Interesting," he said. "And how exactly did I do that?"

"You knew Sandra had killed her father, and you did nothing. You knew something would happen if you sat back and waited," I said.

Doeppers gave me an appraising look and after a moment replied, "Ms. Thies, you seem to like to make accusations. It's a forte of yours apparently, yet rarely do those accusations have any truth to them."

"Well, not this time," I said. "Sandra confessed, and I have it recorded." Both of Doeppers' eyebrows shot upwards; I'd surprised him again. I opened the app on my cell, the one I'd downloaded to record my conversation with Brandi, and hit the play button. The audio was not of the best quality, but you could hear the conversation between Sandra and me. There was no doubt that it was genuine. Once it finished, I sat back and gave my most arrogant smile.

Doeppers looked thoughtful as he stood. He picked up my cell and placed it into a pocket, jotting something down in his notebook. He gestured for me to stand, and when I did, moved to stand beside me. He then looked to me and almost regretfully said, "Ms. Thies, you're under arrest for the assault of Mrs. Sandra Petrovich."

I was so shocked I heard nothing afterwards. I didn't even resist as he dragged me to his squad car and placed me in the back. About the only consolation was that he didn't use handcuffs.

Chapter 18

I'd broken a bone in my hand. The cast extended up past my wrist and the skin beneath itched constantly. I carried a popsicle stick to relieve the itch, but when I tried to surreptitiously meet my need, Mamaw saw me and captured my left hand in her right shushing me to keep still. I glared at Mamaw and tried to ignore the irritant. It did no good; neither the glare nor my efforts at suppressing the constant tingling beneath the cast. Mamaw was too fascinated by the sight before her, and my itch was immune to my efforts. I sighed and tried to pay attention to the ritual before me.

Tina was droning on and on, sometimes in English and sometimes in something that I guessed was supposed to be Celtic. I recognized the names Arnamentia and Brighid, but very little else. Not even the druids of old would have understood her, her pronunciation was so poor. She was standing in the center of a circle of five women, incense burning around her, and waving her arms and twisting like she was dancing the samba in slow motion. The women in the circle swayed, occasionally chanting a phrase back to her, and otherwise watched with vacant eyes. It made me wonder if the incenses were perhaps a bit stronger and more illegal than what I'd originally thought.

"This is fascinating," muttered Mamaw.

I sighed and glanced to Hank, his firm presence a reassurance at this time. When I'd agreed to Tina's request of a cleansing ritual, I hadn't known what it entailed. Oh, it was innocent enough, no icky ingredients or bare bodies, but it was so long. We were already on the second hour and my feet hurt from standing, not to mention the itch that just would not stop. I shifted from one foot to the other, and Mamaw dropped my hand. I palmed the popsicle stick in my left hand and slowly drew my arms together. Before Mamaw could stop me, I had the stick inserted in just the right place. Mamaw threw me an annoyed glare when I let a relieved sigh escape.

The last couple of weeks had been a blur. I'd spent an hour in jail before Emily convinced Doeppers that I needed medical attention. Even then, I was still under police custody, Emily staying by my side while the doctors treated my injuries. Eventually, the charges against me were dropped, once I'd explained that I'd determined Sandra was a killer and my life had been threatened. It helped when Sandra confessed, confronted by the audio recording I'd made. No prosecutor wanted to take that case against me, and so the charges disappeared.

Evan had been devastated, truly torn apart by what had happened. He'd had no idea that Sandra had been the killer, or that she'd fallen so deeply down the rabbit hole of her delusions. It made him reconsider his whole approach to life, and then he came out. He'd even reworked the logo for his business, changing it to a rainbow of colors over a hammer and nails. The repercussions were still being felt around Alpine, with many voicing support, but also those who had started to snub him. I suspected his business would diminish but survive. I was just glad that he'd finished the work on the coffee house, even if the studio apartment was not yet ready.

With Emily's help, Brandi-With-An-I and I had reached an uneasy truce. She agreed to leave my name out of any future newspaper articles, and in return I'd told her about the asbestos in the Carlyle. It had been the talk of the town over the past couple of days, with newspapers as far away as Nashville and Birmingham picking up the story. The mayor and town council had been on damage control, and both Tina and Clyde had been interviewed. Shockingly, both came off in a positive light.

It was a relief when Tina finished. Her circle of friends surrounded her, offering congratulations like she'd just won an Olympic medal. And then Clyde approached, having been invited, but not participating in the ritual. Tina made her way to him and clasped him in a fierce hug, while those around snickered and laughed. I glanced to Hank with a smile, and we approached the coffee bar. Liz was ready for us; I'd hired her temporarily while my hand was in a cast, and this was her first day on the job. Hank ordered a vanilla iced coffee with cream, and I had the same. Mamaw joined us and asked for a straight hot brew. Liz got our drinks quickly——she knew her stuff. I wondered if it might not be better to keep the woman on even after I was out of the cast. She'd been good at her job at The Barn, and if she could handle that rough of a crowd, Gracie's Grounds should be a piece of cake.

"I'm thinking of a bite of pie," murmured Mamaw after taking a seat with Hank and me at one of the small round tables.

"They are Margaret's best," I answered. I glanced to the bar, seeing the space swamped with Tina and her friends asking for drinks. Liz seemed to be in her element, describing the brews even as she made a latte for another customer. "I can't believe the Grand Opening is tomorrow," I said. "And just in time for Oktoberfest."

"I still worry," murmured Mamaw.

"Gracie has it under control," offered Hank. "I'm just amazed that you got this place opened so quickly."

"That was all Tina," I laughed. "She was so anxious to do the ritual that she badgered Clyde and Marion on the permits. All I had to do was insist that the cleansing had to wait until everything was set to open. I might have mentioned that my fire spirit was determined to have it so," I giggled.

"Clever," murmured Hank.

"How was Harry today?" asked Mamaw.

"Ornery but getting better. The doctors at the rehab center said that he'll be released tomorrow."

"I'm just glad he'll be coming home," I said. I still couldn't believe the ole coot had transformed from my onetime nemesis to something of an advocate with Hank.

"You can't continue to leave him alone out there on the farm," badgered Mamaw. "Not with what has happened. What if that miscreant came back?" she asked indignantly. I rolled my eyes and traded a knowing look with Hank. This had become a somewhat common refrain from Mamaw. We could not tell her the truth, and so she'd imagined all sorts of ills just waiting for Harry upon his return home. "I see you two, making googly eyes at each other and thinking I'm just some worrywart of an old woman. I'm telling you, it's just not safe for him there."

"You're right," said Hank. I looked to him, as shocked as Mamaw. I'd been saying for weeks now that something needed to be done with Harry, that a change was warranted. Not recently, mind, the ache from our fight at the cottage was still a bit raw regardless of how we'd moved on since then. "Pop and I've been talking. We'll work something out."

"Well, it's about time," huffed Mamaw. I met her eyes and realized she'd just said that to say something. It wasn't often that you won an argument with a Waderich man. "I think I might just get that pie," Mamaw continued, standing to go get Liz's attention.

"What are you going to do about Harry?" I asked softly.

"I wish I knew," laughed Hank. "I've looked, but there's just nothing. Do you have any idea how hard it is to find a place to rent in this town?" he asked exasperated.

"Tell me about it," I laughed, placing my one good hand upon his.

About the Authors

Doug and Sheryl have been partners in bridge and in life for 28 years with three wonderful children and two spoiled dogs. Originally Midwesterners, they moved south when they got married, and learned bridge while Doug was an impoverished graduate student. Doug and Sheryl began playing duplicate bridge at the Birmingham Duplicate Bridge Club in 2008 after their third child was born in an effort to get out of the house and save their sanity. This plan allegedly worked, at least until the kids started playing bridge as well. Now the whole family enjoys traveling to tournaments around the country as their work and school schedules allow. Doug and Sheryl have been finalists for the NABC President's Cup five of the past seven years. Both are still working towards their Life Master goal. When not playing bridge or writing mysteries, Doug is a mathematics professor and Sheryl is a paralegal.

You can contact them through their website: **https://duplicatebridgeclu.wixsite.com**. While there, check out the bridge hand blog posts.

Dead Dummy is the second in the Duplicate Bridge Club mysteries. The first is Killer Lead.

Made in the USA
Middletown, DE
23 July 2021

44683430R00149